Bogged Down

A Vashon Island Mystery

Charlotte Stuart

Praise for *Bogged Down (A Vashon Island Mystery)*

"*Bogged Down* . . . has everything—an island community that wants to keep their island as it is, eccentric characters, humor, murder, and plenty of mystery to keep you reading."
—Anne-Marie Reynolds, Readers Favorite - 5 Stars

"Readers will love Lew Lewis and her Vashon Islands pals. Stuart writes a vibrant story full of beauty with an undercurrent of treachery."
—Terry Shames, author of the Samuel Craddock series

"Not what you think, page after page. This story has teeth, start to finish. Charlotte Stuart is the best kind of surprise."
—Bob Bickford, award-winning author

"An enjoyable, fast-paced, and well-written mystery set on Vashon Island, Washington, featuring Lavender (Lew) Lewis, a smart, sassy and intriguing protagonist. The author's vivid imagery will transport you to this island paradise and you won't want to leave."
—Cindy Sample, Five-Time Lefty Award Finalist, Best Humorous Mystery

"... a beautifully-written, intricately-plotted classic whodunnit with a heroine (Lavender 'call-me-Lew' Lewis) unlike any I've encountered..."
—Harley Jane Kozak, Agatha, Anthony, and Macavity-Award winning novelist

To the residents of Vashon Island. And to the Vashon Bookshop for providing a hub for reading and support for local authors.

"Now and then we hear the wilder voices of the wilderness, from animals that in the hours of darkness do not fear the neighborhood of man: the coyotes wail like dismal ventriloquists, or the silence may be broken by the snorting and stamping of a deer."

—Theodore Roosevelt

Prologue

The air was still. The silence absolute. The white flowers of a Labrador tea plant growing in the deep peat moss were motionless. Birds were either foraging elsewhere or resting in the red cedars near the edge of the pond. Even the frogs were quiet. A hapless insect broke the silence and landed on the sticky hairs of a hungry sundew. It struggled to free itself but was slowly suffocated and absorbed by the carnivorous plant. Then again all was still.

Until a bubble released a whoosh of air and a body, half submerged in the murky pond, sank to the bottom.

Chapter 1
A Hand Up

Twelve people clustered along a seldom-used path under overhanging conifers. It was a warm day, almost 80 degrees in the sun but 10 degrees cooler in the shade. Most of those present had complied with our suggestion that they wear boots or sturdy shoes. Only one was wearing tennis shoes, a round-bellied middle-aged man in a T-shirt that said, "*Cheat on your girlfriend not your workout.*" I could have mentioned to him that in places along the trail the moss ranged from damp to soggy to downright mucky. He was going to find it hard to avoid sinking to the top of his pristine white Nikes. On the other hand, he'd been warned. And I didn't like his T-shirt.

"You the guide?" a young woman asked me. "I thought Anna was going to be our guide."

"She called in sick," I said, wondering as soon as the words were out whether that was something Anna would have wanted everyone to know.

"Oh," the young woman said, sounding disappointed, even without knowing anything about me. Not only was it my first time to take a group through Whistling Pete Bog, I was a poor substitute for several reasons. First of all, I didn't know much about the bog beyond the few facts I'd committed to memory at the last minute. Second, I'm not a people person. When I agreed to fill in for Anna, I was admonished to be polite and not kid around too much. Apparently, my reputation for being outspoken and at times flippant were not preferred qualities for a bog tour guide. My redeeming quality was that I was available.

There was some chitchat while a young volunteer for the Island Land Stewards passed around the sign-in sheet and collected fees from those who hadn't paid yet. But most of those present had their cell phones out, passing the time by doing whatever it was people do on their cell phones while standing next to someone they could be talking to. A few were taking pictures to document the start of their adventure.

I'm on the board for the Island Land Stewards, the owners of the bog. Our Executive Director twisted my arm to get me to lead the tour. The main instruction I received from him, other than sticking to the script, was to keep everyone on the path. The bog is a unique and fragile ecosystem. Damaged flora could take years rather than days to recover. That's why tours are limited to small groups and only happen once a year. The rest of the time Whistling Pete Bog on Vashon Island is a well-kept secret by those who care about its existence. It is one of only two such bogs on the island, both owned by our organization. It is on a side road toward the south end of the island but doesn't appear on any of the tourist maps. The small roadside sign pointing to the bog is obscured by trees and bushes. Most people, tourists and residents alike, fly past the overgrown path without a clue that it leads to such an amazing place.

When it was time to get under way, I took a deep breath and started the introductory spiel that I'd memorized the night before.

"Approximately 11,000 years ago the glacier that covered this area finally receded and left behind a depression. The land here was lined with glacial till which kept the water from seeping out, so a small pond was formed. Slowly, very slowly sphagnum moss grew outward from the edges of the water. And I do mean 'slowly'–one foot every thousand years.

"So," I ad-libbed, "if you think your tomato plants aren't doing well this summer–." I paused for a few appreciative chuckles before continuing.

When I'd competed my script about the bog's history, I jumped right into an explanation of what they could expect from the path ahead—uneven ground, roots poking up, an occasional detour around trees that blocked the way, soft ground, mud, puddles. From the looks on their faces, you would have thought I was about to lead them on an exotic safari rather than an hour's trek on a tame if uncultivated path. The bog's unique environment and the secrecy surrounding its very existence gave it cachet and an aura of mystery.

We started off through a thick fir and cedar forest. There was no breeze. The large branches overhead were as still as paintings. Except for the muted sound of footfalls and a few hushed conversations, it felt like we were entering another world, a magical place of giant trees and spongy ground. Everyone knew we weren't the first people to journey into the bog. Still, I had to admit, it felt special, even to me.

When we reached the point where the path started sloping downward, the trees opened up, providing a nice view of much of the small valley that contained the bog. This was where we made our first stop. I pointed out a few plants unique to the bog and emphasized that we needed to stay on the path and watch our footing. As we got under way again, a voice yelled a question.

"Will we see any wildlife?"

"Listen," I called back as the group started down the narrow dirt path. "What do you hear?"

As those near the front of the line stopped talking the crackle of dry twigs underfoot seemed louder. A conversation between two young people at the back of the group drifted forward. Someone coughed. Another person uttered an oath when they tripped on a root.

A few people laughed. Someone said the obvious, "I guess we won't be sneaking up on any wildlife."

"Not unless they're wearing headphones and listening to music," I said.

The rich biodiversity on the island included a complex mix of plants and animals, 513 different species at last count. But when referring to the wildlife on the island, most people were interested in catching a glimpse of the solitary cougar, a coyote from one of the four resident families, or a black bear. The island also attracted some rare bird species, but not being a birder, I would have been hard pressed to identify any but the most common of our feathered friends.

We made our way down the hill toward the center of the bog, pausing to wait for the less athletic members of the group as they slowly maneuvered around an angled tree that leaned across the path, while at the same time trying to avoid stepping in muck up to their knees.

"What's the history on the name of the bog?" someone asked.

That was one question I was prepared for. I'd asked the same thing on my first tour.

"The reference to 'whistling' comes from the stories about ghostly apparitions that some claim can be heard moving about at night, especially when there is ground fog." I didn't know what difference ground fog made, but that was part of the legend. "'Pete' was the result of someone misspelling 'peat moss.' And for some reason it stuck. What you will see is actually living sphagnum moss, although the mass is usually referred to as sphagnum peat, and it can be up to eleven feet deep. That's why it feels at times like you are walking on foam rubber."

As we moved down the long hill approaching the pond, I again reminded everyone to stay on the path. Anticipation was building. Whispered comments passed up and down the line: "The ground *is* spongy." "Did you hear that–was that a Common Yellowthroat?" "How much further, do you think?"

We were almost to the center of the bog. The air was still. Everything seemed hushed. Even the frogs were silent. I pointed out white flowers of a Labrador tea plant growing in the deep peat moss and managed to spot one tiny carnivorous sundew, its thin spikes reaching upward as if trolling for prey.

As we drew near the long, flattened deadfall log that spanned the end of the pond, I gave them the safety lecture almost word for word as I'd heard it my first time as a visitor. "The log is about three feet wide," I explained. "Make sure you stay in its center. Although there may be some soft spots, it's the edges that you have to watch out for. The edges are unstable and can slough off if you step on them. You could easily end up in the pond."

Then I told the prescribed story about what had happened on a tour a few years back to a man who had lost his footing and fallen into the water. "If you do fall in, just remember—no swimming allowed." That bit about no swimming wasn't in the script; I thought it was funny, but the line didn't get any laughs.

"Isn't there an easier way into the bog?" one young man asked. He was wearing cargo pants and a sweatshirt and looked fully capable of traversing the log. Maybe he was concerned for some of the older people in the group. The invitation had stressed that only those with "good balance who are comfortable walking on uneven ground" should come. The trail wasn't really that bad, but those organizing the tours didn't want anyone to take unnecessary risks.

"This is the only way in," I said. "We need to protect the land, so we limit access." Looking at the row of expectant faces, it seemed to me that everyone in the group was willing and capable of handling the path ahead. Although I was still hoping Mr. T-shirt was going to soil his Nikes.

When we got to the log, I reminded everyone a second time to avoid the edges. I was looking over my shoulder as the first few started across after me. The man in the lead was in his late twenties. He was wearing shorts and gray wool socks that stuck up over the top of his leather boots. About a third of the way across he stopped abruptly and said in a loud voice, "Very funny." The high school girl who was crossing just behind him suddenly put her hands over her mouth and screamed.

My first thought was that the log was starting to give. I leapt forward toward land, instantly feeling guilty for thinking of myself before considering the safety of those under my care. When I turned back toward the group, the log was still intact. Everyone was standing there, motionless. Staring down at the pond.

That's when I saw a human hand reaching out of the water.

Chapter 2
The Pop-up Face

When no one popped out of the water and yelled, "Gotcha," I had a sinking feeling that my first stint as a tour guide was about to become a part of the Bog legend.

The cell phones had appeared in a flash, as quick as an eagle swooping down from nowhere to seize a herring from the surface of a calm bay. "Stop," I shouted. Then, tempering my tone a bit, I added, "Please don't start sending photos to anyone. We need to call Deputy Grimes before we broadcast what we *think* we're seeing." I knew that everyone, including me, thought it was a hand attached to a submerged body, although I was still clinging to the hope that it was some kind of macabre prank.

"Shouldn't we check it out first?" someone asked.

The young man who'd first spotted the hand was kneeling dangerously near the edge of the log, leaning over, carefully scrutinizing it. "It looks real," he said. "And I can see a bit of the arm. The water is too dark to see more."

"That's enough," I said, reasserting my all too tentative authority. "Everyone off the log. We're going back to the road and wait until Deputy Grimes arrives."

"I'll call him," T-shirt guy said as he started thumbing his

9

cell. He was still on the trail a couple of feet short of the log. As those nearest him obeyed my order to retreat, he took a few steps back to let others pass, possibly crushing endangered foliage. But it was too late to admonish him to stay on the trail. "What do you want me to tell him?" he asked.

"Tell him what we've seen and ask him to meet us on the road at the entrance to the bog trail," I said. Several people continued to stand their ground, mesmerized by the hand poking out of the pond, as if waiting for the magician to reveal the trick. "Now, let's *all* turn around and head back."

"But aren't we going to wait and see what, uh, *who* is in the water?" someone asked.

"No, *we* are going to return to where we started by the road and wait for Deputy Grimes to arrive." I hated having to say the same obvious thing over and over. They were, after all, adults. Then I saw a young woman surreptitiously thumbing her phone. "And I repeat, no photos or calls to anyone. Got that?" I glared at the woman until she rolled her eyes at me and slowly slipped her phone into her pocket. It crossed my mind that someone could already have recorded the event. But even though I was technically "in charge" of the group, I didn't actually have any authority to tell them what they could or couldn't do under the circumstances. Any instructions of that nature would have to come from Deputy Grimes. Nevertheless, it seemed worthwhile to play the bog preservation card to keep things under control.

"One of the reasons we need to stay mum about this is that we can't have people traipsing around here," I said. "We need to protect the vegetation. So please don't encourage any looky-loos, okay? Even good friends. There will be plenty of time later to talk about this. Whatever 'this' is."

There was a lot of grumbling and mumbled conversations as we made our way back up the hill and along the narrow trail to the road, but I didn't see any more cell phones. I suspected that some of the complaining and conversations had to do with me. They seemed to be accepting my leadership, but they didn't have to like it. I'm told I can be intimidating. I not only tend to be assertive and direct, but I'm tall and have pale blue-gray eyes that some say are appealing but others apparently find disturbing. I've had them all my life, so to me they're just normal.

When we finally reached the point at the top of the hill where the trail turned to grass, I wended my way past those in back until I caught up with T-shirt guy. "Did you get through to Deputy Grimes?" I asked.

"No. It's his day off. Deputy Evans was there. He's on his way."

"What did you tell him?"

"Just that there might be a body in the pond."

"And he didn't offer to bring in Deputy Grimes?"

"Nope."

There were only two deputies on the island, Grimes and Evans. I didn't know Evans all that well; he had only been on the island a few months. But I did know that he had almost zero experience in law enforcement, so it seemed to me that, under the circumstances, he should have immediately contacted Grimes. Maybe he saw the discovery of a body as an opportunity to soak up some publicity and make a name for himself. Not a smart move, but then it wasn't my call.

Deputy Evans was just pulling up as we got back to the road. I asked our young volunteer to keep an eye on everyone and make sure they didn't use their cell phones. She reluctantly agreed. Several people trailed after me as I headed over to meet Evans. I didn't bother waving them off. Now that an official had arrived, I was no longer in charge.

"I understand there's a body," Deputy Evans said, as he got

out of his black Sheriff's SUV and looked around as if uncertain who he should be talking to. He was a short man, thin body and thinning hair, with the hint of a belly above his belt.

"Well, we saw a hand extending upward from the pond," I said. "I'm assuming it's attached to someone." The others murmured agreement. "Do you need to contact Deputy Grimes?" I asked. Hint, hint.

"No," he said, figuratively hitching up his pants. "I can handle this." He started pushing past us, then paused. "Ah, can you show me where it is?"

"Have you ever been to the bog before?" I glanced down at his pressed uniform slacks and polished leather street shoes. He apparently took his grooming seriously.

"No."

"Well, you should probably be wearing boots."

"I don't plan on wading in the pond," he said, sounding defensive.

"The bog is a damp environment," I explained. I could have been more explicit, but given his attitude, I was caring less and less about his shoes.

"Just show me, okay?"

"Shouldn't you tell the others what you want them to do while we're gone?" It wasn't my job to tell him what he ought to be doing, but he seemed clueless, and it irritated me.

"They can wait here."

I confess that I was very close to letting him make a mess of the situation. I had to reach deep to find my better self before saying, "You do realize it will take us at least twenty minutes to get there? By the time you check out the hand and we walk back, it will have been almost an hour. Are you sure you want to leave everyone standing around next to the road all that time?" I wasn't at all sure if they *would* hang around on their own until we returned, but they definitely needed some instructions.

"That long?" He seemed to be starting to get the picture. "Okay, they can leave."

"Ah," my better self was struggling with my desire to let this arrogant dimwit ruin his shoes *and* his reputation. "Look, if there *is* a body, then I assume you'll have to bring in people from Seattle. They will probably want to take statements from this group. We already have their names and contact information, so that's no problem. But don't you think you should mention something to them about not saying anything until you know more? We wouldn't want a lot of sightseers showing up here. They could mess up what may turn out to be a crime scene."

Somehow I didn't think he would care about the environment of the bog, but I felt confident that, like me, he'd seen a zillion television shows where someone got in trouble for letting people trample a crime scene.

"Right. Okay, I'll do that." The two who had been standing there listening to the exchange drifted off after him to hear what he was going to say to the group. Meanwhile, I finally did what I should have done earlier, I got out my cell phone and looked up the emergency number for Deputy Grimes.

Deputy Larry Grimes had grown up on the island, leaving to go to college and then through law enforcement training. He married his high school sweetheart, and they moved back to the island about eight years ago when he managed to land one of the two deputy positions. Grimes might be local, but he had a lot of experience with law enforcement and, from my observations, he seemed level-headed and committed to the island community. Evans, on the other hand, was neither local nor level-headed. That, combined with his lack of experience, didn't seem like the right credentials for overseeing the current situation.

He answered on the second ring. "Grimes," he said in his official voice. I'd met him on numerous occasions but didn't know him well enough to be on a first-name basis.

"This is Lew Lewis," I said. Then I quickly summarized what had happened and what was about to happen and was not surprised when he said to wait until he got there before heading back into the bog. Now all I had to do was inform Deputy Evans that I had gone behind his back to notify his supervisor about the situation. It was going to be a bit awkward.

"Who were you talking to?" Deputy Evans asked as he rejoined me. His irritated tone seemed justified since I had encouraged him to tell the others to keep things mum until we knew more.

Trying to keep the self-satisfaction out of my voice, I said, "I called Deputy Grimes. He's on his way and asked us to wait."

Evans' eyebrows became a straight line over his eyes, almost joining in the middle of his face, as his mouth compressed in a parallel line. It was not an attractive look. At the same time that I was taking in his displeasure with what I had done, I was aware of people heading for their cars. Their abbreviated tour and my stint as a tour guide were officially over.

While Deputy Evans prowled around near the entrance to the bog, I got the clipboard with the names of participants from the volunteer, thanked her for her work, and gave her permission to head off with the others. The only tour participant who was still around was T-shirt guy. I couldn't help noticing that his tennis shoes were covered in brown slime and bits of debris. Nice.

He came over to me. "Is there anything more I can do?"

"Deputy Grimes is on his way. Thank you for making the call."

After all, it wasn't his fault that Evans had been on duty at the time. He seemed reluctant to leave but slowly turned and headed away.

Deputy Evans didn't have much to say to me as we waited for his colleague. At one point he muttered something about it being *his* shift, but he left it at that, pacing back and forth as if eager to get going. He didn't ask me anything about the bog or what we had seen, and I didn't offer any details. I was both annoyed with having to hang around and curious about what would be found.

We didn't have long to wait. Deputy Grimes arrived wearing casual clothes and boots. He was a compact man, nondescript but appealing, with neatly trimmed brown hair and a face that looked equally as if it might break into a smile as into a scowl. "I forgot to bring a camera," he said as he got out of his car.

"I have my phone," I said.

"That will have to do, I guess. The camera on my phone isn't that great."

His response seemed less than gracious, but it probably reflected the fact that he was more upset by the situation than his calm demeanor suggested. If that hand *was* attached to a body, this would be a big deal on our low-crime island where minor theft or occasional vandalism to an abandoned house or building were among the worst violations the deputies usually had to cope with.

Grimes glanced down at Deputy Evans' shoes but said nothing. That told me everything I needed to know about their relationship.

I took the lead and started down the trail. Grimes asked me who had been present and who specifically had been on the log when the hand was spotted. Then he asked what they had been told to do when they left.

Evans jumped in. "I, uh, followed procedure and asked them not to speak about the discovery of a body until they were given permission to do so."

His "following procedures" comment made me smile, but I could have cared less if he took credit for doing what he should have known to do in the first place.

Grimes suddenly stopped and turned back to Evans. "I wasn't thinking," he said. "We need to have someone at the road to make sure no one comes down here. You need to go back. In case word spreads in spite of what you told everyone."

"But . . ., was the only word Evans managed to get out before Grimes cut him off.

"If there's a body, we have to preserve the crime scene. If we don't, there will be hell to pay." He turned back to me and indicated that we should continue. Evans' eyebrows and mouth were doing that straight-line thing again, but he turned back as instructed.

"Any chance it isn't real?" Deputy Grimes asked when we were far enough away that his colleague couldn't hear. The island had a reputation for being quirky at times. "Keep Vashon Weird" was a local bumper sticker that most residents considered a great motto for the community.

"It looked real to me," I said.

"Was this the first tour of the year?"

"Yes, but there were several Island Land Stewards' members here the day before yesterday to spruce up the trail. I think they would have noticed a hand reaching up out of the pond."

We walked in silence a while. Then, as if thinking out loud, Grimes said, "We'll have to notify the King County Major Crimes Unit—if it *is* a body."

"Anyone reported missing on the island?" I asked. Assuming the hand was connected to a body, that might provide a clue about the victim's identity. Of course, if the hand was real but there was no body attached, that would still require an investigation. A gruesome one.

"Not that I know of," Grimes said. "Although people sometimes wait a day or two to report that sort of thing."

There were approximately 11,000 people on Vashon Island year-round, but the population swelled to almost 20,000 during the summer. Only a 20-minute ferry ride from West Seattle, our island attracted a lot of visitors. Especially when the weather was nice. The hand could definitely belong to an off-islander, but it seemed to me that it was more likely to be a local. The bog used to be a favorite drinking spot for teenagers before they'd torn down the old shed where they hung out. There was something exciting and spooky about being out in the bog after dark with the whisper of ghosts and closeness of the trees. Like walking through a cemetery at midnight. An occasional group of teenagers still slipped into the bog at night after having a little too much to drink. But if there was a body, and if there had been some kind of accident that happened because of a dare or a mishap during a drinking spree, why hadn't someone reported it?

We maneuvered past the tree that hung over the path, careful not to step in the soft mud, and continued on.

"I moved here just after there was a homicide on the island," I commented. "The landlord who shot his tenant." I remembered reading that the young landlord had claimed that his middle-aged tenant had come after him with a sword, quite an impressive weapon from the pictures in the local paper. The only other homicide on the island that I knew of occurred four years before that when a middle-school custodian strangled his 17-year-old daughter during an argument over her educational future. Both seemed like strange crimes to me. One might even say "weird." And now this.

"It's been that long, has it?"

"Yeah, I've been living here almost ten years." I paused, then added, "And I'm still not considered an official Islander."

"You have to have grown up here." Deputy Grimes smiled. "You might make 'honorary' Islander if you stay around long enough."

We were approaching the log. I heard Grimes take a deep breath as if bracing himself for what was ahead. I wasn't feeling anything but curiosity, but then, I wouldn't have to deal with the aftermath. Once I had shown Grimes the site, my work was done.

The hand was still there, as if beckoning someone to reach down and help pull him out. I hadn't noticed earlier, but the wrist and shirt sleeve cuff were hung up on a limb sticking out of the water. If not for that limb, the hand would most likely have disappeared beneath the surface.

I stood back while Grimes knelt down and examined the appendage. "Well, the hand is definitely real, male, not that young." He leaned over and peered into the pond. "Can't see anything," He stood up and turned to me. "It would be nice to know what we're dealing with here before calling in the County."

"We could probe with a stick," I offered. "That would at least tell us if there's something there."

"I don't want to disturb anything . . .," he said. "But I also don't want to take a chance that this hand slips off and maybe sinks before we check it out. Okay, where do we find a stick?"

I took my collapsible walking stick from my pack and handed it to him. "Be careful kneeling on the edge of the log," I warned. "It could give way."

He nodded. "I've been on the tour," he said as he unfolded my walking stick and locked it into position. Then he got down on his knees and gingerly prodded the water below the hand. I could tell he was moving the stick along something solid, following it down into the depths. "It's definitely attached to a body," he said. He looked up at me. "The pond isn't very deep here. The body seems to be resting on the bottom."

"Must not have been here very long," I said. "Don't bodies come back to the surface in a day or two?"

He smiled. "Watch a few detective shows, huh?" Then he nodded. "That's my understanding. At least in warm weather and in fresh water like this." He stayed on his knees at the edge of the log, considering. "Okay," he said, "think this stick is strong enough to bring the body to the surface so we can see who it is?" He studied the hand. "From the angle of the arm, and the way the body is positioned, my guess is he's facing up."

I nodded, feeling guilty about the twinge of excitement I was experiencing. But if there was a body there, I wanted a chance to see if it was anyone I knew. Partly for admittedly ghoulish reasons, partly to make sure it wasn't a friend or acquaintance.

"Here, hold onto me," he instructed, extending his hand. We locked fingers while he used his other hand to move the stick down along the body's arm and under the torso. Then, straining against the weight of the water-slogged body, he slowly, very slowly, began dragging it to the surface.

I held onto his hand and mentally willed the body upward as Grimes gritted his teeth and struggled to overcome the body's resistance to return to the world of the living.

Finally, a pale face gently broke the surface, open eyes staring at us.

"Jake Williams," we said in unison.

Chapter 3
The Grieving Widow

"Dead," Deputy Grimes added unnecessarily. We stared back at the face a few moments before Grimes, still holding up the body, asked me to take some pictures. I let go of his hand, got out my phone, and quickly took a shot from above, then knelt down and took a couple of close-ups from different angles.

"Hurry," Grimes said, "I can't keep him up much longer."

"Done," I said.

Grimes retracted the stick, and Jake Williams sank back into the pond, his hand still hung up on the limb.

"Damn," Grimes said with feeling.

Jake Williams was a long-time Vashon resident, a fellow board member, and a well-known advocate for various causes. Although well-liked generally, he had recently become controversial for his promotion of the wilding of the island. When a cougar had swum over from the peninsula and taken up residence, Williams had fought those who wanted to capture and remove it. He had also vehemently opposed those who wanted to kill it. In addition, he'd been a strong supporter of leaving the coyotes on the island alone. He'd freely acknowledged that they occasionally went after a chicken or a small pet, maybe even the odd sheep, but believed the fact that they subsisted primarily on small rodents and plants made them acceptable cohabitants. In his opinion, it was up to their owners to take precautions to keep domestic animals safe. Not surprisingly, many of the local farmers and pet owners strongly disagreed.

I helped Grimes to his feet, took back my walking stick, collapsed it, and put it in my pack. As I did so I wondered if I should have kept it away from the other stuff in my pack. The candy bar would have to go.

"You need to see these," I said, holding out my phone. "It looks like he hit his head on something."

Grimes clicked through the pictures I'd taken.

"What do you think?" I asked. "An accident?"

Grimes didn't answer. He had his own cell phone out and was holding it up in different directions and at different angles, trying to get reception.

"I'll send these pictures to you," I said.

"And delete them from your phone," he added, moving a few feet down the log toward solid ground as he continued moving his cell phone this way and that.

"This is a fluky area for reception," I said.

"I need to switch carriers," he complained.

Once we reached the trail he apparently got a few bars because he stopped to punch in a number. He started talking to someone as we walked, pausing to swear and retreat a few steps whenever he lost reception. For the most part I was able to use my cell phone almost anywhere on the island—for the most part. There were blank spots here and there, not always for an obvious reason. It was part of island life, like power outages, horse poop on trails, and waiting in line for the ferry.

When he completed his call, he said, "They'll get a detective and crime scene team over here as soon as possible. Along with some support to cordon off the area and keep the perimeter clear. We obviously can't do even that on our own."

"What about Jeannie?" I asked as I put my arm around the sloping tree and swung to firm ground. "Does the wife get notified by them or by you?" I wasn't exactly a friend of Jeannie's, but we always chatted at events or when we ran into each other in town. She had made me feel welcome when I first moved to the island; I felt a certain connection.

Grimes seemed to give that some thought. "How about by 'us'?" he said.

"Ah, by 'us' do you mean you and me?" I hadn't seen that one coming.

"I want to leave Evans to guard the entrance. The detective they're sending may not like us talking to Jeannie before they do, but I think we need to let her know before the rumors start to fly."

Curiosity struggled with my discomfort. On the one hand, I wanted to know why she hadn't reported her husband missing. Not that it was any of my business. Still, I couldn't help wondering. On the other hand, I'm not very good with people in emotional crises.

"I think it would help to have a woman there," Grimes added, then paused. "Oh hell, I just don't want to do it alone. I've known Jeannie a long time. This is going to be an incredible shock to her. I'd really appreciate you coming with me."

"Sure," was all I could manage. Even though I was anything but "sure" about my ability to provide whatever the "woman along" function might be. I never seemed able to find the right words to soothe people when they were upset. And as a non-hugger, I'm not a natural when it comes to providing physical comfort either. But I could make tea and hand someone Kleenex if needed.

Deputy Evans wasn't at all pleased to be left behind. Especially when Deputy Grimes informed him that he intended to be back in time to lead the detectives and crime scene people to the site. He added that if by chance they arrived before he returned, Evans wasn't to proceed without him.

"I'm just supposed to hang around?" Evans asked, making it clear with his tone that it was an absurd idea.

"Yes. Keep people out of there. And say nothing if someone comes by and starts asking questions. Absolutely no press, you understand? Tell them it's police business, nothing more. And call me if you need help."

———

It was my first time riding in a police vehicle with the word SHERIFF printed on the side in huge block print. I wondered if anyone who saw me would know I was helping out or if they would assume I was under arrest. I supposed being in the passenger seat helped.

"Should I call you Lew or Lavender?" Grimes asked when we got under way.

"Lew, please." I'd always hated my name. Lavender Lewis. My mother was a single mom. We lived in a commune in Alaska when I was young. In some ways it was a great childhood. Except for the strictly enforced gender roles. And the home-schooling. And being stuck with a first name that couldn't be shortened to anything other than "Lav." The other kids loved that. As soon as I started attending a nearby village high school–by order of the state, I tried getting classmates to call me "Lew." Some kids turned Lew Lewis into "Lulu." From my point of view that was barely a notch up from "Lav." A supportive teacher encouraged me to embrace the name rather than fight it. Fighting with the other kids would only encourage them, she'd told me. She was right, of course, but as I grew taller and stronger, I never turned my back on a fight, verbal or physical. By my senior year, no one was calling me Lulu.

"What should I call *you*?" I asked.

"Oh, call me Larry. Everyone does."

I didn't point out that Deputy Evans called him "Grimes." Maybe he was Larry to islanders and near islanders but not to colleagues with less seniority.

"And we don't have to say anything about Jake possibly hitting his head on something. At this point we don't know cause of death, okay?"

"Of course."

"To Jeannie or to anyone else. Let the detectives do their job."

———

The Williams's house was set back in a clearing among the trees down a meandering gravel driveway. It was a two-story Craftsman with a covered front porch and pots of colorful flowers strategically placed to get the morning sun. The tidy house was surrounded by a circle of lawn with a garden to one side enclosed by a tall wire mesh deer fence. Everything looked well-cared for.

There was a dark blue car in the driveway in front of the single car garage. I couldn't help but notice the round sticker on the back window. It was a picture of a coyote with a red line drawn through it. Obviously, Jeannie's car. I wondered if the sticker had been a not-so-subtle message to her husband.

The front door was open.

Jeannie appeared on the porch before we reached the front steps, looking worried

"Larry," she said. "Lew." She stared at us expectantly a moment before inviting us in. Larry looked so solemn that I knew she could guess that we weren't there with good news, but she didn't press for information right away.

"Can I get you something to drink?" she asked as she waved us to some comfortable looking chairs in the sunlit living room.

"No, why don't you sit down with us, Jeannie," Larry said.

Jeannie hesitated a moment, then collapsed into a chair. "It's Jake, isn't it?"

Larry nodded. "He was discovered this morning . . ."

Jeannie started sobbing before Larry could finish the sentence. He glanced in my direction and motioned for me to go over to her. I had agreed to come along for a specific function that I'd been hoping to avoid, but this was the moment of truth. I obediently went over, knelt next to her chair and put my hand on her arm. She reflexively grabbed my hand. "What's happened? Is he . . .?"

Dammit, I wasn't supposed to be the one who gave her the news about her husband's death. But she was asking me directly, fixing me with those oh-so-sad eyes. What choice did I have? "Yes, I'm sorry, Jeannie. He's . . ., uh, gone." Had I really said that he was "gone"? What a wuss.

Larry sat across the room looking uncomfortable. When he didn't say anything, I asked the obvious question: "Do you know where he went last night?" Just as it hadn't been my job to give her the news about her husband's death, it wasn't my job to question her. But it was *my* hand she was squeezing as if it were a flex ball.

"No." She put her head down but didn't let go of my hand.

"Did you call anyone when he didn't come home?" Out of the corner of my eye I saw Larry frowning at me. If he wanted to hold her hand, then he could ask the questions.

Jeannie managed a soft "no" in response. Then she added, "We have separate bedrooms. I didn't know he hadn't come home until this morning." She let go of my hand to take out a Kleenex and blow her nose. "At first I thought he was sleeping in. And when I finally checked and he wasn't in his room, I thought maybe he had gone out early for a cup of coffee. His car was gone."

I gave Larry a few seconds to jump in, but when he didn't, I just had to ask: "Does he often go out early without saying anything?"

"No." She hesitated. "We'd had an argument, about Woody, my cat, and I thought . . . oh, it was so silly." She started sobbing again. I continued kneeling beside the chair, wondering why she hadn't bothered to ask how he had died. I looked over at Larry and raised my eyebrows.

He got up and came over to us. "Can I get you some water?" he asked. She nodded and he left the room. It seemed to me that he was having a serious avoidance issue.

Jeannie looked up at me. "Was it his heart?"

The question seemed a little late to me. And why didn't she ask "where" and "when" it happened? Or was it unfair to expect someone to think rationally when they were emotionally overwhelmed?

"Larry can give you the details," I said. What was taking him so long? "But I don't think they will know the cause of death for a while."

"He had a weak heart," she said. Then she put her head in her hands and cried some more. At that point Larry came into the room with a glass of water. He set it down on the table next to her chair. I stood up and motioned for him to take over.

He nodded agreement but remained standing. After a few moments of silence, he asked, "He drives a Subaru Forester, doesn't he?"

"Yes," Jeannie said softly, straightening up and eyeing the glass of water. Larry picked it up and held it out to her. She accepted the glass as though it were a gift and took a few sips before handing it back to him.

I had seen Jake driving his ancient green Subaru on numerous occasions, but I didn't remember seeing the car anywhere in the vicinity of the bog before the tour. Then again, there had been a string of cars parked alongside the road. Maybe it had been there and I hadn't noticed.

"Can I call someone to come over and be with you?" Larry asked. "Your daughter?"

Jeannie was staring at the hands folded in her lap as if trying to figure out who they belonged to. Finally, she said, "Her number is in my phone." She pointed to the dining room table. "It's over there."

Larry retrieved the phone and conveniently disappeared again to make the call while I kept muttering "there, there," awkwardly living through the time it took for him to return. At that point Jeannie said she needed to go to the bathroom, and Larry and I gratefully stepped outside.

"Thank you," he said to me. "That was tough. But her daughter should be here shortly. She only lives down the road."

"Don't you think it was odd that she didn't ask how it happened or where he was found?" I asked.

"Grief affects people in different ways," he said.

I was mulling that over when we heard a car approaching. A gray Mini-Cooper with red stripe accents flew up the driveway, creating a billow of dust in its wake. It came to an abrupt stop, and a young woman leapt out, leaving the car door open. Jeannie's daughter looked like she had come straight from working in the garden. She was wearing a dirt-smudged man's shirt over an old pair of jeans and had on a pair of bright flowered garden shoes. "Is she inside?" she asked, brushing past us.

"I'll check in later," Larry called after her retreating figure.

He paused for a moment as if considering something. Then he went over and pushed the car door closed. As we walked toward his SUV, he repeated: "Grief affects people in different ways."

Chapter 4
Friends & Other Hazards

When we got back to the bog trailhead, there was Deputy Evans, shoulders erect, still pacing back and forth, Robocop on guard duty.

"I'm supposed to meet some friends at the Roasterie," I said to Grimes, a.k.a. Larry, edging away in the direction of my car, desperate to escape. "Do you need me for anything else?"

Grimes thought for a moment before giving me permission to leave, warning me that the detective from the King County Sheriff's Office would most likely want to talk to me.

To be honest, I hadn't made plans to meet anyone, but I needed a good cup of coffee and the Roasterie was the place to get it. They boasted about specializing in fair trade coffee roasted on site in the *traditional* way. I wasn't entirely sure what that meant. All I knew was that it was really fine coffee.

I found a parking space right in front of the 100+ years old building. My Thermo-Tect Lime Green Prius, a one-time experiment by Toyota to increase a vehicle's solar reflectivity, looked a bit flashy next to the historic white wood-frame structure. You couldn't prove it by me if Toyota's experiment had been successful, but I liked the color of my car. It was discreetly flamboyant and easy to find in a parking lot.

The one-story building that housed the Roasterie looked like an old-fashioned barracks at a summer camp. The outside porch ran the length of the storefront, until the structure gave way to several other businesses housed in the continuation of the long narrow building. To the left as you went up the wide stairs of the porch there was a wooden shelf where those who liked their coffee unadulterated could choose between three different blends kept warm in stainless steel air pots. For those who wanted to sit outside, there were a couple of small tables with mismatched chairs as well as a wooden bench. They were always fully occupied in the summer and used by the more hearty islanders during the winter.

Once inside, it was as though you'd stepped back in time. There was something about the uneven wood floors and the wood walls with open shelves full of glass jars containing coffee, tea and spices that seemed to harken back to a simpler time when everything didn't come in market-tested packaging. I loved the mingling of smells and the old-fashioned look of the place.

I'd barely taken two steps toward the counter when several voices called, "Lew! Over here, Lew!"

Darryl and Lisa Daniels were at a table in the corner by the ornate upright piano, along with my good friend Jay Jackson. All three were frantically waving me over. I'd met Darryl and Lisa, both teachers, at a school fundraiser my first year on the island. We've been friends ever since. JJ and I go way back, to when we were HR professionals in Seattle. JJ moved to Vashon because he had hooked up with a local man who was supposed to be his forever guy. It didn't last, but JJ stayed on the Island. After visiting him a couple of times, I started reading the real estate ads. It didn't take me long to decide that the island was where I wanted to live too. It was just the right blend of rural direct-market farmers and coffee-addicted urbanites.

I gave them the "just a minute" signal and headed over to buy my coffee. In an instant JJ was by my side. "So glad you showed up," he said. "We've been dying to hear all about it."

"About what?" I said, although I had no doubt what "it" was.

JJ poked me in the ribs. "Don't get smart with me, girlfriend."

How long had it been since the aborted tour, a couple of hours? So much for the warning to the participants not to talk to anyone about what they'd seen.

"Coffee first," I said.

"Jan," he yelled past me, "Get this woman some coffee."

Jan pretended to ignore the request, but I saw her start my Americano. Everyone loves JJ and his irrepressible, fun-loving personality. Me, not everyone loves so much. My abruptness and dry humor aren't always appreciated. Although it tends to work to my advantage in the professional arena. Most of my clients have serious problems and expect a no-nonsense approach from their HR investigator. Early on in my career I realized that my skill set wasn't in people management. What I liked and was good at was figuring things out, interviewing people, questioning them to get at the heart of a complaint. Being somewhat aloof doesn't mean I can't read people, and my demeanor often causes them to tell me more than they might normally share or confess to.

"Word has it that you were on hand–no pun intended—at the bog tour." JJ gave me a big smile. He has a wide mouth and an even row of white teeth, so his smile is impressive.

"The participants were warned not to talk about it," I said, a bit peeved that word had spread so quickly. Although I wasn't actually surprised. It was hard to keep anything under wraps on the island.

"And who thought a warning to stay mum was going to work on Vashon Island?"

Jan glanced in my direction as she continued working on my Americano. "I heard about Jake," she said. "That's a shame. He was a nice guy."

"Jake!" Jay said. "Not Jake Williams."

Even though word travels fast on the island, I was surprised that Jan knew who the victim was already. "Mind if I ask where you heard that?" It didn't really matter to me, but I was curious about the grapevine.

Jan hesitated, then apparently noticed that JJ was also interested in her answer. "Megan at the pharmacy. She over-heard her boss talking on the phone with Jeannie's daughter who called about getting a sedative for her mother."

My guess was that the authorities didn't expect to keep the victim's name secret for long in this close-knit community, but it seemed to me that the speed with which the victim's name had become public knowledge might have set some kind of record. At least I didn't have to worry about being blamed for blabbing the news.

"Jake Williams," JJ repeated as I picked up my coffee and we headed to the table in the far corner. "Damn. The hand belonged to Jake Williams."

I sat down in front of the glass enclosed shadow box that displayed all the items the store's coffee purchasers had found in the burlap bags of coffee beans they'd imported between 1985-1989. Nails, screws, buttons, cotter pins, bottle caps, rocks. Everything imaginable. Even though the process for detecting foreign objects in coffee beans was undoubtedly better these days, seeing that display always made me uneasy.

"You won't believe it," JJ said, taunting Darryl and Lisa with a "guess what I know" tone.

"Sooo . . .?" Lisa said, looking at me with her clear hazel eyes. She and Darryl fit right in with the outdoorsy look of so many on the Island. Casual clothes, practical shoes, and healthy complexions.

When I didn't respond right away, JJ asked, "Aren't you going to tell them?"

"You go ahead," I said, taking a sip of coffee, breathing in the rich aroma as the hot liquid slid down my throat.

"No, you were the one there," JJ said. "You should tell them."

Darryl jumped in: "One of you just spit it out!"

I wasn't trying to be evasive, but in that moment, the discovery of Jake's body felt somehow personal to me, more than just fodder for local gossip. On the other hand, if the situation had been reversed, I knew I would have been asking them about what they had seen. "It was Jake Williams," I said finally.

"No!" Lisa sounded sincerely shocked. Then, "Oh, poor Jeannie." It was too bad that Grimes had taken me instead of Lisa to tell Jeannie about her husband's death. I had no doubt that Lisa would have known the right words. She would have rubbed Jeannie's back and murmured "there, there" in a gentle and comforting way. That was the kind of person she was.

"What happened?" Darryl asked. "Did he fall into the pond? Why didn't he just climb out? Did he hit his head on something?"

"So many questions," I chided. Then added, "They don't know yet. The county detectives are on their way to investigate."

"It's strange," Lisa said. "I mean, why was he in Whistling Pete Bog in the first place?"

"What if it wasn't an accident?" JJ said, raising his eyebrows suggestively. He hadn't interacted with Jake much, so he was obviously thinking of Jake's death as a mystery rather than as a personal loss.

"What do you mean?" Darryl said.

"What if someone . . . pushed him in?"

Darryl scoffed. "Come on, get real."

Then we all stared at JJ, waiting for him to defend his suggestion.

"Well, it's always the spouse, right? And it's rumored that Jeannie has been upset with Jake because of his stand on the wilding of the Island. Her beloved cat Woody disappeared about a week ago. There are signs up everywhere asking if anyone has seen him. Jeannie's convinced it was either the cougar or a coyote that got him."

"No one kills their spouse over a cat," Darryl said.

"I said *beloved* cat," JJ emphasized. "She doted on it. They got it just after the last kid left the nest."

"Woody was a nice cat," I offered. I liked cats. They didn't demand much from you and never expected you to say the right thing.

"You're a cat lady," Darryl said to me, "would you murder someone over a cat?"

I felt myself bristle. I gave him the stink eye and said, "Depends. I might be tempted if someone started referring to me as a 'cat lady.'"

Darryl leaned back and pretended to be scared. "Remind me not to ask you to babysit," he said. I didn't point out that they never had.

In spite of feeling bad about Jake's death, once they started talking about it, even I couldn't resist speculating about whether it was an accident or a deliberate act of violence.

"If he was murdered," JJ argued, "it must have happened at or near the pond. No one could have hauled a body that far into the bog."

"Someone could have forced him at gunpoint," Lisa said.

Darryl nodded agreement. "In that case, the most important question is who wanted him dead."

"It could just as easily have been a heart attack," I offered. I didn't mention that it looked like he had been struck from behind. That didn't prove it wasn't an accident, and besides, it was up to the police to determine and announce cause of death.

"Let's hope it was something like that," JJ said. "If it was murder, then there's a murderer at large on the island."

Finally, I changed the subject. "So, has your sister had any luck finding a place to live, Lisa?"

"Nothing yet. But Marie is working on it."

Marie had been my realtor when I moved to the island. Although we weren't good friends, we kept in touch. "She's good; she'll find her something."

"I hope so. The prices, you wouldn't believe how expensive houses are now."

A lot of islanders felt there was a housing crisis. The foot ferry to downtown Seattle had made commuting viable, and vacation homes that had been in families for generations were being sold to professionals who worked in the city.

"We're actually lucky there's limited water on the island," Darryl said. "Otherwise there'd be houses and apartments springing up everywhere."

We were interrupted when my cell rang. Well, rang might not be the right word. I had a recording of coyotes barking and yowling as my ring tone. I liked it, but some people found it unnerving.

"You may want to change that," JJ whispered, glancing around at the people seated at nearby tables. It had definitely caught their attention. I hit "answer" and mouthed "sorry" as I got up and headed outside to take the call. The caller identified himself as Deputy Grimes. Given how formal he sounded, I assumed someone was standing next to him and that saying it was Larry didn't seem appropriate. He informed me, somewhat stiffly, that I was wanted back at the bog. The King County detective, Harlan Crane, had some questions for me.

——————

Grimes was waiting for me next to the road when I pulled up. He indicated I was to join a group of men standing near the entrance to the trail and mumbled something about Crane from major crimes being in charge of the investigation. He hit the words "in charge" as if to say that not only was Crane taking over, the Vashon deputies were not considered part of the team. Deputy Evans was standing near the entrance to the trail, arms crossed, still on guard, and not looking at all happy.

"Thought you might want to know that we found Jake's car," Grimes said. "It was parked on the highway."

"So, he either walked to the bog from the highway or went with someone," I said, thinking out loud. That suggested he may have gone willingly. But it didn't eliminate the possibility that he was brought to the bog under duress.

"Looks that way."

"That reminds me, I should mention that word has spread; everyone knows the victim was Jake Williams."

"It figures," Grimes said. He nodded in the direction of a tall thin man whose jacket sleeves were too short for his long arms. "The tall one is Harlan Crane, the King County Detective—with a capital 'D'—the one assigned to the case."

At that moment Detective Crane turned toward us, and I couldn't help but think of another Crane, one from a story I had read over and over as a child. We had a tiny library in the commune where I'd grown up, mostly classics, very little specifically for children. We were supposed to *do* things, not sit around and read. But I managed to steal away with a book often enough to indulge myself without getting into too much trouble. One of my favorites was Washington Irving's *The Legend of Sleepy Hollow*. His description of Ichabod Crane as an "old scarecrow who has escaped the cornfield" was a perfect fit for Detective Crane. None of his parts seemed proportional. He had a smallish head on a long neck above narrow shoulders. As we drew near, I saw that his large nose dominated his face, although it was rivaled for attention by huge ears that stuck straight out from his head.

After we were introduced, he perfunctorily thanked me for coming and asked if I would mind walking back to the scene of the crime with him. It almost sounded like I had a choice, but I knew I didn't. Grimes wasn't asked to join us. It was just Crane and me. He took the lead and set a fast pace, picking up speed when he saw that I was keeping up. With my long legs there was no problem matching his stride.

On the way, I answered a few questions about the island and about the victim. It felt like he was sizing me up rather than gathering information. I had a million questions of my own but was reluctant to ask them. I sensed he wouldn't be forthcoming, and that would tick me off, and then I would say something I'd regret, and that, in turn, would close off any possibility of a good relationship with him or his team. It wasn't worth taking the chance. Especially at this point when I probably knew as much as they did.

When we got to the log, there were crime scene people all over the place. A young man with a fancy camera was pushing his way through the thick brush surrounding the pond, apparently to get yet another angle on the spot where the body was found. Someone in a wetsuit popped out of the water and started making his way toward the log. The body itself had been removed and was lying on a canvas alongside the trail.

"This is a very fragile bog," I said to Crane, unable to keep the disapproval out of my voice.

"Sorry, but we do need to search the area."

I started to say something more, then clamped my mouth shut. They would do what they had to do. And nature would heal its wounds in time. A long time.

"I understand you knew Jake Williams," Crane said.

"Yes." Although I was staring at his body, it seemed strange to hear Jake referred to in the past tense.

"Any thoughts on what happened?"

"Depends on whether it was an accident or not." Take that, Mr. Detective with a capital "D."

He smiled, or grimaced, it was hard to tell which.

"Deputy Grimes tells me that there are few secrets on the island." He looked at me for confirmation and I nodded. "I would rather everyone didn't know it was a homicide until we have a chance to talk to a few people...?" He ended the statement as a question. I nodded again, although there was no way I could promise anything would remain a secret, even if I kept my end of the bargain.

"Is it a homicide for sure?" I asked, hoping for more details.

"Yes," he replied. "As I'm sure you've surmised. You're the one who took pictures of the deceased's head, correct?"

"Yes." I wanted to ask if they knew whether a blow to the side of the head was the cause of death, but it seemed to me that they were only guessing at this point. Unless there was something he was holding back, like a bullet wound to the heart. Grimes had exposed most of the torso when he'd brought Jake's body to the surface, however, and I hadn't noticed any damage to the front of the body. That didn't mean there wasn't some hidden injury.

Changing the subject, he said, "Deputy Grimes told me

that you are a member of the group called the Island Land Stewards?"

"Yes. I'm on the board." I knew where he was going with his question, but I could also keep information close to the chest, unless he asked something specific.

"And so was Jake Williams?"

"Yes."

He smiled again, and this time it seemed to reach his eyes. Did he know I was deliberately being succinct, and did he find it amusing because he knew I couldn't keep it up under the circumstances? Or was that giving him too much credit?

"And this, uh, swamp belongs to them?"

"Yes, they bought the *bog* and the surrounding land to *preserve* it." Hint, hint.

"Can you tell me a little about the group and whether there were any tensions between Jake Williams and other members?" No short answer to *that* question. "And his relationship with the community in general—."

Since Crane really was in charge, and since I didn't want to be seen as uncooperative, I gave him what I considered to be an accurate high-level overview of Jake's position in the small community and within the Island Land Stewards. There was one salient piece of information that I passed along. As far as I knew, Jake was almost universally well-liked. Until recently. Once he became the symbol for the wilding of the Island, he had become a flashpoint for those opposed to it.

"Is there anyone in particular I should talk to?" Crane asked.

In spite of the open hostility around the wilding issue, I couldn't think of anyone I would place high on a suspect list.

"There is a quarterly membership meeting this evening that I plan on attending." I didn't have to tell him that there would undoubtedly be talk about what had happened.

"Would you mind keeping your eyes and ears open, maybe take a few notes if anything comes up that we should pursue?" Crane asked.

"Sure," I said. Why not? I wanted Jake's killer caught as much if not more than he did. Whoever had done this had made the island—MY island–feel a little less safe.

And I didn't like that one bit.

Chapter 5
A Close-knit Community Unraveled

The Island Land Stewards rented an older building near the center of town that had once been a small grocery store. It still had that corner grocery look, with a flat space above the door where the name had once been painted. Now there was a large wood sign hung there with the name of the organization engraved between carvings of two evergreens on the left and several birds in flight on the right. In an attempt to modernize its appearance, the building had been painted dark green and the old moss-covered composition roof had been replaced with green metal.

Inside, the main floorspace of the former store had been turned into three offices and a large meeting room. There was also an ample storage area for tables and chairs, a small kitchen and a bathroom. The three offices were for the Executive Director, Andy Barnett; his admin and right hand, Kelly Davis; and their development and outreach associate, Liana Hines. There was also a spare desk for the occasional intern at one end of the storage area.

The Island Land Stewards had 11 board members, a core group of 25 or so who regularly attended quarterly membership meetings, a fair number of volunteers who participated in specific projects, and hundreds of donors. When I first moved to the island I was attracted to the group because of its mission to preserve land for public use and for its environmentalism. I liked to run on trails when not doing my woods version of parkour, so the group seemed a natural fit for my interests. I'd volunteered for a variety of projects and regularly joined work parties to develop and maintain trails. Eventually I found myself on the board.

One thing that initially surprised me about the group was how much they did for the community, in addition to buying and facilitating the preservation of parks and trails. Anything related to the environment or sustainability seemed to fall under their mission. For example, they were dedicated to maintaining threatened ecosystems, everything from salmon streams to farm fields used by migratory birds. Each time a new issue popped up, everyone was willing to jump on board. Until Jake Williams started pushing for the protection of all forms of wildlife as part of Vashon's "natural state."

Then talk of predator control and human-wildlife conflicts became regular topics of discussion. The once convivial gatherings where neighbors caught up on what was happening, ate store-bought cookies and drank lukewarm tea and coffee had turned, more and more frequently of late, into heated arguments about whether cougars and coyotes could coexist with people and their pets and farm animals.

What it meant to stay "wild" on a semi-rural island that had limited public land overall was an interesting and challenging question. Especially when one of the goals for the Island Land Stewards was to strive for food sustainability. You can't do that without farms and farm animals. And once the wild animal population discovered how easy it was to prey on fenced-in livestock and pets for food rather than chasing down a fleet-footed deer, it had become increasingly more difficult to protect the domestic animal population.

The turnout at the quarterly meeting was larger than usual, a mix of members, board members, and volunteers. There was the usual small talk while milling around the snacks table, but I hadn't heard anyone mention Jake until just before people started moving toward the chairs in the main room. At that point an unpredictable lull in conversations caused one person's comment to rise above the shuffling of feet and movement of chairs.

"Jake Williams was asking for it." The indictment reverberated throughout the small room.

After a brief moment of stunned silence, Kelly Davis, Andy Barnett's admin, spoke up in a voice that was much louder than her usual measured speech. "No one deserves to be physically assaulted for taking a stand on an issue."

Andy had been talking to someone at the back of the room and quickly moved forward to call the meeting to order, encouraging people to take their seats. But before he could officially get under way, one of the newer board members made another provocative statement.

"There's no way it's safe to have wild animals on this island."

"There have always been wild animals on Vashon," another member countered.

It went on from there, slowly escalating into sharply divided camps of opinion about wilding and about Jake Williams, with Andy trying and failing to take back control of his meeting and Kelly looking flushed and miserable.

Amazed at the passion and partisanship being displayed by people I thought I knew, some better than others, I started covertly taking notes. Crane would have a lot of suspects from this group alone. And if this was any indication of the depth of feeling in the community as a whole, the list of suspects would grow exponentially.

Unfortunately, someone noticed I was unusually quiet, and I was suddenly in the spotlight—and caught red-handed.

"Lew," a board member seated behind me and one seat to my right said. "What are you doing? What are you writing down?" It could have been an innocent question, but it sounded accusatory.

"Just keeping track of the pro and con arguments," I said. The lie came out before I had time to think about it. Since I'd known and worked with these people for quite a few years, the lie felt like a betrayal.

"We're just voicing our opinions. Some venting. Nothing new," a woman from the front row said, turning around to stare at me.

"Well, a few of us do seem, well, a bit emotional," someone else pointed out.

"That's because we're all on edge. With Jake dying like that."

"Dying 'like what'? That's what we ought to be asking."

Suddenly everyone was looking at me, expecting an explanation because they apparently knew I had been present when Jake's body was discovered.

"That's something I can't tell you," I said truthfully.

"Can't or won't?"

The tone was neutral, but I sensed some hostility behind the question. Before I could answer, someone else asked, "You're not working with those detectives, are you, Lew?"

"Why would you think that?" It was the type of response I typically used in my work to stall for time.

"You talked quite a bit to that tall guy from the county."

That damn small-community grapevine again. They had eyes everywhere. "I was leading the tour group that discovered the body," I pointed out. "Of course, they wanted to talk with me."

"You went with Larry to break the news to Jeannie," someone said.

"And . . . you're taking notes," the person seated behind me repeated. The young woman next to me leaned over and tapped the last thing I had written and asked, "What are those initials?" I'd thought I was being subtle by not using actual names in my notes, but apparently that made me look even more guilty. I felt as though I was on trial and the evidence was mounting fast. At this rate I would never make "Honorary Islander."

"Look," I said, trying to sound reasonable. "No matter which side of the policy argument you're on, we all want to find out what happened to Jake, right?" There were a few nods of agreement, but given the level of energy in the room, no one was quick to let me off the hook. The pack was starting to circle. It was probably easier to be mad at me than at each other.

"So, back to those notes you're taking," my original accuser said.

"By writing down what individuals were saying for and against wilding, I thought I could follow up after the meeting," I ad-libbed. Did what I had said even make sense?

"Why?" My accuser sounded sincerely puzzled.

"Well, I'm hoping the police figure out what happened to Jake. But they don't know the community, and we do. Someone in this room may know something that could be helpful." Someone in this room could even be a murderer, I thought but didn't say it out loud. "They, um, may not realize that what they know is important or even that it's connected to Jake's death. I might be able to surface that information by asking a few questions."

"If you aren't doing this *for* the police, are you trying to play detective on your own?" The question felt both condescending and unfriendly.

Before I could respond, Kelly came to my rescue: "It would be better for us and for the community if we volunteered information rather than looking like we're resisting police efforts." She glanced around at the circle of faces. "And Lew is a trained investigator."

"Well, not exactly," I said quickly. They all knew my consulting work focused on HR investigations, but researching harassment, discrimination and worker misconduct complaints was a long way from investigating a homicide. "I investigate potential HR violations, that's not the same thing."

"But you know how to ask people questions to find out what's going on, right?" Kelly persisted.

What could I say? Asking questions to get at the truth in a situation was at the heart of my profession. "The police don't need my help," I said. "Or want it," I added quickly.

"But didn't you just say you were taking notes because you were going to talk to some of us individually?" someone asked.

They had me there. "We-e-ll, yes. But unofficially. Just to encourage everyone to think about whether they know anything that might be helpful."

Andy looked around the room at the angry faces of his membership. "Keep in mind, we own the bog," he said. "And Jake was a board member. We're already involved in this."

People were eyeing each other, as if trying to get the sense of the group before adding their two cents' worth.

A long-time resident and former board member said, "Larry is a great deputy, but he doesn't have the same authority as a county detective. And people over in Seattle don't understand Vashon. They never have. They think we're a bunch of hippies."

"Hippies and misfits." There was a lot of head nodding in agreement.

A silent consensus seemed to be gaining momentum.

"Lew lives here. She knows the community."

"She can help those detectives see it from our perspective."

I had gone from villain to good guy and liaison to the police without saying a word. It seemed like they were unofficially appointing me to be the designated investigator for the Island Land Stewards. It wasn't a role I wanted, but it was better than being the enemy.

No matter how hard Andy tried to get the meeting back on track, he only partially succeeded. The main issue on the agenda was to discuss whether we should be trying to purchase the Winchell properties. They had been on the market a while, and both were adjacent to land already owned by either the county or the Island Land Stewards.

The general consensus was that we should make an offer on the two side-by-side properties. The appraised value was reasonable enough. The question was whether we could interest the county in partnering with us. There was nothing particularly special about the land other than its location. We were trying to create a trail from one end of the island to the other. The Winchell properties were on that route.

The meeting slowly limped to a close. Then Kelly was suddenly passing around a sheet for everyone to write out their telephone numbers and email addresses. I knew she already had all of that data online, but by having them write down their information themselves, it confirmed that they were agreeing to the interview process. My ad hoc role as their investigator had become official.

Nonetheless, I knew it wasn't a task I should take on without running it past Grimes. Maybe he would want to join me when I met with people, or at least with some of them. Or maybe he would tell me to keep my nose out of police business. Or warn me off because of Crane. I wouldn't know until I talked with him.

––––––

It was dark as I made my way down the path to my walk-in waterfront cabin. There are quite a few walk-in waterfront homes around the island. Usually that's because the hillside behind is too steep to build a road. You can only get to these homes by trail or by water. It was the only way I could afford waterfront, and I liked the idea that my living arrangement was a little offbeat. Besides, the beach in front of my place was all sand, stretching for a quarter of a mile in either direction. A great place to walk. And to swim, if you didn't mind the cold water. And the occasional jellyfish.

My 950 square foot cabin was basically a box snuggled into the wooded hillside. There was 500 square feet on the main floor and 450 above. The second-floor deck gave me access to a small flat area of land in back where I had just enough sun and dirt to grow a few tomatoes, two kinds of lettuce and some padrone peppers. The deck went from the north side of the house around the back, ending at the southeast corner. The cabin was old and not particularly attractive as a structure, but I'd painted it a lovely cobalt blue, and I was pleased with the overall effect. I especially liked the inside where the walls and cabinets and built-in couch were all cedar.

Only about eight of the twenty-five houses and cabins on my walk were owned by full-time residents. The rest were vacation properties, several that had been owned by the same families for generations. The houses on either side of mine belonged to people who showed up sporadically during the summer, usually on weekends, and sometimes they rented out their houses during the winter. At times like tonight, with the houses on both sides dark and empty, it could be a lonely place.

When I stepped inside and my two cats didn't come running up to say hello and start demanding something to eat, I was immediately on guard. I normally never worry about leaving my door unlocked, but tonight things felt different. Not just uncomfortable, but actually a bit scary. I didn't own a gun, but there was a piece of decorative driftwood by the shoe rack next to the door. Since I was feeling spooked, I picked up the piece of wood before going further into my house. It wasn't much of a club, but it was something.

A quick search revealed there was no one on the ground floor. I was about halfway up the steps to the second floor when I heard a noise. My instincts had been right on, there was definitely someone or something, an animal perhaps, but definitely *something uninvited* in my house!

My first impulse was to shout out that I knew there was someone there and that I had a weapon. But before I could open my mouth my brain kicked in and I had second thoughts. A piece of decorative driftwood might be effective against an unarmed intruder if taken by surprise, but it might not be a good match against someone forewarned, especially if they had a real weapon.

Another idea was to go back downstairs and call someone to check out the rest of the house with me. But I couldn't think of anyone nearby that would be helpful under the circumstances. Retreating and calling the police was also an option. Then again, I would feel incredibly stupid if my dangerous trespasser turned out to be a venturesome raccoon. The absence of my two cats didn't really prove anything. They could be staying out of sight because of a human intruder, or they could have gone into hiding to avoid tangling with another animal that had invaded their territory.

In the final analysis, it seemed to me that my best option was to proceed alone and take whoever or whatever by surprise —assuming they hadn't already heard me come in.

When I reached the top of the stairs, I took a deep breath, slipped off my shoes and started a room-by-room search.

There was no one in the hall.

No one in my office.

No one in the bathroom.

One room to go, the small rectangular spare bedroom that I used as a reading room at the south end of the house. I stood to one side and pushed the half open door a few inches wider. Weak moonlight filtered through the pollen streaked window. The sofa bed along the far wall was empty, but I could see a pair of feet hanging over the edge of the couch just around the corner.

When I heard a cat purring, I reached inside and flicked on the switch, turning night into day. There, big as life, was JJ, stretched out on the couch, his feet propped on the arm. My two fickle cats lay on his chest. Dilly, my orange tabby rescue cat, stretched his paws and looked like he was considering getting up, then thought better of it and found a new position on JJ's lean body. Natasha, my lovely Russian blue, didn't even bother opening her bright green eyes.

But JJ's eyes blinked open. "Hey," JJ said, his voice thick with sleep. "It's about time you got home." He looked at me for a moment as I stood there trying to get control of my racing heart. "What's with the stick?" he said.

"I wasn't expecting you," I said, lowering the piece of wood.

JJ eyed my driftwood club. "And just *who* were you expecting?"

"This thing with Jake has me on edge," I admitted as I put down my makeshift weapon and sat on the arm of the couch. "What did you do to my cats?"

"I gave them a few of the cat treats from the cupboard in your kitchen," he said, slowly sitting up. He shifted Dilly to one side and picked up Natasha and set her down gently next to him on the couch.

Dilly apparently didn't like the change in location, leapt down and came over to say hello to me. I picked him up and ruffled the fur on his back. Natasha opened one eye to check out her new location and promptly went back to sleep.

"I could use a cuppa," I said. "Want one?" JJ nodded. We were about to get up and head downstairs when we both heard a sound from below. JJ held a finger to his lips to indicate we should be quiet, grabbed my piece of driftwood and motioned for me to follow him. I wanted to protest that the driftwood was *my* weapon, not his, but he was already heading for the stairs.

Chapter 6
Threats and Zombiez

B efore we got halfway down the steps, a timid voice called,
"Anyone home? Lavender, are you here?"

"Be right there," I yelled. It was my neighbor from two
doors to the north, an elderly woman who insisted on calling
me Lavender because "it's such a pretty name."

I slipped past JJ and switched on the kitchen light. Beatrice
was standing there just inside the door in a long, flowered
nightgown, blinking against the sudden blare of light, her hands
outstretched in front of her, gripping a Lone Wolf Glock 19L
that was pointed at my chest. And her hands didn't seem too
steady.

"Beatrice," I shouted, "don't shoot!"

She blinked a few more times.

"Oh dear, don't worry. It isn't loaded." She looked at the
pistol in her hand as if surprised to see it there and slowly
lowered it. "It was my late husband's, and, well when you came
home and went inside but didn't turn on your lights right away
like you usually do—." She hesitated before continuing. "I'm
sorry, it's just that I was worried. What with this murder and
all."

It was both disconcerting and comforting to know that I

was being watched over by a neighbor and that she knew I always flicked on the light the minute I stepped inside. The thought that she was willing to come to the rescue, albeit with an unloaded weapon, was touching. It was sad though to think that Jake's death was undermining the security most of us had always felt living on the island, making us nervous and quick to suspect the worst. I waved her into the kitchen and explained that JJ and I were just about to have a cup of tea and asked if she would join us.

"I wouldn't want to intrude..." She left the sentence hanging and glanced over at JJ, apparently trying to decide if there was perhaps another reason for me leaving the lights off.

"No," JJ jumped in, reading her thoughts. "She isn't my type." Then he laughed. "Now, *you* on the other hand—." He smiled charmingly at her.

"Here," I said, handing her a sweater from the rack near the door. "Please come on in." I pointed at the Glock. "Maybe you can leave that there, on the counter."

In spite of the fact that Beatrice had seen JJ coming and going often enough, exchanging pleasantries from time to time, they had never sat down and had a conversation together. They quickly bonded as we drank tea, and inevitably the conversation drifted to speculation about possible motives for murder. Beatrice had heard all about Jake's demise at the grocery store, where a group of Islanders she knew were standing around talking about *the murder*. I wondered if there was *anyone* on the island who hadn't heard about what happened and who didn't assume it was a homicide.

We also chatted about mutual acquaintances and debated the pros and cons of the wilding of Vashon. When she decided it was time to go, I finally approached the topic of the Glock. "About that pistol," I began. Before I could complete my sentence, JJ jumped in and said,

"Next time put in the bullets first."

"No," I said firmly. "Next time, leave it locked up and call the police if you seriously think something is wrong."

When I lived in the commune, the elders had insisted that everyone, even young girls, be trained to use rifles to protect themselves against wild animals. And when I ran away at seventeen and lied about my age to join the army, I received lots of weapons training before ending up in administrative personnel support in Afghanistan. I knew how to use a firearm, but I had consciously sworn off owning a gun after returning to civilian life.

"We aren't in the city, you know," Beatrice said. "When things go wrong, the police can't always get here in time."

JJ started to say something but made the mistake of looking at me first and quickly shut his mouth.

"Beatrice," I said gently. "I can't tell you how much I appreciate you trying to protect me. But you can imagine how awful I would feel if something happened to you because of me."

Reluctantly, very reluctantly, she promised not to act rashly in the future. "And *you* need to lock your door when you go out," she said with feeling. Then, softening her tone, she added, "Just until things are back to normal."

JJ spent the night on the lumpy sofa bed in the spare room. It was my way of accommodating guests without encouraging them to stay for long. I need my space and time alone. That's why JJ usually checks in with me before coming over. And after tonight, it would probably be a while before he surprised me again with a visit.

Over coffee and toast the next morning, we talked some more about Jake's murder. Jake had actively supported a number of controversial projects and policies in recent years, but none where emotions ran so high as with the wilding issue. Still, no one stood out as a strong suspect. And even though JJ theoretically leaned toward the wife as being somehow involved in the husband's death, neither of us could imagine how or why Jeannie would have lured Jake to the bog at night and then managed to overpower him.

"Maybe it's as simple as someone forcing him into the bog so that his body wouldn't be discovered right away, if ever," I suggested. "And the fact that Jake's hand got caught on a branch was just bad juju for his murderer."

"You mean he—or she—didn't notice the hand sticking up?"

"It's possible. Especially if it was at night. Or if they thought the body would sink and didn't hang around to see if it did."

As he was leaving JJ asked if I wanted to have dinner later. I thanked him but explained I was going out to eat with Andy and Norm. Norm is a long-time friend of Andy's and an Island Land Stewards' volunteer.

"Dinner with *two* men, huh? Not bad."

"The three of us are going on a coyote count run tonight," I said.

"Andy isn't bad looking," JJ mused. "You could do worse." JJ was always encouraging me to get out more. And he was right, Andy was single and not bad looking—if you liked the macho type, big shoulders and muscular arms. JJ does. I don't necessarily. Norm was also single and similarly muscled, but shorter than Andy who was about my height. I don't mind a man being shorter than me—most are—but although both men were comfortable to be around, neither one got my juices flowing.

"On second thought," JJ said, "maybe you shouldn't be going out on a coyote count right now. Until the police find out why Jake was killed."

I was torn between being touched by his concern and irritated with him for cautioning me about what I should or shouldn't do. "It's been on my calendar for a month," I said testily.

"One month, two months—that doesn't matter. You're already in the spotlight, why call more attention to yourself? Andy and Norm can do the count on their own."

"I *want* to go," I said. I was fairly certain my tone clearly indicated that was the end of the argument.

JJ hesitated, then smiled. "You are a stubborn woman."

"Almost as stubborn as you," I countered.

Then I, too, smiled and JJ threw his hands in the air in defeat before grabbing me and giving me a hug. My body stiffened, and I gave him a limp squeeze back. I was never sure if JJ hugged me in spite of my awkward response or just to tease me. Maybe a little bit of both.

"Just promise me you will be careful. Don't go wandering off on your own." JJ stepped back from me and grinned. "Maybe you can borrow Beatrice's gun." With that he headed off down the path, waving at me over his shoulder.

When I went back inside and sat down at my desk, I felt conflicted. There was a long to-do list right on top of a pile of folders next to my laptop. I was well aware that I needed to spend some time on my consulting work, but because I was seen taking notes at the Island Land Stewards meeting, ostensibly for myself and not for Detective Crane, and because I'd promised to do some follow up, I felt like that should be a priority. Besides, exploring motives for murder was a lot more intriguing than writing a report on the findings from a case I'd recently completed. And even if everyone on my list was innocent or clueless, I would get a checkmark for trying.

As I scanned the list of names, no one jumped out as a possible killer. I decided to start with those I considered most passionately opposed to wilding. It didn't take long to set up a couple of meetings for late afternoon as well as several for the following day. I also called my realtor friend, Marie, and arranged to have coffee with her. We were about due to get together, and besides, Marie was well-connected on Vashon. She might be able to suggest some avenues of investigation that I wouldn't think of. The downside was that, if I drank coffee with everyone I met with, I was going to be wired.

Then I called Grimes and left a message. I didn't specifically invite him to join me, but I mentioned the possibility in case he was interested. Since Crane was in charge, it was possible Grimes would tell him what I was up to and Crane would in turn tell me to butt out. Of course, the interviews weren't official, so I wasn't sure he could stop me from meeting with people I've known for some time, even if the ostensible purpose was to talk about a homicide.

To ease my guilt and perhaps put some money in my bank account, I spent the rest of the morning writing the report for the sexual harassment investigation I'd done the week before for a small Seattle company. There was no doubt in my mind that the person accused was guilty as charged and should be fired, but it wasn't my role to act as judge and jury. Rather, my job was to gather all of the facts and leave it up to the client to decide what to do with the information. I had interviewed everyone involved, studied the company policies, and laid out the context as clearly and concisely as possible. Now it was up to management to do the right thing. They usually did. Not always because it was the right thing to do; sometimes they just wanted to avoid a lawsuit.

Early afternoon I took a break and did my personal version of a parkour session up through the woods behind my cabin. We didn't have team sports in the commune when I was a kid, but we spent a lot of time outdoors, and I'd developed a habit of regular outdoor exercise. In the army I was taught self-defense skills. Then, when in Afghanistan, one of the sergeants introduced me to parkour. I immediately liked the combination of running, climbing, jumping and vaulting through an obstacle course. And I liked the philosophy that went along with it, the idea that there is no obstacle in life that can't be overcome. That there is always a "way through."

After the army I'd attended college and tried my hand at gymnastics. The moves were consistent with what I had learned through parkour. But doing the same things over and over in a gym didn't appeal to me. Nor did competing with others. I wasn't in it to be the best. I just wanted to do it for myself.

The woods that afternoon flashed golden in the sunlight as I ran and leapt and tumbled my way over logs and around trees. At one point I sat on a moss-covered log to catch my breath, inhaling the sweet scent of decaying pine needles and listening to a crow complain about my presence. Exercising in the woods always made me feel so alive, physically and mentally. Unlike workouts in fitness centers where the smell of body sweat hovered in the air and heavy breathing echoed off institutional walls.

After my run I took a shower and was getting ready to leave when my phone started howling. It was Andy. He sounded upset and asked when I could drop by. I explained that I had two meetings scheduled at the Roasterie but could stop by briefly on my way there. When he didn't say that it was okay to wait until after my meetings, I knew something serious was up. I hurried down the path to the parking lot and drove about ten miles over the speed limit all the way to the Island Land Stewards' office.

Andy and Norm were both in Andy's office when I arrived. And they were both wearing the same grim look on their faces. Without any fanfare, Andy handed me a piece of paper. "I found this on my desk when I got here about an hour ago."

The computer-generated message was as ominous as it was succinct: "Stop *counting* those devils and *shoot* them or you'll end up in the bog with your friend."

"That's not good," I said as I handed the note back to him.

"Not good?" Andy shook his head. "'Not good' is an understatement, I'd say."

"I assume no one saw who left this here?" I asked.

"No, the office was locked until Kelly came this morning. But I'd left my window cracked open because of the heat. With all the bushes alongside the building, no one would have seen someone from the road if they'd climbed in that way."

"Have you shown this to Deputy Grimes?"

"No, we've been trying to decide what to do."

"How many people have handled the note?"

Andy and Norm looked at each other. "Damn," Andy said. "Fingerprints."

"Well, we can still have Grimes pass it along to Detective Crane to have it analyzed."

Andy and Norm were staring at the piece of paper as if it were about to burst into flame. I took out a Kleenex, grasped one corner of the note with it and said, "Do you have a large envelope I can put this in?" Andy jumped up to get an envelope while Norm continued to stare at the paper in my hand.

"It sounds like a serious threat," Norm said as Andy came back with a large manila envelope.

"Could be," I said. Then, glancing at my watch: "Sorry, but I need to go. Why don't you drop this off at the Sheriff's office; Grimes needs to know about this right away." As I headed for the door I added, "See you at Zombiez." Zombiez was a local diner that described itself as "more Scooby Doo than Walking Dead." It wasn't fancy, but it had atmosphere and great comfort food.

"Wait," Andy said.

I paused in the doorway.

"Do you think we should reconsider going out on the count tonight?"

I didn't hesitate. "No," I said, "This count needs to be done. But I do think we need to talk about taking precautions."

Andy and Norm exchanged glances and then both nodded in agreement. "See you at Zombiez," Andy said. His words were certain, but his voice wasn't.

———

Marie was waiting for me at the Luna Café. She waved me over to a two-person table along the wall. There was already a cup of coffee waiting for me.

"Glad you called," she said. "I've been wondering how things are going."

"Are you talking about my failed attempt as a bog tour guide, or just in general?"

She laughed. Marie is an attractive, fashionable woman and a very successful realtor. "Okay, you caught me. A little of both."

"In general, great. But you probably know as much about Jake's demise as I do."

She laughed again. "We realtors do keep up with the local gossip." She got suddenly serious. "But how are *you* doing? It must have been difficult for you given your friendship with Jake."

She knew I'd been in Afghanistan, but I'd never talked about my experiences there. And now didn't seem like a good time to do so. "Death is never easy," I said.

We chatted a bit more about Jake's death, but she didn't mention anything that I didn't know. Then we turned to how our jobs were going. When she mentioned that the real estate business was booming, I brought up the Winchell properties and asked if she knew whether anyone other than the Island Land Stewards were showing interest.

"Funny you should bring that up. I talked with Annie Regis earlier today. We were discussing the need for low-income housing, and she said something about a client who thinks the Winchell properties might be suitable for that."

"Well, that could be good and bad—for the Island Land Stewards, that is."

"Let's see, good if the purchaser agrees to an easement, bad if they drive up the price and aren't flexible about an easement. Do I have that right?" She smiled.

"You know the goal—tip to tip walking trails."

"And I support that."

"But you realtors do love a bidding war."

Marie rubbed her fingers together. "A little extra money is always nice."

We had to cut our coffee short because she had a client appointment and I had two interviews to do. I thanked her for the information about the developer and headed down the road to the Roasterie.

My first two interviews were with board members who were not only outspoken about their negative views on wilding, but had engaged in heated, public exchanges with Jake about the issue. At the top of my list was the man who'd made the injudicious remark at the meeting about Jake "asking for it." *That* comment alone wouldn't have earned him the number one spot on my list, but he'd also argued about wilding with Jake on more than one occasion in the past. The other interviewee was upset because his pet llama had been attacked by the cougar. The incident was followed by an uncomfortable confrontation between Jake and him at our last quarterly meeting. Although the two men weren't the only people passionately opposed to the wilding of the Island, it seemed like a good enough place to start.

Unfortunately, two hours later I was none the wiser. Neither conversation had produced anything useful. Both men had expressed what seemed like sincere sadness over Jake's death. Both had acknowledged that Jake's demise wasn't going to resolve the wilding issue or change the debate. Both had displayed sympathy for Jeannie, someone they both knew well. Unless all of my instincts were dead, neither man should be considered a prime suspect. And, neither had any ideas about who might have done it.

I didn't mention the note Andy had received to either of my interviewees, but as we talked, I tried to picture them writing the note and climbing in through a window in the middle of the night to deliver it. It didn't make any sense. But then neither did Beatrice waving her husband's Glock around. Given the right circumstances, people can do strange things.

Andy and Norm were already at Zombiez when I got there. They were seated on chairs with bright green vinyl cushions, facing a picture on the wall of Mona Lisa with a skull face. Their small square table was directly under the end of the toy railroad track hanging from the ceiling with the train that always seemed to be running. Around and around, the same old track. I liked the idea of it as part of the decor, but sometimes I felt sorry for the train, always just out of reach of eager kids, never varying its route.

Grimes was seated at the table with Andy and Norm, his back to me as I approached. When I reached the table and asked if they had already ordered, he turned to me and said, "Sit down, Lew. We need to talk."

Chapter 7
Counting Coyotes

G rimes got straight to the point. "I don't think doing the count tonight is a good idea, but Andy thinks it's necessary, and Crane actually wants it to happen. He's going to send over two men for back-up." He paused briefly, then said, "Lew, I think you should go home."

"And lock my door and never come out again."

"That isn't what I mean."

"I know what you mean. Let the men take care of this."

Grimes rolled his eyes. "Dammit, Lew. You're smarter than that."

"Tell you what," Norm said, smiling at me, "*you* can go on the count. I'll go home and lock *my* door."

"Look," Andy said. "The note was on *my* desk, but anyone who goes with me tonight could become a target. Why don't I go alone with the two back-up guys?"

"What if the two back-up officers are women?" I said.

Andy actually smiled. "Better yet."

Grimes held up his hand to stop the talk, just like he was directing street traffic. "Okay, I've said my piece. You do what you want. Just make sure you take the threat seriously. Don't take any unnecessary chances." He stood up. "Hope to see you all tomorrow."

After Grimes had gone, Andy turned to me. "I gave the threatening note to Grimes. He's going to pass it along to Crane to have it checked for prints. But no one is hopeful that they'll find anything."

We avoided talking about the coyote count until we had ordered. I got my usual ZAT salad with crispy cod, and both Andy and Norm got a Zombiez Scary Good Burger with fries. I was definitely going to snitch a couple of fries.

"You're convinced that we should do this tonight?" Andy asked me while we waited for our food.

"Uh huh. If we roll over, we're saying he wins."

"Or she," Norm said with a grin.

"Or they," Andy added.

"What good would it do to postpone for a couple of days?" I asked. "Do you really think those detectives will figure out who left you the note that soon? Besides, you've told me that the best time to do this count is when the pups are just beginning to vocalize. And didn't you say that should be happening about now?"

"Okay, we need to get this done fairly soon," Andy said. "I guess it might as well be tonight." He sounded resigned but not happy about it.

"So, what's the deal with these backup people Grimes mentioned?" I asked. "They going to be with us or just somewhere nearby? Are we talking about officers in uniform, or what?"

"You know as much as we know," Andy said.

"Do you think they'll have weapons? Like, real guns? Or are they just supposed to be there to take a bullet for us?"

"No need, I can do that." Norm leaned toward me and pretended he'd been shot.

"This isn't fun and games, guys," Andy said.

Norm straightened up in his chair. "We know that, Andy. But I agree with Lew; we can't just run and hide."

"Seriously," I said. "Why do you think Crane wants us to go ahead with the count tonight? Because we'll be safe as long as they are there to protect us? Let's face it—we're bait. They're obviously hoping the note writer, and possible killer, will come after us."

"On the plus side," Norm said, "We'll probably have him, her, or them outnumbered."

Andy shook his head. "Okay you two. I get it. But I just can't believe this is happening. I've always thought this was a close-knit community."

"Well, there's definitely a frayed end out there somewhere," I said. "It does seem to me that it has to be someone local. Who but a local would know about the coyote count project and where your desk is? And not that many outsiders know about the bog."

"I've been thinking about that."

"Who exactly *did* know about tonight's plan for counting coyotes?" I asked. "You didn't post the schedule anywhere, did you?"

"No, but I haven't kept it a secret either. Any number of people could have heard about it. And if they know about the count, they probably also know we tend to go to the same locations every time."

Our meals came and we interrupted our conversation to concentrate on the food. Norm playfully slapped my hand when I grabbed one of his fries, and then he offered me a few, like we were sharing a last meal.

"You could get a side of fries," Andy suggested.

"Way too fattening," I countered as I dipped one of Norm's fries in Andy's catsup.

After dinner we returned to Andy's office and planned our route for the coyote count, otherwise known as the howling survey. Coyote counts are done by playing recorded coyote howls on a loudspeaker and counting the replies. It's all done in one night, moving quickly from one spot to the next to ensure that you are hearing separate families.

We went out to set up the speakers in the truck and were just finishing when Detective Crane and a young sidekick arrived. I was surprised to see Crane. It didn't seem like an assignment for the person in charge, but then, maybe he thought counting coyotes would be interesting. You never knew.

We did introductions. The young man with Crane politely shook everyone's hand and introduced himself as *Detective* Forester, as if "detective" was his first name. He was sharp looking in a barely out of college, crew-cut sort of way. Spit polished and eager.

"Is that with one 'r' or two?" I asked. Not that it mattered, but there was something about him that rubbed me the wrong way; it made me want to poke at him a little.

"One. Like the author." He said it like he might be C.S. Forester's grandson.

"I have all of his books," I offered, making an effort to put aside my irritation and appear friendly. "I've always loved sea adventures."

"Really?" He sounded surprised.

Norm jumped in. "If you're about to suggest that not too many women read sea adventures, I'd stop while I was ahead if I were you."

"It's just that . . .," Detective Forester said, then paused.

"Norm's right," I said firmly, ending that conversation by turning to Detective Crane and asking, "So, what's the plan?"

Crane's dark eyes roamed over us. "First," he said, "I want

to be clear that you don't need to do this." He paused as if to give us time to reconsider before charging into battle. More for show, I thought, than because he expected us to change our minds. "If you want to go ahead with it, then I suggest you proceed with your count as you normally do."

Norm and I turned to Andy to answer for the team. He said, "We'll do it."

"Do you think the note writer will come after us?" Norm asked.

"We'll be ready if he does." Crane gestured toward Forester to indicate they were there for us. "You do understand that it's a good possibility that the note writer and the murderer are the same person," he added.

We all nodded. Why else would the two detectives be using us to smoke him out?

"Forester and I will follow in my car," Crane said. "We'll stay back a way so as not to scare him off, assuming he shows up."

It didn't feel like much of a plan to me, but using bait to catch a bigger fish *was* a proven formula.

Neither Andy nor Norm mentioned our speculation that it might be a "she" or a "them," and I didn't bring it up either. To me gender wasn't an issue; men and women could be equally dangerous. And it seemed likely there was only one stalker. We were probably fine with or without backup. Unless the stalker had a gun. That was something I didn't like thinking about. But I had already noted that at least Detective Forester, with one "r," was carrying.

"No one knows our specific route," Andy said. "Although we go to the same general locations each year, we just decided this evening where we're going first. If the person who wrote the note comes after us, they'll either have to wait for us to show up at a particular spot or follow us from here."

"We'll have it covered," Crane said, sounding confident.

I wasn't sure what having it "covered" meant. But I would have felt better if they'd mentioned having in-ear audio transmitters and night vision glasses. Maybe an on-call SWAT team. Or a sharpshooter in place. Knowing we had that kind of back-up would have made me feel secure. Being covered by two detectives without much of a plan didn't.

Crane asked if there were any final questions or comments, and when there were none, he said, "Okay then, let's go."

We got in our respective vehicles and headed for the area where the widest ranging coyote pack was located. It seemed to me that if the note writer intended to follow us, perhaps having a police escort, even in an unmarked car, would discourage him from actually taking action. With any luck, we could complete our count and get through the night without incident. Although that would undoubtedly disappoint our two bodyguards.

Our first stop wasn't too far north from where I lived, a small park on the beach surrounded by fairly dense woods. The hillside to the south was relatively steep, but the area around the creek was flat with a gulley cutting through the hillside, eventually disappearing at a forested bluff. The sound of running water muffled other night sounds.

Lone coyotes didn't howl. But you could tell where mating pairs and families were by counting the vocalizations of their pups. When combined with individual sightings, encounters with domestic animals, and scat analysis in known locations, you could get a pretty good picture of the coyote population.

Norm got out the clipboards for taking notes while Andy started the recording. Crane and Forester remained in their car about 200 yards from where we were parked. Not quite out of sight in the moonlight. If someone approached by road, either in a car or on foot, they would see them. But they would also be seen. If the goal was to capture the note writer, it didn't seem like a very good strategy. At best they might get a license number. But it was their call.

To be honest I didn't really expect anything out of the ordinary to happen. Nor did I believe the others thought the writer of the note would actually make a move. In spite of our expressed concerns, the likeliest outcome was that we would make our three stops, record what we heard, and return to the Island Land Stewards' office in the wee hours intact.

So, when the first shot rang out, we all froze in place. For just a second. Then I yelled for everyone to take cover, and we all dropped like stones.

For me it was a flashback to Afghanistan. That part of my life was buried in the past, but not so deep that my body didn't react. Although I'd been initially assigned to administrative duties, there were times when I'd definitely needed the skills I had learned in basic training. Even though my survival instincts might be dulled by time, they were still present.

While Andy, Norm and I made our way to the far side of the truck, Detective Forester suddenly leapt out of Crane's car and sprinted, hunkered over, in the direction of the shot.

"Stop, Wyatt," Crane yelled after him from the safety of their car. But Detective Wyatt Forester, now an officer with a normal first name, kept running. Brave or foolhardy, who knew.

Another shot hit the dirt near the front of the truck, and we all crouched lower. Out of the corner of my eye I saw that foolhardy detective continue zigzagging toward the woods. Damn. Was he hell bent on being a hero, or was he prepared to shoot our attacker as well? That question was answered when I saw him raise his hand and heard him returning fire into the woods.

I had no choice. I knew I was the person best qualified to tackle the island terrain at night. Not only because of my regular parkour exercises in the woods, but because of my combat experience. Even after years as a civilian it was ingrained in my U.S. Army DNA.

"I'm going with him," I yelled to everyone as I got up and started running after the detective.

"No," Crane shouted out his car window. Was he staying behind to call for back-up? And, if so, who was he going to call? Grimes and Evans?

"I'll go," Andy yelled. But I was already halfway across the clearing, gaining rapidly on the young man I now thought of as Wyatt, wondering if the shooter was retreating or taking aim for another shot.

Wyatt plunged into the woods like a charging bear. I followed, my eyes struggling to adjust to the darkness under the trees. While exercising at night in the woods, I never had to worry about getting shot at. Nor was I ever rushed. There was always time to assess the lay of the land and make informed decisions. This was taking the nighttime in the woods experience to an entirely new level.

Thankfully, there was a bright three-quarters moon and no clouds. But the high forest canopy blocked most of the light. The moon's wavering glow peeked down intermittently through the trees revealing scattered, surreal glimpses of the landscape contours ahead. This close to the creek the underbrush thinned out, but there was enough to make running in the shadowy darkness challenging. The usual deadfall and small clumps of bushes obscured the forest floor. Ferns and wild huckleberry bushes lashed out at me. A blackberry vine scraped along my sleeve. Even for someone used to running through the woods at night, it was tough going.

I was being cautious, careful of my footing, but I was still gaining on Wyatt. He was screaming for whoever had shot at us to stop in the name of the law. In my opinion we would have been far better off to have pursued the shooter as silently as possible. Instead, the noise of the detective crashing through the brush and his on-going demands that the shooter reveal himself made Wyatt an easy target—*if* the shooter was nearby. What I wasn't at all sure of was whether Wyatt was actually on someone's trail. For all I knew, the shooter had run off in another direction and was long gone.

Wyatt was just a few feet ahead of me when he stumbled and fell. His gun went off, and I did a quick assessment to make sure he hadn't shot me by accident. Then I knelt beside him and asked, "Do you know which way he's headed?"

"No, dammit. But we need to go after him." He scrambled to his feet and looked around as if expecting to get clues as to which way to head from the trees or the night sky.

"I don't have much hope," I said. "Why don't we just go back?"

"No, you can go if you want, but I'm going to keep looking."

It didn't seem to me that I would be able to change his mind, and we hadn't been shot at while standing there, so I felt reasonably confident the shooter had made tracks. To assuage Wyatt's need to demonstrate his bravery, I made a suggestion that I hoped was a safe one. "We could fan out and scout the area" I said. "Then if we don't find him in say fifteen minutes, we probably won't. Agreed?"

He seemed to consider my idea, then asked, "Do you have a gun?"

"No," I said, wishing like hell I did, "but if I catch up with him, I'll shout. Until then, it might be a good idea to proceed quietly, okay? Try and sneak up on him, take him by surprise." Not that I thought Wyatt had a ghost of a chance to sneak up on anyone used to being in the woods at night, but it seemed a better option than having him continue to shout out threats. And he didn't have to know that I had no intention of revealing my position by shouting for help if I somehow managed to locate our shooter. I would assess the situation in the moment and decide what to do if and when it happened.

"Okay," Wyatt said, "you go east and I'll go west." I wasn't sure he could tell directions in the woods, but I agreed anyway. "And shout if you come across him. Don't take any chances."

I didn't point out that we had already taken a huge chance by hanging around and talking after being shot at. "If we don't find him in fifteen minutes, we're heading back, agreed?" I said to confirm the time limit.

"Agreed." He sounded almost relieved that we had a deadline, and he could always blame me for giving up.

When he headed off in a westerly direction as planned, I was almost surprised. I quickly sprinted off to the east, leaping over a fallen log so I could put some distance between myself and Wyatt before he got off course and shot me by mistake. After a few minutes I slowed down, scanning the trees, moving as quietly as I could through the underbrush, stopping every few feet to listen. The shooter was either nearby or, more likely, no longer in the area. I just hoped Wyatt didn't get lost. Fifteen minutes could be a long time in a dark forest for a city boy.

Even when you're used to being in the woods at night and know generally where you are in relationship to the rest of the island, it can be easy to get turned around. I was consciously keeping track of which way I was heading when I heard movement off to my right.

An animal perhaps? Or had I been lucky enough—or unlucky enough—to actually catch up with the shooter? Standing as still as possible I held my breath and listened. Whatever or whoever was headed in my direction. Damn!

Chapter 8
A Lucky Shot?

Crouching low behind a bush that was far too scant for real cover, I waited, listening for all I was worth. It crossed my mind that the shooter might have a pair of night vision goggles. You could buy them anywhere these days, even Walmart. I wasn't sure who the target customer for night vision goggles was at a big box store, but I had considered buying myself a pair to use at night in the woods. Now I wished I had. Even though my eyes had adjusted to the dim light that barely reached the forest floor, I couldn't make out anything more than a few feet away.

For the longest time there was no sound other than my own controlled breathing. Then I heard it again, coming closer, slowly. An animal stalking its prey? Or a shooter? Two voices in my head were fighting each other. Run, one said. Stay put, the other said. I could think of reasons to do both. Indecision kept me glued to the spot.

Then I heard the crack of a branch in the distance from behind. Whatever it was, it too was headed in my direction. Two animals? Two shooters? An animal and a shooter? I felt trapped, trapped by the situation and by lack of a weapon to fight off predators.

I had just about decided to make a run for it when I realized that whatever was coming from behind was making a lot of noise. Too much noise to be an animal or the shooter trying to creep up on me. It had to be Wyatt.

There was no choice: I had to warn him. "Wyatt," I yelled. "Get down!"

The words were no sooner out of my mouth than a shot rang out. There was no time to think about tactics; we both made tracks at the same time.

I could hear bushes rustle and twigs snap as someone or something fled to the south, while I went west, toward what I assumed was Wyatt's location. It suddenly occurred to me that Wyatt might mistake me for the shooter, so I dropped to one knee and shouted, "Wyatt, it's me." When no one answered, I tried again, "Wyatt?" Could I have been wrong about what I thought was a person coming my way?

Then I heard the moaning and slowly moved forward. "Wyatt?" I called softly. "Is that you, Wyatt?"

"Over here," he said finally. He sounded strange.

I headed in the direction of his voice and found him sprawled on the ground, legs outstretched, with a dark splotch of blood on his left pant leg. "I've been shot," he said. He sounded surprised and angry at the same time. "The bastard shot me," he repeated. His gun was lying on the ground next to him. I picked up his gun and put the safety on before tucking it in my pocket.

"Quiet for a moment," I ordered, listening for sounds of the shooter. When I heard nothing for several minutes but Wyatt's ragged breathing, I felt relived. But it still seemed unwise to hang around any longer than necessary. The shooter could be out there somewhere, waiting for the right opportunity.

There wasn't enough light to assess how bad Wyatt's wound was. Rather than wasting time on first aid in the dark with a potential shooter lurking nearby, it seemed like the better option was to get him back to the road as quickly as possible. "Here," I said, reaching down to give him a hand. "Let's get you up."

"I can't," he said.

"Yes, you can." It came out as a command, and Wyatt meekly obeyed. "Can you put any weight on that leg?"

He tried and gave out a yelp of pain.

"Okay, lean on me. We can do this." He draped his arm around my shoulder, and I steered him in the direction we had started from.

"Isn't the car back that way?" he asked, nodding toward the northeast.

"No, it's this way." No wonder he'd ended up where he did.

Wyatt leaned more and more heavily on me as we slowly made our way back to the car. I was concerned about blood loss, but now that we were almost there it made sense to keep going. "Coming out," I yelled as we approached the road.

"Is that you, Lew?" Andy yelled back.

"Yes, and I could use some help."

Seconds later Andy and Norm appeared, gasped and, looking at Wyatt, simultaneously said, "You're bleeding." At that, Wyatt almost collapsed, and I gladly turned him over to the two men.

Crane was waiting for us at the tree line, looking very worried, a pistol in his hand. In the pale moonlight his eyes looked large and dark as two lumps of coal.

"Wyatt," he said, when he saw Wyatt being supported by Andy and Norm. "You're hurt?"

Wyatt groaned.

"If taking a bullet constitutes being hurt, then yes, he's been hurt," I said.

"Shouldn't we call for an ambulance?" Andy asked.

"Bring him over to the car," I said. "Let's take a look."

In the glow of the headlights Wyatt's leg wound didn't look life threatening, but there was a fair amount of blood. Norm got a towel from Andy's car and wrapped it tightly around the wound to stem the flow.

"There's no medical care here on the island for a gunshot wound," I explained to Crane. He'll have to be taken to the mainland for treatment." I had several emergency service numbers in my phone. "Let's call for a helicopter. At this hour it would be faster than calling for an aid car and waiting for a ferry."

Crane said he agreed, and I made the call. When they answered I explained the situation and was told we should meet them in twenty minutes at the airstrip at Misty Isle Farms. Crane had a blanket in his trunk. We put that over the back seat of his car and helped Wyatt inside. I got in beside him. Andy was to lead the way with Crane following. As we started off, Wyatt turned to me. "Am I going to die?"

I'd seen more than my share of gunshot wounds when I was in the army, but I hadn't actually taken the time to look carefully at Wyatt's injury. All I had seen was the tear in his pants and the blood. But the modest blood loss and the fact that he had remained conscious and had been able to hop back to the car made me think his injury wasn't all that serious. Still, he could have been operating under an adrenalin rush. I wasn't a medical professional; what did I know? Even so, for once I knew the right words: "You're going to be fine," I said. "We just need to get you to a hospital."

While we were waiting for the helicopter, Crane came around to the side of the car to talk to Wyatt. "What happened?" he asked.

Wyatt nodded in my direction and said, "She yelled at me, so the shooter knew where I was. And he shot me."

I still had his gun in my pocket and was tempted to shoot him right then and there myself. Instead, without a word, I pulled out Wyatt's gun and handed it across Wyatt to Crane. Then I got out of the car and walked a few feet away to collect myself and avoid saying something I shouldn't.

The helicopter showed up minutes after the exchange. Crane went with Wyatt on the helicopter, and I drove Crane's car back to the Island Land Stewards' office where they could deal with it in the morning. Then I joined Andy and Norm in Andy's office. "Wish I kept a bottle of Scotch here, or any liquor for that matter," Andy said. "I could use a drink."

"Too bad the town closes up so early," Norm said.

"Did I hear Wyatt correctly?" Andy asked.

"You mean what he said about me shouting at him?"

"Yeah."

"You bet I did. He got turned around and was headed straight for the shooter. What was I supposed to do?"

"You two caught up with the shooter?" Andy sounded surprised.

"Well, I'm not sure that's accurate. It's more like we may have stumbled across him. Unless it was an animal in the bushes—someone or something was headed straight for me. If it was the shooter, he probably sensed I knew he was there and guessed that I was unarmed."

"Why do you say 'if'? He shot Wyatt." When I didn't say anything, Andy continued. "Do you think he was only trying to wound him? Or was his aim off?"

"I can't imagine that he was able to figure out exactly where Wyatt was and aim accurately enough to wing him under those conditions. It was a lucky shot. Unless—."

"Unless what?" Andy asked.

"To be honest, there's something bothering me."

"This doesn't sound good."

"No, it's not good at all." I hesitated, but I needed to tell them. "I'm pretty sure the shot didn't come from a location near me."

"You mean you think there were two shooters?"

"Either that . . . or . . ."

"No way," Norm said.

"Huh?" Andy said. "What do you mean?"

"She thinks Wyatt shot himself. Don't you, Lew?"

"I think it's a possibility." I really hated to say it out loud. "He could easily have stumbled and discharged his weapon by accident. The safety was off. It happens."

"But he must have known it if he shot himself," Andy said.

"He might have been in shock," I said.

"If that's the case," Andy said, "won't they figure it out at some point?"

"When they take a closer look at the wound and remove the bullet, either or both ought to be a pretty good clue."

"Is it called friendly fire when you shoot yourself?" Norm kidded.

I hit him in the arm with my fist. "Funny guy," I said.

By the time we finally called it a night, I was feeling the low that often follows an adrenaline high. Norm offered to see me to my place, but I informed him that I wasn't going home; I was going to a friend's house and didn't need anyone to drop me off.

JJ answered after three rings. He sounded like he'd been asleep.

"Tonight I sleep on *your* extra bed," I informed him. "But first I need a drink."

Chapter 9
You Were Warned

When I returned to my place the next morning, I wasn't surprised to see a note on my door. I was irritated, however, that it was pinned there with a small knife. Whoever it was could have shown more respect for personal property.

Taking the note by the corner, I ripped it off the door, leaving the knife in place, and quickly went inside. Dilly and Natasha immediately made it known that I'd been neglecting them. Because of the coyotes, I'd been keeping them inside more than usual, definitely not a popular decision. I always worried about them when they were outside because of the eagles and hawks, both serious threats to small animals. But, of late, the coyotes seemed to present a more immediate threat. Maybe it was just the hype in the community. Whatever the reason, all Dilly and Natasha knew was that I had failed to give them their late-night snacks and denied them the pleasure of hounding me awake when they were ready for breakfast.

The note confirmed what we already knew—someone was trying to prevent us from doing the coyote count. "You and your friends were warned," it said. It didn't mention shooting a police officer. I wondered if he, or she, had been responsible for Wyatt's gunshot wound, or if I was right to suspect that Wyatt had shot himself. I also wondered if anyone had seen who'd put the note on my door. With most of the houses near me empty during the week, it was unlikely, unless Beatrice had noticed a stranger on the walk. I would check around just in case, then turn the note over to the authorities as we had with the one left on Andy's desk. Maybe we'd get lucky.

My phone rang while I was pouring cat food into their individual bowls, apologizing for the delay, as if they could and would acknowledge my contrition. If they weren't such food focused creatures, I'd leave food out for them instead of doling it out at mealtime. But their breeds and their personalities tended toward over-indulgence, especially when it came to food. I was determined to keep them healthy by controlling their diet.

"Did you get one?" Andy asked when I answered my cell.

"If by 'one' you mean a note from our harasser, then yes. I assume from your question that *you* did?"

"Yes, at home this time. And Norm got one too. Both of ours were pinned to our doors with kitchen knives. And yours?"

"The same," I said. And then added: "Hopefully you avoided touching the knife and the note."

"Yes, this time I remembered. But I'm not sure about Norm. Anyway, I've called Grimes. He and Crane will be at my office at 11:00. Can you be here?"

I had several meetings scheduled with Island Land Stewards' members, including one at 11:00, but I said I'd be there.

"And don't forget to bring your note," Andy said. "And the knife."

I immediately got on the phone and made arrangements to meet my 11:00 appointment at 1:00 instead. That meant I'd have back-to-back meetings in the afternoon, but I could cope. I had just enough time to put the knife and note in an envelope, make a few calls to neighbors to see if anyone had seen anything, respond to a few emails, review and re-prioritize my to-do list, and put on a fresh shirt. Fortunately, I didn't have any pressing client needs. Unfortunately, no one had seen anyone put a note on my door.

———

Andy had brought in some uncomfortable metal folding chairs for the meeting. Norm was standing off to one side thumbing his phone. Crane was seated, looking like a bird perched on a pile of sticks. I went over and handed him my envelope. There were two others on the table beside him. He nodded but didn't say anything. Nor did he offer an update on Wyatt until I broke down and asked.

"He'll mend," was all he said. I couldn't tell if his brief comment was bravado or if he blamed me for what happened. Maybe they'd figured out that Wyatt had shot himself and he chose not to elaborate.

I took a seat and tried to get comfortable. The chair was flimsy and leaned to the left. "But no permanent damage?" I asked. I really did want to know.

"The shot didn't hit anything vital," Crane said. "Didn't splinter any bones. He was lucky."

There was something about his dismissive tone that made me think Crane had accepted Wyatt's version of events. I wanted to point out that if Wyatt hadn't circled back around ahead of time he wouldn't have been shot. Whether by someone else or by himself. In retrospect, however, I was grateful for his miscalculation. If he'd done as he'd said he was going to do, then the stalker might have attacked me. *If* that was what I'd been hearing in the nearby bushes.

Grimes came rushing in, looking harried, and said, "Sorry for being late."

Crane frowned at him as if the two minutes made a difference in his life. Then he took out a pad of paper and said: "Here's what we know so far . . ."

It wasn't much. The only prints on the note left on Andy's desk belonged to people who had handled it in the office. No one had seen anything. There were no real leads. No primary suspects. Just some lines of inquiry. It occurred to me that I was going to have to be vigilant for some time, unless there was an unexpected breakthrough soon. If I wanted my normal life back it might be time to up my game with the interviews I was conducting.

Crane ended with, "So it's my recommendation that you all back off, and if we need anything from you, I'll let you know."

"'Back off—what does that mean?" I asked.

"Just what it sounds like. Go about your lives and leave the investigation to us."

"When can we finish the howling survey?" Andy asked.

"Let's wait and see how the case progresses, okay?"

"It needs to be done in the next couple of weeks," Andy persisted. I was surprised. I didn't think he would want to go out again after what happened.

"I can't force you to postpone your activities. But it seems to me that the risk outweighs the outcome."

"Our work is important," Norm interjected. More defiance? Where was this coming from? Were they feeling like I was, that not enough progress was being made? Or was it just talk? Macho a macho.

"What about you, Lew?" Andy asked. "Want to wait until they catch the person threatening us?"

"I'm game to try again whenever you are. If someone wants to shoot us, there are more convenient times and places to do it." And next time I would have a weapon of my own, I decided. And I was pretty sure that Andy and Norm would also be armed.

"Come on, you guys," Grimes said. "We can't protect you, you know that."

"We aren't asking you to," Andy said.

"It doesn't sound as if you are anywhere near identifying Jake's killer or the guy who shot at us," I bluntly pointed out. "We can't put our lives on hold indefinitely."

Crane shifted in his chair, looking even more uncomfortable, if that was possible. "We have a team out combing the woods at this very minute," he began.

I interrupted, "How do they even know where to look?" He was really pissing me off. "I know where it happened; they don't."

"They should be able to tell from the . . . um . . . the foliage." It was clear he hadn't spent much time in the woods.

"No offense," I said, obviously intending offense, "but without knowing where we were, they won't find much. And they'll just destroy any evidence that may be there."

Grimes jumped in. "She's right, Crane. Lew spends a lot of time in the woods around here. You ought to take advantage of that." Andy and Norm were nodding in agreement.

Crane didn't respond right away, staring at the wall, not looking at us. Then he said, "All right, you may have a point. I'll call them and tell them you're on your way. Ask for Detective Cannella."

I was up and out the door before he could change his mind.

Ten minutes later I was parked next to an unmarked tan sedan on the road close to where we'd been the night before. There was no one around, but before I could get out of the car, an officer came out of the trees and headed in my direction. He looked like he was a couple inches shorter than me and had straight dark hair brushed back off his face. As classic Italian looking as his name. And very handsome. He flashed me a toothy smile and extended his hand. "Lavender?" he asked as he checked me out. I was quite sure he hadn't missed a thing.

"Lew," I corrected.

"You don't look like a Lavender."

I wasn't sure if that was a compliment coming from him or not. Most people expect someone with my name to be light-skinned, but my mother's brief fling with a northern Ukrainian student had left me with an olive complexion, light hair and pale eyes. I'd never met my father, never even seen a picture of him. But mother always told me I looked just like him, usually when she was mad at me for something I'd done. And she'd always called me "Lavender," maybe because she knew I hated the name.

Ignoring his comment about my name, I asked, "How many people do you have with you?"

"There's three of us."

"Are they nearby? I can take you to the place where the shooting happened."

"It was pretty dark last night, wasn't it?"

"Yes, a three-quarters moon, a waxing gibbous moon to be specific. And no clouds." Why had I named the phase of the moon? Acting defensive like that just made me sound pretentious.

"And you think you can find your way back to the exact spot?" He didn't seem convinced.

"I'm here, aren't I?" I turned and started walking toward the woods, slightly to the left of where he'd come out.

"Hey, wait up." Detective Cannella hurried after me. With my long legs I can cover a lot of ground quickly when I want to, without appearing to hurry.

"Give me time to call the others," he said, sounding more

amused than annoyed. Since he wasn't being a complete jerk, I stopped and waited.

"I've never been on the island before," he said after calling his two colleagues. "I'm amazed at how much undeveloped land there is here."

"Yes, over fifty percent of the undeveloped land in King County is on this island, and some of us want to preserve as much of it as possible. Others don't share that point of view. That's one of the problems we face."

"Kind of like the cowboys and Indians," he said. I didn't like the comparison, but in some ways, he was right. Should we try to live in harmony with the land or domesticate it? I knew it was too late to return it to its original state, whatever that was. For that reason, I wasn't really sure where I stood on the wilding proposition, whether related to animals or to native species. Thoughtful, fact-based decision making to determine what to preserve and what to develop seemed like the best approach to me. For that to happen we needed both facts and conversations.

"That analogy may have some merit," I agreed, "but it over-simplifies the situation and brings up other baggage." What was it about this man that made me push back on everything he said?

"Hey, I'm just a simple fellow," he said with a disarming smile that probably worked on the majority of women. "Cut me some slack, okay?"

Fortunately, his two cohorts appeared before I had a chance to come up with the putdown he deserved. I have a thing about men who think every woman should fall all over them because of their looks and their charm.

"Len . . . Dave . . . this is Lew, short for Lavender." He just couldn't let it rest. And he had the disarming smile down pat.

We shook hands, I took the lead and they followed me into

the woods. When you entered at the right location, it was actually fairly easy to see the way we'd come the night before. Not only was there the occasional footprint, crushed debris and bent limbs, but there were also smears of dried blood here and there. In spite of the fact that Wyatt blamed me for what had happened, I probably needed to send him something while he was in the hospital. Candy. Or flowers. He would probably prefer candy, so maybe a nice floral bouquet, whatever pink flowers were in season.

When we neared the place where I'd been trying to stay out of sight, I stopped and pointed. "I was over there. Someone or something was about sixty feet in that direction." I pointed again, then turned to my right. "Wyatt was coming from this direction, the southwest, when I shouted for him to get down."

"Someone or 'something'? It was the shooter, right?" Ray asked.

"All I knew for sure was that either a person or an animal was headed toward me. When I heard Wyatt I tried to warn him."

"He's under the impression that was what called attention to his presence."

"If I knew he was there, the shooter knew he was there too." I didn't think it was necessary to spell out other possibilities.

"Can you take us to where he was shot?" Canella asked.

I headed in what I hoped was the right direction. If they hadn't been there with me, I would have taken a few minutes to reconnoiter, but there was no way I was going to let them think I had any doubts. Fortunately, I'd made a sound guess, and a few minutes later they were examining the blood on the ground where Wyatt had been shot.

"What kind of gun were you carrying?" Len asked.

"I didn't have a gun." Did he think that I might have shot Wyatt?

"You were out here hunting for a shooter with no weapon?" Len said, sounding like he didn't believe it.

"It wasn't a choice I would have made under other circumstances. But I didn't think Wyatt should be out here alone." I hesitated. "He didn't know the area."

"And Crane stayed behind?" Ray said.

"Look, it all happened very quickly. Wyatt instinctively went after the shooter. Maybe he shouldn't have. I don't know. But someone needed to back him up." I wanted to say that what Wyatt had done was stupid and that Crane had been right to stay behind, but I kept my mouth shut.

"But you didn't stay with him." Len was headed somewhere with his questions, but I wasn't sure where.

"No. To be honest, I thought we'd lost the shooter."

"Who made the decision where to look?"

I hesitated again. What was this line of questioning all about? "Wyatt did. I suggested we split up and circle around, and he said that he'd go west and I should go east. I told him I'd give it fifteen minutes before heading back."

"And why were you calling the shots?"

"I wasn't."

"Sounds like you were."

I looked at each man in turn. "As I said before, I know the area; he didn't. He wanted to keep looking; I didn't. So I told him what I was willing to do. After that it was up to him to decide what *he* wanted to do."

"Why do you think the shooter ran after hitting Detective Forester?" That question came from Dave who had been silent up to this point.

Maybe the shooter didn't run away, I wanted to say. Maybe he limped off with my help. Instead I said, "Maybe to get away." I knew my tone had a sarcastic edge, but I was getting tired of the grilling.

"And you decided not to pursue him." Dave again. Were they each following up on a different theme? I should have been paying more attention. But I'd been under the impression I was simply providing them with location details, not a defense of my actions.

"I didn't have a weapon, and I didn't know what had happened to Wyatt. Wyatt was my first priority." Argue with that. "We through here?"

Dave and Len looked at Ray. Ray said, "Sure. You guys take a look around. I'll walk back with Lew."

I deliberately walked as fast as I could, enjoying listening to Ray struggling to keep up. Back at the road Ray made one more attempt at charming me, but I managed to resist. He really was attractive. But his flirty manner wasn't in synch with the way the three of them seemed to blame me for last night's events. Whether I had called attention to Wyatt's whereabouts or not, what had happened was not my fault. I understood their desire to support a colleague, but they didn't have to go out of their way to discredit me. And what if my suspicions were right and Wyatt had shot himself? Weren't they going to be surprised.

If I was right. That remained to be seen.

Chapter 10
No Laughing Matter

I barely made it to the Snapdragon restaurant in time for my one o'clock meeting with Helen, a long-time resident and farmer with strong views about the rights of domestic animals. She was waiting for me in the enclosed courtyard at the back of the building when I arrived, her gray-streaked hair piled in a precise knot on the top of her head, her shabby but clean jeans and olive plaid shirt the epitome of Vashon chic. She smiled when she saw me, a warm smile that made me immediately smile back.

The courtyard was surrounded by a weathered wood fence with a few trees drooping gracefully over the fence from the other side. There was a dry fountain in one corner that had the look of an abandoned work of art. The tiny metal tables were inevitably tippy on the stone pavers, but they matched the ornate chairs and gave the area a European flavor. It was a pleasant place, and both the coffee and the pastries were excellent. I was addicted to their rhubarb scones but didn't want to be distracted by food during our interview. Maybe I would purchase one to go on the way out.

Although I was supposed to be asking the questions, Helen jumped right in and started telling me all of the reasons Jake

Williams had been on the wrong side of the issue related to the wilding of the Island. Each point was accompanied by vigorous hand gestures. I moved my coffee back to avoid having it knocked off the table.

"If the cougar limited its diet to deer and other wild animals, I might not be so concerned. But how do we protect our livestock?" Helen raised both hands in the air, palms up.

"And Goldie, just think about Goldie." Goldie was the llama that belonged to the board member I'd already interviewed. The llama had fought back and escaped from the cougar, but it had several deep claw marks to show for the encounter.

"And don't forget the sheep." She slapped the table with one hand. I wasn't sure what that meant, but I nodded vigorously in agreement. I definitely wouldn't forget the sheep. And I wasn't about to point out that some people were under the impression that the sheep might have been killed by dogs rather than by the cougar.

"I read about a cougar in northern California that had to be put down because it was chasing bicyclists," she continued. "It may even have mauled one or two cyclists, I can't remember. The bottom line is that we can't be sure the cougar won't attack a small child. How can we possibly take that chance?"

I wanted to interrupt and let her know I'd heard both pro and con arguments many times before, but she was on a roll, so I just waited. The coffee was quite good, hot and strong, the way I liked it. But I kept thinking about that scone.

When she finally paused, I asked if she knew of anyone in favor of getting rid of the cougar and who might have wanted to see Jake out of the way. Since she had just made it abundantly clear that she vehemently opposed his views on the wilding of the Island, it was a very loaded question. Although it seemed to me that she wouldn't have been quite so candid if she had been responsible for his death. Unless it was a very clever cover. Somehow, I didn't think so. I had already mentally crossed her name off my suspect list. Three down.

"No one in our group would do such a thing," she assured me.

"If not one of us, then is there someone else who you think might have wished him harm?"

"I have no idea." She took a sip of her own coffee. It was probably cold by now. "It must have been someone from off-island."

"But why do you think Jake would go into the bog with someone from off-island?" I asked. "There had to be a reason."

She thought about the question for a moment. "I don't know," she said. "I guess that's for the police to figure out."

"You don't think that someone who has lost an animal they cared for might have been angry enough to get in a fight with him? Maybe there was a fight and what happened to Jake was an accident." I could imagine a blow to the head occurring during a fight, but unless Jake was dead when he fell into the pond, the other person had left him to drown. *That* wasn't an accident. Still, I was hoping that by suggesting it *could* have been an accident Helen might be less resistant to naming someone.

"I know all of the people who've lost animals, and I can't believe that any of them would have physically fought with Jake about it."

"What about the guy whose llama was recently attacked by the cougar? He's new to the island, isn't he?" Maybe she would give up a newbie if not a long-time resident.

"Well . . ." She tilted her head to one side as if considering the possibility. Then she sighed. "I just can't imagine it. He's got a wife and kids. Sure, they loved their pet, but they're good Christians."

I didn't point out that sometimes good Christians do bad things; instead I decided to try a different tack. "How about someone who is opposed to the coyote packs on the island. Anyone object to studying them rather than rounding them up?"

Again, she hesitated. "There are several people who think they should be eliminated."

"Does anyone you know object to Andy's work? Specifically, the howling surveys?"

"You should ask Damon about that."

Damon was my next interviewee. I would take her advice and do just that.

I barely had enough time to grab a refill before Damon arrived. The rhubarb scones were sold out.

Damon was short and stocky and walked with a rolling gait, like he rode horses a lot. Maybe he did; I had never talked to him about anything personal. There was something off-putting for me about the man. And I suspected he was on the opposite end of the political spectrum from me. On the rural-but-liberal Vashon that would put him in the minority.

After we shook hands I dove right in and mentioned that I was going on the coyote count outings with Andy and Norm and had heard that he disapproved of Andy's project. Did he mind telling me why?

"We should put a bounty on them, not count the damn things. You can count them after they're dead."

Well, that was clear enough. I remembered him speaking out against wilding at meetings, but I didn't remember him being so specific.

"Have you made your feelings known to Andy?" Was he the source of the threatening notes? Could he possibly be the shooter?

"You bet I have. Andy knows I'd shoot any coyote I came across."

"Did you know that I went out with Andy and Norm the other night on a howling survey?"

"No." He looked me over carefully as if seeing me for the first time. "You one of them coyote lovers?"

"I just want to know how many there are on the island. Do you really think we shouldn't be counting them?"

"Like I said, I'd count them as the bodies piled up. But you're welcome to do whatever you like." His eyes became intense. "What does any of this have to do with Jake's death?"

"Well . . . Jake was a strong advocate for the coyotes on the island."

"So? You don't think I had anything to do with what happened to him, do you?"

He sounded angry, really angry. I sat there, not responding, waiting to see if he would whip himself into a frenzy. But he didn't. Instead he immediately calmed down.

"I know any of us could be a suspect," he said. "But I can assure you that I didn't do it. I liked Jake. We had the occasional beer at Sporty's. When his wife let him out of the house, that is." He frowned. "That Jeannie is a piece of work."

"What do you mean?"

"Nagged him all the time. About him not helping her son enough. About going out with the boys. About that damned cat of hers disappearing. I'm against keeping the coyotes around, but bitching at her husband all the time cuz some coyote may have got her cat, well that's plain stupid."

"You don't think she had anything to do with his death, do you?" I wondered if he was trying to deflect my questions about his relationship with Jake.

"No, of course not. I can't picture her doing him in. Kicking him out, maybe."

"You mentioned she wanted him to help her son. I didn't think her son was around anymore."

"He isn't. But when he was living at home Jake was always complaining about him. Drug use, money problems, the usual. It caused a lot of tension between him and Jeannie."

Our conversation ended by me asking if he had any idea about who might have wished Jake harm, and him saying that he didn't. Like June, he was convinced none of the Island Land Stewards was involved, and he couldn't think of anyone else in the small island community that he wanted to see on a suspects' list. It was as if everyone on the island was family, united by invisible bonds even when they disagreed with each other.

As I waited for my last interviewee to show up, I drew a line through Damon's name. I couldn't prove he wasn't the killer, but my gut said he wasn't. But then, what did my gut know?

My final interview wasn't any more productive. Raymond had made my list simply because he was a complainer. And because I had sensed in the past that he was jealous of Jake's popularity in the group. When I asked him about possible suspects, he pointed a limp finger at the owner of the llama that was attacked. Another at the owner of a pig that had recently met an abrupt end to life. He added that the cougar could have avoided becoming the center of a controversy by dining on the excessive deer population instead of targeting domestic animals. As if the cougar were to blame for Jake's death. He concluded that someone should have shot the cougar, not Jake.

"Have you heard that Jake was shot?" I asked, surprised by his comment.

"Yes, wasn't he?"

"I don't know." Far be it from me to quash a rumor. Unless Raymond knew something I didn't. If Jake had been shot and it wasn't common knowledge, then Raymond might have to go back on the suspect list. I would follow up with Grimes just to make certain.

I bought a few pastries on the way out as an excuse to drop by and see Jeannie before heading home. Crane had probably asked if her husband had any enemies, but I wanted to hear for myself what she had to say. But first I stopped by Annie Regis's office to find out more about the developer Marie had mentioned.

Annie was all smiles when I poked my head in and found her at her desk. "Come on in," she said warmly. "I have a few minutes before my next client."

"It's about the Winchell properties," I said right off. "You may know that the Island Land Stewards are interested in either purchasing the properties or maybe getting an easement through the land."

"You've heard that I have a client who's looking at them?"

I nodded.

"That was fast. Well, I'd be happy to mention the easement to her. Since it's for low-income housing that could be a win-win for everyone."

"Great. Thanks." Mission accomplished.

"She's also asked me to show her some houses on acreage today. Something she and her family could use on weekends. Said she's never been here before. Her daughter likes horses. You know how that goes. It's a great place for that sort of thing."

The receptionist appeared and said that Annie's next appointment was early. Annie turned to me and said, "This is her now, Rene Hubbard. Want to meet her?"

Moments later, the receptionist showed Rene Hubbard in. She was shorter than me, and classy. My guess was that her designer jeans cost more than all the jeans I've ever owned put together. Her navy-blue blazer boasted "perfect pairing" with expensive jeans. As Annie introduced us and we shook hands, I noted the firmness of her grip at the same time I was admiring the Southwest silver earrings peeking out from under her perfectly sculpted hair. A mover and shaker if ever there was one.

We exchanged pleasantries and I mentioned that I was a board member with the Island Land Stewards.

"Oh, I'm not familiar with the group."

"Basically, our mission is to preserve undeveloped land and habitat on the island."

"That sounds admirable," she said with an impatient smile. I decided to wait on talking about easements. If she bought vacation property on the island, she might be more receptive to our goals. Most of the trails we cultivated were open to horse-back riding.

"Well," Annie interrupted, standing up and turning toward her client. "I have some great places to show you today."

I took the hint. "Ah, I was just leaving," I said. "It was nice to meet you." I didn't add that I hoped she found what she was looking for, because I wasn't sure I did.

———

When Jeannie answered the door, my first thought was that she looked terrible. Like she hadn't been sleeping or eating. She accepted my offering of Snapdragon pastries with a weak smile.

"I don't want to interrupt . . ." I hesitated, hoping she wouldn't turn me away.

"Come in," she offered. "Would you like a cup of tea? I seem to be drinking a lot of tea lately."

"No thanks, I'll only stay a few minutes. I just wanted to see how you were doing."

We sat in the living room. For a moment neither of us said anything, then we both spoke at once. She thanked me for being there for her the day she learned of Jake's death while I said how sorry I was about his passing. Then we both stopped talking.

"I know it isn't easy for you to talk about this," I said. "But do you know if there was anyone in particular who was upset with Jake about his views on wilding?"

She thought for a moment, then shook her head. "No, no one in particular. Even I disagreed with him about it. I blamed him for Woody's disappearance, but not enough to . . ." She looked like she was about to cry.

Not enough to kill him? Or not enough to want him dead? I waited a moment, but she didn't finish her sentence.

"What about some other issues he was involved with–anyone angry with him about something other than wilding?"

"No, not that I know of."

We sat in silence for a few minutes. Then we picked up the conversation by chatting about the weather and how her garden was doing. In the end, I was glad I had stopped by. Not because I had learned anything related to Jake's death, but because she seemed to appreciate me having done so.

———

That evening I was headed to a comedy potluck in a friend's basement. Nigel Moore loved his own name because he thought it sounded theatrical. He had a mini theater in his basement, complete with stage, painted backdrop and curtains. The comedy routines he performed with several other friends could be downright low-brow and vulgar, as were the videos they made. Sometimes they were hilarious, other times not so much. But he had a following that loved him and his events, and I counted myself among his fans.

By the time I arrived with my chips and dip, an unimaginative offering that I quickly slipped onto the table, the room was full of people. I grabbed a paper plate and loaded it up with other people's goodies. Each time I came I promised myself to bring something homemade, but so far that hadn't happened. I always, however, appreciated what others brought. Nigel supplied the drinks and the laughter, asking for a small donation from those attending to cover costs. I dropped a five into the bowl at the end of the table and looked around to see who was there.

Only one face surprised me: Morey Lawton, Jeannie's disreputable son by her first marriage. No one had mentioned he was back in the area. We'd never actually met, even though he was still on the island when I first came. I recognized him from a picture Jeannie had on their mantle. He hadn't aged much in the eight years he'd been away. The question was why he had chosen this particular time to return. Had the prodigal son come home to console his mother over the loss of her husband, his stepfather? If so, it seemed odd that Jeannie hadn't said something when I'd dropped by earlier. Or, was it possible he had come by for another reason, *before* Jake was killed?

At first glance he wasn't unattractive, tall and broad-shouldered with light brown hair and a square jaw that proclaimed virility, but at the same time there was something soft about him. He stood slightly stooped, like he was tired or lacked confidence. I stayed to one side, waiting for a chance to join in the conversation he was having with one of the more flamboyant young women in the group. The first strike against him was that his eyes seemed to be lasering her chest while they talked. To be fair, there was plenty of chest showing.

Strike number two against him was that he sounded high to me. There was something about his speech and demeanor that was off. But then maybe he was always fidgety and slightly incoherent. Maybe he always tilted slightly when standing.

Maybe he always cast his eyes downward and therefore couldn't avoid staring at people's chests.

When he finally turned in my direction, I didn't get a chance to introduce myself. But he didn't look at my chest. He looked me right in the eye. "Hey, I know you. You're that do-gooder from the Island Land Stewards. You want to save Wile E. Coyote." He sniggered and said, "Beep, beep." Then he added, "Let them eat cats. Get it, Princess?" I couldn't remember anyone ever calling me Princess before. And I didn't think my island reputation was as a do-gooder.

"Sure, I get it." I didn't add "jackass," but I thought it.

"It's people like you that . . ." He paused to belch loudly and pound his chest with a fist. "You, you're to blame for my mother's cat. You and your wilding buddies."

"My name is Lew," I said, trying to sound civil. "And I'm sorry about your stepfather's death." He not only sounded high but like he was more concerned about the cat's disappearance than his stepfather's murder.

A couple of other people joined us, whether hoping to see a fight or to keep Morey under control wasn't clear.

"Well, *Lew,* I hope you're proud of yourself," Morey said, emphasizing my name in a way that made it sound like a curse.

"I'm not sure I know what you mean."

"It's people like you who sucked Jake into getting all excited about those damnable coyotes and cougars." Morey leaned toward me, our noses almost touching. "You'd better watch your back," he said. There was a whiff of something medicinal mixed with alcohol on his breath.

"That sounds like a threat," I said, holding my ground. I could feel the anger building in me, like a wave of heat almost to the boiling point. It would have been satisfying to take him on. But I didn't want to ruin Nigel's party, so I finally took a step back and said, "It was nice meeting you, Morey." It should have ended there. But he grabbed my arm, and I instinctively took another step back, rotated my wrist to break free and then had to consciously stop myself from kneeing him in the groin.

Nigel suddenly appeared and put his hand on Morey's shoulder. Laughing heartily to ease the tension, he said, "I wouldn't do that if I were you, Morey. Lew's a, um, feisty lady."

Feisty lady? I raised my eyebrows at Nigel and he grinned. "Come on, Morey, let's get you a plate of food." He steered him away, and I felt my shoulders relax. The others drifted off, except for the young woman Morey had been talking to. "Thanks," she said. "I thought he was going to fall into my shirt."

"I was just trying to offer my condolences," I said, consciously calming myself. It was scary how quickly I fell into combat mode even after all these years.

"That may have been what set him off. A few minutes ago he was going on and on about how Jake didn't deserve his mother. Seems to have a mother fixation. And a love-hate thing for his stepfather. Weirdo."

Suddenly there were loud voices at the far end of the room. Morey was resisting Nigel's attempts to get him to settle down. There was a crash as a plate fell to the floor. "It's okay, everyone," Nigel said loudly. "Morey is just leaving."

A couple of other men went over to help, and the three of them firmly escorted Morey to the door. The two other men disappeared outside with him while Nigel turned to the group gawking at the scene. "Show starts in five minutes. Get some more food and drink and take your seats, please."

Five minutes to the second later the show got under way. It was a combination of stand-up comedy, improv skits, and a couple of short videos. Nigel was in top form for his stand-up routine. It was more political than usual and wouldn't have played well to a more conservative audience, but everyone seemed to love it. The skits were local humor. As were the videos. Everyone laughed and catcalled when appropriate. The incident with Morey seemed to have been forgotten. Although not by me. I kept wondering whether Morey was the note writer and whether he was the one in the woods taking shots at us.

When the show was over, I didn't hang around to chat. It had been another long day. I gave Nigel a kiss on the cheek, told him he'd been great, and that I was leaving. He put his hands on my shoulders and held on for a moment, looking far more serious than normal. "Be careful," he said. "Morey is a strange dude. We don't know what he might be capable of."

Chapter 11
Lights Out

There are times when I wished I drove a silver Toyota, like it seemed half the people in the world did, instead of my lime-green stand-out. As I left Nigel's, it felt like I was an easy target for anyone crazy enough to try to follow me.

By carefully monitoring my rear-view mirror, I was fairly certain Morey hadn't tailed me from Nigel's. But then, that didn't rule out the possibility that Morey or someone else knew where I lived and was waiting for me at the other end.

It was late when I finally got home, or, more specifically, to the parking area at the head of the community walkway. The sky was hazy, blocking the wedge of moon that should have been my streetlight for the parking area. The darkness at night was just one of the many reminders that the island was more country than city. There were few streetlights, even on the main roads. For the most part residents relied on moonlight, the stars, headlights and flashlights.

One side of the parking lot was shrouded by trees, but the other side had a few spaces facing the water. There was more light on the water side, but those spaces were filled. I pulled into a spot under the trees and groped in my glove box for the flashlight that was supposed to be there. I finally found it under a pile of manuals that I never used. When I flipped the switch the light flickered then went out. I swore and shook the damn thing.

When it was clear that no amount of shaking, twisting or swearing was going to revive the flashlight, I put it in my pocket so I would remember to replace the battery. My only option was to make my way down the narrow path with my night vision and the thin light from my cell phone to protect me from the shadows and my own imagination.

I normally enjoyed the walk to my cabin along the familiar path. Especially at night. I liked the feeling of being alone with the water and scattering of small homes that front the path as it hugs the shoreline. But when clouds blocked the stars and moon and most of the houses were shut up for the night, *and* there was the possibility of a hostile druggie or a killer lurking around the corner, the walk wasn't all that appealing.

When I got close enough to see that the floodlight over my door was out, I turned around and went back to Beatrice's. A flashlight with a dead battery and now this. I wanted to sleep in my own bed, and I didn't want to call someone to come over and check out whether I was facing a burned-out bulb or something more sinister. With a working flashlight and fifteen rounds of defense at my disposal, I was confident I could handle the situation on my own. It was just hard to accept that it had come down to that.

When Beatrice didn't peek out her window as I approached her door, I guessed she was probably asleep. I had to knock long and hard to rouse her. But she finally came to the door and seemed more than willing to loan me both a flashlight and her Glock. She didn't even remind me what I had said about waving a gun around when you didn't intend to use it. I didn't intend to use it, did I? I made sure it was fully loaded, just in case.

As I approached my cabin with the flashlight in one hand and the Glock in the other, I had an argument with myself about the wisdom of my actions. On the one hand, if it was just a burned-out bulb I would feel foolish if I called Grimes or even JJ at this hour. I knew either one would gladly come if called. On the other hand, if it was Morey in a hopped-up state or the person who had been stalking us—maybe also Morey, did I really want a confrontation that could end in a shoot-out?

I didn't turn on the flashlight right away, hoping for the element of surprise *if* there was someone there. Quietly and cautiously I crept toward the door. My heart was beating even faster than it does when I exercise. I could almost sense the blood coursing through my veins. To calm myself, I took a deep breath and slowly exhaled. Once, twice; my combat training started to kick in.

Just short of the door I felt and heard glass crunch under-foot. I paused and turned on the flashlight, looking first down at the floor of my porch, then up at the light above my door. The bulb had been broken. I quickly switched off the flashlight, reached for the doorknob, slowly turned the handle and pushed. Nothing happened. I'd locked the door when I left, and it was still secure. I tried again just to make sure and breathed a sigh of relief. Someone had knocked out my flood-light, but they hadn't broken in. Maybe it was a kid with a bb gun or a rock. Or maybe it had been a faulty light. I'd heard of them exploding.

I got out my key, slipped it into the lock, pushed the door open and, after a short pause to listen, stepped inside.

Instead of an intruder, what I found just inside my door were my two cats, pacing back and forth, looking more hostile than friendly. Probably wondering what was taking me so long to get inside. I switched on the interior light and paused again to listen while Dilly and Natasha impatiently urged me forward. Sometimes it was hard to accept that they liked their food more than they seemed to care about me, but tonight their mere presence was comforting. I would be happy to feed them, pet them, give them anything they wanted in exchange for their company. First, however, I had to check out the rest of the house, just in case.

It didn't take long to ascertain there was no one else there. It was just me and my two hungry cats.

I knew Beatrice was probably still up, waiting to make sure I was safe, so I called her and told her everything was fine. She said not to worry about bringing back the flashlight or the handgun tonight. Tomorrow was soon enough.

When I was ready for bed I put the gun in my nightstand drawer for safekeeping. I was about to turn in when I remembered the broken floodlight. It would only take a few minutes to replace the bulb, and it would be reassuring to know I had a porch light on.

When I got down the box of bulbs and batteries in my tiny pantry-storage area, I noticed that it was my last replacement bulb, so I stopped in the kitchen and added it to my grocery list. I was feeling mellow and tired, but I still paused to listen before opening the door. Then, flashlight in hand, I stepped outside.

Even in the dim light of the night sky I could see something straight ahead, a large dark object hanging next to the entry gong beside my porch. It must have been there before, when I first came home. From the other direction it probably blended in with the shadows from the trees. But I should have been paying more attention to my surroundings; I shouldn't have missed it, whatever it was.

I flicked on the flashlight. Even knowing there was something hanging there, I was unprepared for what it was. Someone had hung a dead coyote by its hind feet from the post next to my gong.

It didn't take much to figure out the intended message.

Chapter 12
A Coyote, a Dog, and a Couple of Chickens

J's phone went to voice messaging, so I hung up and dialed again. And again. Dammit, I didn't want to leave a message–I wanted to talk to him. After four tries, he finally took the hint and answered his phone.

"Lew, did it ever occur to you that when someone doesn't answer their phone there's a reason?"

"I need to talk."

"I figured that out. And for the record, I will always call you back as soon as I can."

"I need to talk NOW."

"Okay, give me a minute. I'm headed into the living room."

"Oh," I said, suddenly getting the message. "Sorry."

"No, you aren't, or you wouldn't have been so persistent."

"I need advice. And you're the only one I can count on to be both honest and rational."

"Next time I need a reference letter, I'll call on you. Okay, I'm sitting down, hit me with it."

I filled him in on the dead coyote and the confrontation with Morey and asked if he thought I should call Grimes or Crane or both right away or wait until morning. We tackled the question from several different angles and finally decided that there was nothing they could do that evening, in the dark. The coyote was a message, another warning, not an attempt on my life.

"I don't want you out walking around though," JJ said.

"Really?" I said. "You're telling me what I can and can't do?" I immediately regretted my tone, reminding myself that I had called him for advice, and at an awkward time.

"I wouldn't dare," JJ countered. "Just make sure your door is locked and stay inside, okay?" He paused. "Want me to come over?"

"No, that isn't necessary," I said firmly. I'd already interrupted his Friday evening. "I'll lock myself in. And I have Beatrice's Glock."

"Well . . .," he said slowly, obviously weighing his options. "What if I come over first thing tomorrow morning?"

"Hey, no need. Enjoy your Saturday morning. I'm sure Grimes will be around early. And Crane will probably send someone." I thought for a moment. "Let's meet for lunch at the Hardware Store. Would that work for you?" The Hardware Store was the oldest commercial building on the island. Once a real hardware store, it was now a popular restaurant with comfortable seating and an eclectic menu.

When the call ended, I sat there a moment, trying to dredge up some guilt for breaking in on whatever he'd been up to, but selfishly I was pleased I was able to get through. Some friend I was. But he had calmed me down and helped me decide how to handle the situation. I needed to do something nice to make it up to him.

I made sure the cats were locked in, gave them an extra treat that they immediately devoured, and locked myself in my bedroom with a book, a glass of wine, and a gun. I thought there was no way I would sleep. I kept seeing Morey's angry face and remembered him telling me that I'd better watch my back. Nigel's assessment that he was a strange dude didn't help.

At some point I must have nodded off. I woke up with the sun in my eyes, an empty glass of wine on my nightstand, and my book beside me on the bed with its pages all twisted.

It was almost 8:00. That's later than I usually sleep. Maybe it had something to do with the fact that I had locked the door to my bedroom and the cats hadn't been able to come in and demand that I get up and serve them breakfast. I could hear one of the cats scratching my bedroom door, its nails undoubtedly making tiny grooves in the wood. Cat owners have to get used to working that sort of thing into their décor.

I dragged myself out of bed, stretched, pulled on some clothes, stretched some more and decided I was ready to face the day. When I opened the door, Natasha wound herself around my legs, looking up at me with her piercing green eyes. I couldn't help myself; I picked her up and started making those stupid sounds people make when talking to their animals. Dilly came racing over to make it clear that he too deserved attention and that it was about time I got up. Or at least that's what I imagined he was trying to say as he vocalized what clearly sounded like a complaint. It was probably all about food.

It wasn't until I had my coffee on and the cats fed that I called Grimes. I hadn't looked to see if the coyote was still there, but when I told him about it, he asked me if it was. The cats wanted out, demanding their freedom by running back and forth between me and their closed and securely locked cat door. Using my foot to ward them off, I managed to keep Natasha and Dilly inside while I opened the main door a crack, just enough to peek out. The coyote was still there, its scruffy fur moving slightly in the breeze. It looked like it had been shot in the head, and one of its legs was bent, as if it had been caught in a trap before being shot.

From experience, I knew it wasn't all that easy to come across a coyote. But given how much online information there was about the locations of the various families on the island, it wouldn't have been that difficult to set a few traps. But why break my light? Was it to avoid being seen when they were hanging up the coyote? Or did they think that it was a more sinister message if viewed by the narrow beam of a flashlight? Like kids around a campfire telling ghost stories in the dark.

I reported to Grimes that the body was still there.

"I'll call Crane to see if he wants to send someone over," he said. "Meanwhile, stay inside and don't contaminate the area near the coyote. Better yet, why don't you go out the back and block off that entrance so no one else walks around there and destroys possible evidence."

My back door was on the second floor and opened onto a deck with a gate to the small back yard between my cabin and the trees. From the yard I made my way down the hill on the narrow trail on the opposite side of the house from the main entrance. On the path at the bottom of the hill I had a shed where I kept miscellaneous things, some useful, some not worth keeping. I found a piece of rope and an old stool in the shed and used them to create a barrier to keep people from trying to get to my front door, which was actually on the north side of my house, not in front. Then I wrote a note that said to "call me if you need to get in touch," wrote out my cell number and hung the note from the rope with a clothes pin.

Instead of going back into the cabin I sat down on one of the old plastic chairs by the firepit in my tiny front yard and called Andy. He sounded out of breath when he answered.

"What's going on?" I asked.

"Boner's missing," he said. Boner was his dog, a mixed

breed with mottled brown and white fur, floppy ears and big soulful eyes. Originally called Duke, Andy had changed his name to Boner because even when he was a pup he'd humped everything in sight. Andy had never managed to break him of the habit, but his friends had learned how to shake the dog off. Except for that quirk, he was a great pet.

"What does 'missing' mean? How long has he been gone?"

"He's always here at breakfast time. I've been scouring the neighborhood, but he doesn't seem to be anywhere."

"Has he wandered off before?"

"No, he doesn't roam. He's a homebody."

"Well, maybe he was lured off by some bitch in heat." Maybe he was off somewhere humping something that actually wanted to be humped for a change.

"It just isn't like him. And then there's what happened to Norm."

"What happened to Norm?"

"Someone opened the door to his chicken coop and all of the chickens got out. He's rounded most of them up, but a couple are still missing. And there were a lot of feathers near the woods. He thinks a coyote or hawk may have made a meal of them."

I took a deep breath. "Well, something happened to me, too." I started telling him about the dead coyote just as I saw Grimes heading in my direction down the path. I explained that Grimes had arrived, and I would call him back later with the details.

"Hey, Lew," Grimes said, stopping just outside the barrier I had erected. I joined him and together we stared at the coyote.

Seeing it hanging there reminded me of a book I'd read that had outlined our country's long history of trying to eradicate these resilient animals. Coyotes have been trapped, poisoned, and shot for their pelts and even for sport. They have faced species cleansing programs and habitat destruction. They've been strung up on fence posts as a "lesson" to other coyotes and as a way for their human enemies to boast about how many they had killed. But no matter what we've thrown at them, coyotes have adapted and survived. When their numbers are threatened, they actually increase the size of their litters. It has been said that when the world ends, only rats, cockroaches and coyotes will remain.

But not the one hanging by its hind feet from the post next to my gong. His species might survive, but he had been killed as a message to me. Collateral damage of sorts.

"Crane is sending over a couple of guys to check out the scene. They'll probably take down the coyote."

"Well, I hope they come soon."

"If you have someplace to go, I'll hang around until they get here."

"No, pull up a chair," I said. "Want some coffee or something?" He said he would love a cup of coffee, so I went around the side of the house, up the hill, across the deck, and down to the kitchen to get one for him. As soon as I entered the house Natasha and Dilly were on my heels the whole way, occasionally yowling in protest about their unfair imprisonment. Next to their food they loved roaming the neighborhood best. My guess was that some of the neighbors gave them treats in spite of my requests not to do so. They could be charming when they wanted something.

When I got back with Grimes's coffee, I found him talking to Beatrice. She was quite upset by the dead coyote and couldn't understand why anyone would do that to a poor animal. I pulled up another chair for her, and Grimes tried to calm her down by explaining there were a lot of crazy people in the world. I wasn't sure why his saying that helped, but she seemed reassured. Personally, thinking about all the crazies out there made me even jumpier.

"Speaking of crazies," I said. "I had an unpleasant encounter with Morey, Jeannie's son, last night at Nigel's comedy potluck. He got right in my face and threatened me, after calling me a do-gooder and blaming all of us do-gooders for getting his stepfather involved in the wilding movement. I think he was either drunk or high, not sure which, maybe a little of both. They had to forcibly remove him."

"Do you think he is responsible for this?" Beatrice asked, tilting her head toward the coyote without actually looking at it.

"I've been thinking about that. I ran by the grocery before the party, but it would have been a stretch for Morey to come here, hang up the coyote and then beat me to Nigel's. He was there when I arrived. I suppose he could have done it after he left the party, but in the dark and in a hurry?"

"So, you can't eliminate him, but you still think it's unlikely to have been him?" Grimes said.

"That's about it."

Beatrice wasn't convinced. "When Jeannie remarried everyone talked about what a horrible time Morey gave her. My understanding is that he never accepted his stepfather. Jake kept trying to get Morey to shape up. They had one fight after another. Then Morey ran away. Good riddance, I thought at the time. And now he's back and all of this happens."

"What about the daughter?" I asked. I didn't actually know her except to say hello.

"She's about ten years older, so she was already gone when Morey started having problems. As far as I know, she was fine with her mother remarrying."

It occurred to me that I might want to find an opportunity to chat with Jeannie's daughter. She hadn't come up in any of my conversations with Island Land Stewards, but I could fudge that a little if Crane found out and didn't approve.

Two of my part-time neighbors stopped to look as they headed down the path toward their weekend residence. They asked about what had happened and seemed concerned, not for me necessarily, but perhaps wondering whether they should turn around and go back home. Earlier they might have walked by without so much as a glance in the coyote's direction. There was something about seeing a barrier that made you stop to check things out.

Beatrice finally accepted a cup of tea, Grimes and I finished off a pot of coffee, and the three of us ate an entire package of pecan shortbread cookies before Crane's men showed up. I recognized the two men from the first day at the bog. It surprised me that Crane had sent crime scene specialists to check out my dead coyote, but then, if the two "murders" were connected, they might learn something helpful.

The crime scene men didn't spend much time looking around. They took a lot of pictures, asked me a few questions, then took the coyote down and put him in a plastic bag. I tried not to look, but it almost felt like I owed it to the coyote to acknowledge its death. As a species they had suffered so much at the hands of humans, and although I wasn't quite the coyote lover Morey thought I was, I felt bad that one had been sacrificed to scare me off.

One of the crime scene men mumbled something about the only good coyote was a dead coyote, and his somewhat more sensitive colleague glanced in my direction and said, "He didn't mean that."

"Yes, I did," his colleague said.

"Well then, you need to do some reading about coyotes," I pointedly suggested. "They are smart, adaptable, eat a lot of mice and rats and don't harm the landscape or people."

"Thought they went after chickens and cats," he said.

"Unfortunately, that's true," I reluctantly admitted. "But so do some dogs. Do you have a dog?" He looked like someone who would have a big aggressive dog.

"Yes, but he wouldn't harm another animal. And I bet you have cats, don't you? They kill birds."

"He's got you there," Grimes said. He'd been listening to the exchange, a faint smile on his face."

"Okay, truce," I said, raising my hands in the air. I had enough enemies without making new ones over an issue that could be argued on many levels.

"The one thing we all agree on," Grimes said, "is that it is some kind of sicko that leaves a dead coyote strung up as a message. Right?"

We all nodded. Then I thanked them for coming by and taking the body with them.

Just as he was about to leave, Grimes's phone rang. He listened for about thirty seconds and then said, "I'm on my way."

"An emergency?" I asked.

"A neighbor reported what sounds like two people fighting at the Williams's. Evans is headed there now. Have to run—."

I wanted to ask if Morey was one of the two people, and if so, who he was fighting with, but Grimes was already making tracks. Poor Jeannie. She had enough on her plate already.

After removing the barrier, I decided to clean up the broken glass before taking off to meet JJ for lunch. Even facing away from the post, the image of the dead coyote hanging next to my gong was burned into my brain. I had always loved that gong, but maybe I could buy a flower pot or piece of art for my small porch to draw attention away from it until the image faded, if it ever did.

Since I was still uneasy about what had happened, I

refused to let Natasha and Dilly out when I left. They made their feelings known, but this was one fight I couldn't let them win. To make up for it, I would give them supervised prison yard time when I returned.

When I arrived, JJ was already in one of the booths along the wall at the Hardware Store. He was leaning over the menu, his longish blond hair tucked back over his ears. At first glance, some people think we look alike. Except for my darker skin tone. And our eyes. Whereas mine are almost colorless, his are a lovely chocolate brown.

"I thought you had that menu memorized," I said as I sat down across from him.

"Almost," he said with a smile.

"How was *your* evening I asked," raising my eyebrows suggestively.

"Not as good as I'd hoped."

He was always on the lookout for a permanent partner, but so far he hadn't found the right guy. Since I hadn't found anyone I wanted to spend the rest of my life with either, I could appreciate his frustration. At the same time, what I found difficult to understand was why he kept trying so hard. It would either happen or it wouldn't. And life as a single had its advantages.

"You could say that about *my* evening too," I said. "In fact, I'd say mine was downright scatological."

"I was hoping for something more imaginative."

"Would you prefer offensive, vulgar, lewd or just plain foul?"

"That's a hard choice. I think I lean toward lewd, but I'm always a sap for vulgar."

"Sap? Does anyone say sap these days?"

"You're just trying to change the subject because you're too la-di-da to use the word 'shitty' to describe your evening."

I suddenly got serious. "They took the body down this morning. It was sad, really sad. It reminded me of the time a kid I knew at the commune cracked open a squirrel's skull with a rock."

"Sounds like a charmer. Where is he now?"

"I don't know. Probably a scientist who does animal research."

"Hey, be nice, we need animal researchers."

"It's like eating a hamburger. I'd rather not think about the cow who gave its all as I'm chowing down."

The waiter came over to take our orders. He was young and athletic looking with bright colored tattoos peeking from under the short sleeves of his T-shirt. I'm always tempted to ask about someone's tattoos, but since I've handled a number of Human Resources' complaints where comments about tattoos have figured prominently, I hesitate to do so. We both ordered one of our favorites, the Baja Tacos with a side salad, and chatted about random topics while we ate. After the waiter brought our bill and a mint in a cigar box, an interesting tradition, we lingered over coffee. It was calming to be there with JJ. But I needed to get going and touch base with Andy to find out whether Boner had returned.

Chapter 13
Alma Mater

As I pulled into the driveway, I saw Andy and Norm sitting on the front porch of Andy's rustic log house, with a bowl of chips and two cans of beer on a small table between them. "Pull up a chair," Andy called as I got out of my car. "Want a beer?"

I said yes to the beer and sat down next to Norm. Andy reached into a small cooler beside his chair, pulled out a can and handed it to me.

"Man, that's an ugly vehicle," Norm said, eyeing my car. He considered my Prius a symbol of a liberal urban lifestyle that he found distasteful. He was always quick to needle me about it.

"It gets a damn sight better mileage than that ancient truck of yours. Which I might add isn't exactly easy on the eyes, you know. Maybe if you washed it occasionally."

"I'm saving the planet's water for better things," he countered.

Andy wasn't joining in and didn't look very happy. "No sign of Boner?" I asked.

"No. And Crane still wants us to hold off doing the coyote count, at least for a couple of days."

"Did he mention whether they got any prints off any of the notes or knives?"

"Wiped clean."

"Of course."

"Why wait a couple more days?" Norm said. "It isn't as if they're going to catch the guy who killed Jake and shot at us any time soon."

"I agree," I said. "We have to make some decisions."

"About what?" Andy asked.

"How we are going to deal with the threats against us."

"I don't see what we can do," Andy said.

"Well, we can't just sit around and wait for something to happen," I said. "I don't know about you, but I don't like constantly wondering when some wild-eyed nutcase is going to try to run me off the road or leap out of the shadows with a gun."

"What do you suggest?"

"Well, we could run an ad in the Beachcomber announcing that we've decided we don't really care about the coyotes after all."

"Not funny," Andy said, sounding defeated.

"I agree with Lew," Norm said. "We can't just sit around and do nothing."

We sat there a few minutes without speaking, each of us lost in our own thoughts, Norm munching loudly on chips.

"Oh, by the way, I got the name of the developer who's been looking at the Winchell properties, apparently as a location for low-income housing. Rene Hubbard. Met her, in fact. I suggested to Annie that we would be interested in potentially purchasing an easement if Hubbard moves forward and makes an offer."

"Low-income housing seems compatible with an easement," Andy observed.

"She's also looking for a vacation home on the island."

"Better yet."

"Ironic actually. Another wealthy city dweller willing to pay big bucks for a vacation home while also looking for property to build low-income housing."

"You can't stop progress," Andy said.

"But I don't have to like it."

"Hey, Lew, didn't you come from the big city?" Norm raised one eyebrow.

"I'm a homesteader, not an interloper." Changing the subject, I asked, "Any chance either of you know Morey, Jeannie's son?"

"I know who he is, but that's about it," Andy said.

"Same for me. Why?"

I told them about what had happened at Nigel's and that Nigel had warned me Morey was a strange dude. "The question is whether he's strange enough to have written those notes to us and whether he is responsible for the dead coyote at my place."

"Well," Andy said, "back when he left town, the rumor was that he'd had a falling out with Jake. Jake was really bothered by his drug use. Morey was unstable even back then. Stole from his family to support his habit."

"Everyone says he's an unpredictable hothead," Norm offered.

We speculated for a time about the logistics of killing and positioning the coyote at my place, either before the party or after he was kicked out. Given the state Morey was in, I was doubtful that he'd been capable of it, but Andy and Norm had him tried and convicted in short order. Stealing from his family apparently meant he was capable of anything in their eyes. Not that we had proof of any of it; just local scuttlebutt.

"Can either of you think of anyone who would know

Morey well enough to render an opinion on his state of mind and motives?" I asked.

Andy and Norm had both gone to school on the island, but they were older than Morey and couldn't remember who his peers had been.

"What about his sister?" I asked. "Did you go to school with her?"

"She was a few years ahead of us," Andy said. "Nice girl. But I'd hate to bother her now, while she's dealing with her mom and her stepfather's death."

"We could check the school annuals." Norm said. "I know they keep copies at the high school."

"And we could talk to a couple of his teachers," Andy said. "They always know the gossip on the Island."

"Since it's Saturday, maybe we should start by trying one of his teachers," I suggested. "Any ideas?" I had planned to go home and work on a couple of consulting projects, but I could always work on them later. It wasn't as if I had any Saturday night plans.

Andy and Norm started talking about teachers who had been around long enough to have overlapped with their school years as well as with Morey's. As they talked about their high school days, I could tell that Andy had been the "good student" and Norm the "typical jock." In spite of those differences the two had obviously become lifelong friends.

In the end they agreed that the place to start was with Mrs. Grange, their former English teacher. She retired about four years ago but was active in the community and, according to the two men, knew everybody. Andy remembered her fondly, but Norm seemed to have mixed feelings. "She still looks at me as if she wants to slap my hands with a ruler."

"Come on, she never did that," Andy countered.

"She *wanted* to," Norm said.

They both laughed. Then Norm got serious, "We could also talk to a local drug supplier. Maybe he'd be able to fill us in on whether Morey is using."

"You have one in mind?" I asked.

"Well . . .," Norm hesitated. "It depends on Morey's drug of choice. You can buy pot at the local store that opened recently, but there's also a guy on the island who sells a little to friends." Andy and I exchanged looks. "It isn't as if marijuana is illegal anymore."

"It is if you aren't licensed to sell it," I pointed out.

"Well, it isn't illegal to talk to him," Norm said. "And he might know if there are other drug dealers on the Island. I can reach out to him on my own if you don't want to."

"No, we're in this together. If we learn anything helpful, we can tell Grimes, and he can pass it along. We don't have to implicate any . . . friends," I said. "Or suppliers," I added, laughing at the look on Norm's face. "Don't worry, I can keep my mouth shut."

Andy got on the phone and looked surprised and pleased to have Mrs. Grange answer on the second ring and say she was available and willing to talk with us. We were welcome to come by any time. When Andy suggested we could be there in about twenty minutes, she agreed without hesitation. That's true island hospitality.

———

I'm not sure what I expected, but it wasn't the Mrs. Grange who met us when we pulled into the driveway. She was tall and slim, her suntanned face taut beneath a scattering of wrinkles. She was wearing snug jeans and a tie-dyed shirt that I recognized as the product of a local crafts person. I owned several myself.

"I thought we might have something cool to drink out here." She pointed to a table with a yellow and green striped umbrella overhead. It was surrounded by a lovely garden of flowers in pots of various sizes and colors strategically placed to provide variety and dimension. Ground cover—woolly thyme, baby tears and blue star creeper—filled in the spaces between the pots. On the table was a pitcher filled with a pale-yellow liquid with lemons floating in it, four glasses, a stack of napkins and a plate of cookies that looked homemade.

Andy introduced me to Mrs. Grange and we sat down. "You can call me Cynthia," she said to all of us, smiling a smile that radiated warmth. "It's good to see you," she said to Andy and Norm. "Norm, I assume you are staying out of trouble these days." Norm actually blushed. I flashed on an image of a young version of Norm, swaggering down a locker lined hallway headed for a lunchroom food fight.

"It's been a long time," Norm said a bit defensively.

Cynthia laughed. "Don't worry. I know you're no longer the same mischievous kid you were back then." She laughed again, a soft sound of amusement. "You were a real rascal, you know. Or, maybe I should say you liked a bit of fun. It's all how you label things, isn't it?"

We chatted and ate a few delicious peanut butter cookies before she brought us around to the point of our visit.

"I heard that you've been targets of someone opposed to the coyote survey," she acknowledged.

"We aren't accusing anyone," I said, "but we think Morey Lawton might have a motive for threatening us, at least from his point of view."

"Morey." Cynthia said, looking thoughtful. "I'd heard that he was back in town."

"We were wondering if you could tell us your impressions of him," Andy said. "From his school days."

"Off the record," I added. "We don't want to cause him any trouble, but we need to figure out who's behind the threats that have been made."

"I assume the police are investigating," she said.

"Yes, but we're a bit uptight about what's happening and feel like we might be able to move things along more quickly . . ."

"By talking to a local gossip," she filled in for me with a low chuckle.

I took a sip of lemonade. "You make this with real lemons, don't you?" It was delicious.

"Now that I'm retired, I have time to indulge in some of life's little pleasures." She waved her hand to indicate her beautifully cultivated yard.

"It's lovely," I said.

"Colorful," Norm added.

Cynthia looked at each of us in turn. "I can understand why you're nervous. I would be too in your place," she said. "I can give you some background on Morey. And I'm more than willing to share my opinions with you, but you should talk to a few others to get a broader perspective. Each of us thinks we see the 'real' person. Deal?"

We all murmured assent.

"Morey has a troubled history," she said. "He was a handful when he was young, before Jeannie divorced her first husband, Frank. It was rumored that Frank beat Morey for the most minor infraction, sometimes for no reason at all. You'd have thought Morey would have celebrated when she married Jake. But he didn't. By then he was drinking and probably using drugs. At least that's what everyone thought at the time. Jake tried to help, but Morey was perhaps too far gone by then. They fought, and Morey ran away at the end of his junior year. I heard somewhere that he went to Wyoming to live with Jeannie's sister and finished school there. I'm not sure what he did after graduation, but it was rumored that he turned his life around, got a job, settled down. The only thing I know about those years for sure is that he didn't come back here. Until now."

"Do you know if he kept in touch with Jeannie?" I asked.

"You'd have to ask her. We all assumed that the reason she never talked about Morey after he left was that it was either bad news or she never heard from him. I didn't press the issue with her because I didn't want to pry. But I've been curious. I like to keep up on what happens to the students I've had in class." She smiled at Norm.

"What about his sister? Do you think he kept in touch with her?"

"I doubt it. She was too much older than him for them to be close. And although I don't think she had a particularly bad relationship with her father, she was gone before he started taking his own frustrations out on Morey."

"Based on what he was like back then, could you picture Morey being violent?" I asked.

Cynthia frowned. "I just don't know. He was a bully and quick to take offense. Got in a fair number of fights. But nothing serious. Kids can grow out of behavior like that."

"That hasn't been my experience," I said, then, feeling like my statement had been rude, added, "But as a teacher, you probably see the bigger picture."

"I always hope," she said, smiling. "I suppose if I'm being honest, it's not often kids change when they grow up. They mature, they become capable of making better decisions, and the troubled ones sometimes succeed in spite of themselves. But if they start out messed up, it isn't easy to get back on track. Not without some help. I'd like to think that the time Morey spent in Wyoming made a difference to him."

"He had to be escorted out of Nigel's comedy night on Friday," Norm said. "He threatened Lew and complained loudly about do-gooders and coyote lovers."

"Really?" Cynthia sounded disappointed. "I suppose he wants someone to blame for his stepfather's death. And maybe he feels guilty about not being here for his mother."

We drank some more lemonade, finished off the cookies and politely declined her offer to get us more.

When Andy asked if there was anyone from Morey's class that she thought he might be in touch with, she said she would have to tickle her memory a bit. Then she explained that she had kept annuals from every year she had taught. It hadn't occurred to me that a teacher would keep them as a history of a life's work, but it made sense. Annuals were very concrete keepsakes, not like pictures from office events or conferences that you invariably forgot to label.

"Let me get the annual from his last year with us," she said. "That might help me remember who his friends were. Although I think he was pretty much a loner."

"Really good cookies," Norm said when she was gone. "Love those cookies."

"You need a wife," Andy said.

"I need a lot of things, but that isn't one of them," Norm retorted.

"I'll bake you some cookies," I offered.

"You don't strike me as the domestic type," Norm said.

"I'm not." We all laughed. "But growing up female in a commune you learn how to bake. I can even make butter."

"Now that's a useful skill."

"It's on my resume. Along with a picture of me in an apron and a white ruffled bonnet sitting on a stool next to my churn."

Cynthia returned with the annual, thumbed through the pages and came up with a few names of people she thought were still on the Island who had at one time or another palled around with Morey. "And I seem to remember that Paige Thoreson had a crush on him. She was a couple of years behind him in school." She shook her head. "I thought about warning her off at the time, but then he left town. You all probably know her—she clerks at the grocery."

"*That* Paige?" Norm said.

"Yes," Cynthia confirmed. "She always liked the bad boys." She smiled knowingly at Norm, and he quickly turned away.

We thanked Cynthia, a.k.a. Mrs. Grange, and headed back to Andy's. We now had the names of several past pals of Morey's to talk to, as well as Paige. Then there was Norm's marijuana friend. It felt good to be doing something rather than sitting around waiting for the next thing to happen.

Andy and Norm had plans for the evening, so we decided to wait until the next day to follow up on our list. I was quite certain that their "plans" involved socializing and drinking. Mine didn't. I had to set up meetings with a few more Island Land Stewards' members and get some consulting work done so I could bill a few clients and keep my cats in their fancy cat food.

As I pulled out of Andy's driveway it occurred to me that I could stop by the grocery and pick up a few things for my home alone evening party. Not that I minded being alone on a Saturday night. Spending some time with my cats, snacking on junk food and getting a little something done sounded just fine to me.

Maybe I had the grocery store on my mind because Cynthia had mentioned that Paige once had a crush on Morey. But I did need to pick up a few things. And if Paige happened to be working, well, that would be a serendipitous bonus.

When I entered the store and saw Paige behind the counter, I was at first pleased, then uncertain. There were more shoppers than I'd anticipated. It would be hard to talk to her without someone overhearing our conversation. On the other hand, there she was, right in front of me, an opportunity waiting to be seized. Maybe by the time I'd picked up my groceries there would be fewer people around.

I went down the familiar aisles, looking for food items that were healthy but satisfying and that didn't require much preparation time. Fresh olives. Cheese. Whole wheat bread. Tomatoes. A couple of overpriced apples. And a Lindt dark chocolate bar. As I put the chocolate bar in my basket, I silently thanked the nutritionists who had labeled dark chocolate good for you.

The crowd did seem to have thinned out a bit by the time I was ready to check out. Unfortunately, there were two people in Paige's line and the clerk in the next line over was just finishing up with someone. When the other clerk said she could help me, I pretended to be studying the items in my basket until the person behind me took advantage of her offer instead. Luckily there was no one behind me when Paige started processing my purchases.

Paige had pretty light brown hair with dark roots showing at the part down the middle of her head. The roots were most noticeable when she bent over while positioning items in the cloth bag I had for once remembered to bring with me. With her checked blouse and freckled nose she looked more like someone who would enjoy a square dance rather than a dark bar with a bad boy companion. Maybe that had been a phase and she had long since moved on.

Paige and I had exchanged pleasantries in the past, but we had never had a real conversation. So when I asked if she had a break coming up because I had a few questions I would like to ask her, she justifiably looked surprised. Especially since I'd kept my voice low as if I were suggesting something illegal.

"Questions about what?" she asked, leaning forward and keeping her voice low to match mine.

"Someone you used to know," I said.

She straightened up and looked suddenly defiant. "Why not just ask me now?" I glanced around to see if anyone was paying attention; no one seemed to be.

"I'd rather talk in private." I said, softly but firmly.

For a minute I thought she was going to refuse altogether, but she turned to the checker one counter over and said, "I need to take a quick break. Cover for me, okay?"

She waved off an elderly man who had come up behind me with a basket full of frozen Lean Cuisines, put a "register closed" sign out and quickly finished off my order. I picked up my cloth bag full of groceries and we went outside. There was a bench to our left in front of a blank wall between the grocery and a suite of small offices. I'd often thought it was a strange location for a bench, but it seemed like a good, if public, place for our chat.

I didn't know where else to start, so I hit her with the bottom line: "You may have heard that Morey Lawson is back in town." She didn't indicate one way or the other whether she knew he was back, just sat there waiting for me to get on with it. "Anyway, he and I had an uncomfortable, uh, exchange at Nigel Moore's on Friday evening." I paused to see if she was going to comment. When she didn't, I decided to get right to the point. "That same night someone left a dead coyote at my place. And I think it could have been Morey. Since you knew him in school, I was wondering if you think Morey is the kind of person who might do that sort of thing." It came out perhaps too blunt and a bit awkward. But there it was.

"Why are you asking me?" She sounded wary but not particularly surprised.

"You went to school with him, didn't you?"

"That was a long time ago."

"You haven't seen him since he came back to town?" The question seemed to make her uncomfortable, but she didn't admit to having seen him. Instead she dodged my question by saying,

"We weren't friends or anything back then."

"So, you don't have any opinion about whether he's capable of killing a coyote and hanging it up on a post as some sort of message?"

She blinked a few times and stared straight ahead. "He's been gone a long time. And I didn't really know him all that well." Then she stood up. "If that's all, I need to get back to work." Before I could say anything more, she turned and headed off, leaving me with lots of unanswered questions. Why had she been so reluctant to talk about Morey? Had they been better friends than Cynthia had known? Had they kept in touch after he left town? And, most important, had she been in touch with him recently?

On the way home I mulled over whether I should have let Norm and Andy talk to Paige before approaching her on my own. I was the outsider, after all. On the other hand, they could still talk with her, and I would be able to suggest some things they might want to ask. Maybe she would open up to them. Maybe they would be able to uncover what she didn't want to tell me.

———

The cats seemed pleased to have me to themselves for the evening. They cuddled, purred and begged me for food. Natasha sat on my lap while I worked on my computer. Dilly kept jumping on my desk, and I repeatedly had to shoo him off. It probably didn't help that I intermittently gave him treats. If he connected the treat with jumping up on my desk, then I was in for problems in the future.

When I went to bed I again locked my bedroom door and kept Beatrice's Glock handy. I had intended to give it back to her but was glad I hadn't. I didn't know if Morey was responsible for the dead coyote or not. But someone had hung it there to make a statement. Either way, I wasn't taking any chances.

Chapter 14
Kidnapped!

I woke up with a start, my heart racing. There were coyotes howling and barking. It took me a moment to realize it was my phone.

A glance at my clock told me it was only 7:00. On a Sunday morning. If it was JJ I was going to give him hell for waking me up. But, no, my caller ID said it was Andy.

"Andy," I mumbled. "Is something wrong?"

"Did I wake you up?" he asked.

"It's Sunday morning at 7:00 a.m.—what do you think?" I knew I sounded rude, but I couldn't help it.

"Sorry, I assumed you would be up."

He didn't sound sorry, but by then I was awake, so it was useless to keep complaining. "You must have called for a reason," I said. And it better be a good one, I added to myself as I staggered over to my door and let my insistent cats in before crawling back into bed.

"Yes, I called because I have news."

It was at that point that I realized he sounded happy, really happy. "*Good* news?" It had been a while since there was much of that around.

"Really good news."

"Do I have to guess?"

"Drum roll . . ." He made a trilling sound, ending with a "ta da."

"Do I have time to make coffee?" I was awake, but I wasn't feeling up to playing word games. Besides, my cats were crawling around on my bed, nosily letting me know it was time for their breakfast.

"Okay, okay, I'll get to the point. My news is that Boner's been returned."

I felt a wave of relief wash over me. "That *is* good news. And worth being awakened for," I admitted, petting Natasha as she snuggled up against me. Despite his one idiosyncrasy, Boner was a nice dog, and Andy had been really upset when he disappeared. Then his wording struck me. "Been *returned?*"

"Well, it isn't all good news," he said.

"What does that mean?"

"I thought maybe you and Norm could come over for breakfast and we could discuss this."

"Please, just tell me what *this* is."

"Boner was kidnapped," Andy explained. "And his kidnapper attached a note to his collar when he returned him. That's what we need to talk about."

"Another threat?" The relief I'd experienced moments ago was quickly being replaced by a new sense of dread.

"Yes, another threat."

"Okay," I said, pushing Natasha away and throwing back the covers. "When do you want me to be there?"

"As soon as you can. I'm going to make some scones. That's one of your favorite things, isn't it?"

I was touched. "You can make scones?"

"Well, to be honest, I have some from the Snapdragon in my freezer. But I'll warm them and whip up some eggs to go with them."

I went downstairs and fed my two feline companions. They gave me a fleeting glance of thanks before digging in. Then I got into the shower and, in spite of the fact that our ordeal wasn't over, I found myself singing, off-key perhaps, and loud enough for anyone passing by to hear. I really was pleased to learn that Boner was okay. Pleased for Andy and pleased because I had grown fond of Boner over the years.

———

Norm was already there when I arrived. The smell of bacon cooking was almost overwhelming. "Hey," I said. "Haven't you two heard of stove fans?"

"Good point," Andy said, flicking on the fan.

Boner was suddenly in front of me, excited by the scent of cats on my clothes or the cloying smell of bacon in the compact kitchen, it was hard to know. Maybe both. I knelt down and gave him a good rubbing all over. "It's good to see you," I said as if talking to an old friend, but in the human-to-animal voice I can't break myself from using.

Andy was humming as he handed Norm a bowl of eggs and pointed at a fry pan on the stove next to the huge pan of sizzling bacon. "It's time," he said.

"Want me to do anything?" I asked.

"You can set the table. It's almost ready."

Minutes later we were all chowing down. The scones were a bit dry, but still good. The bacon and eggs were done to perfection. And the coffee was a perfect match for the hearty fare, a dark roast called Abbot's Blend from our local coffee-making monastery.

By silent agreement we weren't discussing the latest note or what we were going to do about it until after breakfast. As I ate, I occasionally glanced over at Norm and Andy. The events of the last week had brought us closer together. We had bonded in adversity and friendship. We hadn't come up with any answers yet, but after what we had gone through together, it seemed to me that we were better equipped to work as a team to pursue leads.

After we had finished breakfast and put the dishes in the dishwasher, we went into the living room and Andy showed us the note that had been attached to Boner's collar with a large safety pin. The note was in a plastic bag, but the large black print was still easy to read: "Now you know what it feels like to lose a pet. You were lucky . . . *this* time."

"I thought about fingerprints right away," Andy explained. "I removed the note from Boner's collar with gloves on. The safety pin is in another bag."

"Did Boner just show up at your door?" I asked.

"Yes. I heard a dog barking and knew it was him. My first thought was that maybe he *had* wandered off on his own after all and had finally managed to find his way home. Then, when I opened the door, I realized he was tied to the porch railing with an old piece of rope. Before I saw the note, I thought maybe someone had found him and brought him back. Then I read the note and realized someone had taken him to make a point."

"Better than a dead coyote," I couldn't resist saying.

"Makes it pretty clear," Norm said. "Someone doesn't like the island wildlife but didn't want to hurt a pet."

"They obviously took care of him," Andy commented. "He wasn't even all that hungry this morning. And he seems just fine."

"It's too bad Boner can't talk," Norm said as Boner rubbed up against his leg in a suggestive manner.

'Yeah," I agreed. "There are a number of things we'd need to discuss." We all laughed.

Andy called Grimes to report that Boner had apparently been kidnapped for two days and returned with a threatening note pinned to his collar. Grimes asked if the dog was okay and seemed relieved to find out that Boner was none the worse for his experience. He then said he would be by shortly to pick up the note.

Norm had gone back into the kitchen for another cup of coffee. I could hear Andy's Keurig making its water-filling-reservoir noises. I'd already had two cups of coffee, but the sound was to me like the can opener was to my cats. "Make one for me," I yelled to Norm.

"Me too," Andy shouted.

"Lew, you take it black, right?" Norm yelled back.

"Right."

A few minutes later Norm came in balancing three cups of coffee. I've never understood why people, myself included, try balancing acts like that when it would only take a few seconds to run back and get that third cup or whatever it was that made it difficult to carry everything at once. I can't count all the times I've sloshed coffee or spilled something by trying to limit myself to a single trip from one room to another. But Norm managed just fine.

When Grimes's official SUV pulled into the driveway, Andy went to the door to let him in. Boner rushed forward to greet him, jumping up and down on Grimes's leg until Andy pulled him away.

"Glad you got him back," Grimes said. "But can't you train him not to do that?"

"You just need to push him away," Andy said, sounding slightly defensive.

Grimes accepted the offer of coffee and sat down to study the note. "Pretty clear," he said. "Don't know why people can't just talk things through instead of making threats."

"Or why they have to use innocent animals to make a point," Norm said. Boner was sprawled across Norm's feet while Norm rubbed his head.

"At least they didn't harm him," Grimes said.

"No, but I'm not a wilder," Andy pointed out. "I'm running a science project to find out how many coyotes we have on the Island. Whoever kidnapped Boner isn't going to get what he wants by targeting me." He looked at Norm and me. "Or them."

"Well," Grimes said, "look at it this way. Let's assume Jake's death was a crime of passion, someone obsessed with making the island safe for pets and livestock. Your program is visible. And it seems coyote friendly. That may be all they need to convince themselves that you're responsible, at least in part, for preserving the wild animals on the island." He pushed Boner away with this foot and said, "It's too bad your dog can't talk."

Grimes looked puzzled when the three of us laughed.

Chapter 15
Sit Tight

Grimes finished off his coffee and declined an offer of more. "I need to call Crane and let him know what's happened and get this evidence to him. I'd be surprised if there were any fingerprints on the note, but you never know."

"Before you go, we wanted to let you know that we've been discussing what we can do to speed up the investigation."

Grimes held up a hand to stop me from saying more. "Last time I talked to Crane I mentioned that you were meeting with some of the locals about the murder as well as about the threats. He told me to tell you to 'sit tight and stay safe.'"

"That's really what he said?" I asked. "*Sit tight and stay safe?*"

"It's their jurisdiction. He wants us to let them handle this."

"Meanwhile we let whoever is threatening us continue doing whatever they feel like?" I looked at Norm and Andy for support, and Norm jumped in.

"We can't just sit around and wait for this lunatic to pull another stunt—or worse, another murder. We know the people on the island, Crane and his team don't."

"So, what are you going to do?" Grimes asked. "Maybe I can help." His offer made me wonder whether he too was losing faith in Crane and his team, or if, like us, there was the urge to do something, anything, to either make progress or to create the illusion of progress being made. Illusions were better than inaction.

"For one thing, we're going to talk to some people who knew Morey back when," Norm said. "We got their names from his former teacher, Mrs. Grange." Norm was apparently unable to call her Cynthia when she wasn't right in front of him insisting that he do so. "We know there are some issues with the timeline for him as a suspect, but he's the one with the strongest motive. We feel it's worth the effort to look into his past and see what we can learn about what he's been up to lately."

"I agree," Grimes said without hesitation. Then he looked at each of us in turn as if trying to make a decision about something. We all waited. Finally, he said, "Look, I don't want to tell you what you should or shouldn't do, especially since you are being directly impacted by what's going on. But if you're going to be out there talking to people, I need to share some information with you that I normally wouldn't, okay?"

We all nodded.

"That call I got about the fight at the Williams's place Saturday night? Well, it was Morey and Jeannie screaming at each other. Nothing physical as far as I could tell, but a real loud exchange. The distance between houses in that area is enough that no one would have noticed the fight except that one of the neighbors decided to take over some cookies to Jeannie. Thinking that with Jake gone, maybe she could use the company. By the time I got there, Morey had run off and Jeannie was in tears. Really broken up. It took me a while to get out of her what had happened."

"And?" Norm said when Grimes paused.

"This is off the record. Not to become part of the island

grapevine, got that? I'm only telling you because I think you need to know what you might be up against."

We all nodded again.

"It seems that Morey has relapsed and is using again, big time according to his mother. And he wanted money. Or something to sell to get money. And when she said no, he started going through drawers and looking in closets for cash and valuables. She tried to stop him, but he wouldn't listen. Then when he grabbed some of her jewelry, she physically tried to get the stuff back from him, and he pushed her aside. It was about that time that the neighbor heard them yelling."

"What did he take?"

"About $300 in cash and most of her jewelry. She said it isn't worth much, but some of it has sentimental value."

"What a lowlife," Andy said.

"That's a generous assessment," I said.

"If he can do that to his mother . . ." We left the thought out there to be massaged and poked at. It was difficult to know just what Morey might do if he was that desperate.

"So, I assume you're looking for him."

"Yes, I've called for help from the Fourth Precinct. They're our back-up for crimes like this."

"You're treating it as a separate case from Jake's death." It was part statement, part question.

"Crane's team is focused on the homicide investigation. It seemed like a good idea to bring in a team that knows the local drug scene. With luck, we'll catch up with Morey before he fences all of his mother's jewelry."

"Poor Jeannie," Andy said.

"Does she suspect Morey of her husband's murder?" I asked.

The question seemed to surprise Grimes. He had to think a moment. "No, I didn't get that impression. Of course, I didn't ask her directly. But from what she did say, my guess is that she's blaming Jake's death on some anti-wilder."

"But what if Morey isn't thinking clearly? Who knows what he has already done or what he might do to get enough money to buy more drugs." I could still see the anger in Morey's eyes when he leaned into me and whispered his threat.

"I can't say. What we do know is that he didn't get along with Jake, he's apparently an addict, and he robbed his own mother. That's why he's on the suspect list. When we catch up with him we'll sort everything out."

"Is he on Crane's suspect list too?" I asked.

"I'm not sure, but I would think so. My first priority is to find him, then to figure out what he's done. The lawyers and the courts can take it from there."

"But about what's been happening to us," Norm said. "What do *you* think about whether Morey's behind it? And if he is, why do you think he's doing it?"

"I'm not sure if it's Morey. What's happened to you seems more calculated than the other things we know he's done. But I'm not ruling it out." He shook his head and frowned. "Now you know that I'm going to do everything I can to stop this madness. And technically I should be telling you to stay out of all this. But I understand how you feel. You've been threatened, and Boner was kidnapped." He paused. "That said, I don't think Crane's advice to sit tight and stay safe is that bad. There's a murderer out there, and he may be the same person who is doing all this to you or not. We can't know at this point. But we do know that someone is playing hardball. As a law enforcement officer and a friend, I strongly recommend that you don't go off on your own or take any chances. And don't hesitate to call me . . . day or night."

Both his assessment and his advice seemed sound, but we all knew that the only way we would really be safe was to catch whoever was responsible for Jake's death and the threats against the three of us. With that in mind, there was one thing I'd been meaning to ask but hadn't gotten around to. Now seemed like a good time.

"Have any other Island Land Stewards' members been threatened or had acts of violence committed against them? I haven't heard of any, but I've been wondering if anyone has complained to you."

"No," Grimes said. "Nothing."

"What about Jake's friends? Other wilders?"

"Not a peep."

"Why us?" Andy asked. "It just doesn't make sense. We try to get people to discuss the issues; we aren't partisans."

"Did any of you ever work with Jake on anything related to wilding?" Grimes asked.

I shook my head "no," and so did Andy and Norm.

"Have you spoken out at any meetings or public events in a way that someone might assume you're pro-wilding?"

We gave him another chorus of negative head nods.

"How about going to coffee or out to eat with Jake recently, some place where you might have been seen by someone who assumed you were working together on something."

"I sat at his table at a recent fundraiser," Norm said. "But we didn't talk much separate from the group."

"I met with him over coffee not too long ago," Andy said. "And we did talk about coyotes. But I can't think why that would have been considered a big deal by anyone. He was always at the Roasterie having coffee with someone. He was a networker."

"Maybe we're just symbolic," I said. "Because of the coyote count project."

"That seems likely to me," Grimes said. "But I don't want to overlook the possibility that someone else might be in danger. I'll ask around. Meanwhile, haven't you interviewed some of the members?" Grimes asked me.

"Yeah. I've already talked to several who attended the last quarterly meeting. So far, I've come up with nothing. But you know Raymond, don't you?" Grimes nodded. "Well, he referred to Jake being shot. He's the only one I've heard that from. Anything to it?"

"Not that I know of," Grimes said. "And I think Crane's team would have told me something like that."

"Well, then it's probably just some screwy rumor, something someone said to sound like they knew what was happening." I thought for a moment, then asked, "One more thing, have you talked with Paige Thoreson about Morey's whereabouts? I talked with her last night, at the grocery, and I sensed she was holding something back."

"You've already met with her?" Norm said, sounding both surprised and disapproving.

"I needed some groceries, and she happened to be clerking. It was too convenient to pass up."

Andy looked skeptical, like he couldn't understand why anyone would go shopping on a Saturday night.

"What did you learn?" Grimes asked.

"Nothing, really. But she seemed evasive when I asked her if she had seen Morey recently. There was just something about her response—. I know there isn't much history there, but there's some. And it strikes me that she might be vulnerable based on past feelings and her current circumstances. It's hard to know."

After Grimes left, we continued drinking coffee and hanging out. Norm called the two guys from Morey's class that we wanted to talk to and managed to get through to both of them. He asked if they had seen Morey lately. They confirmed that they hadn't seen him in years, but they were willing to talk to us, so Norm arranged for us to stop by later that afternoon. One thing about living on a small island, life is a bit slower, and nothing is too far away.

During a lull in the conversation I called Beatrice and asked if she minded if I hung on to her Glock a little longer and if she would please go over later and give my cats something to eat. In case I was late getting back. She said "yes" to both. Natasha and Dilly would undoubtedly be delighted to see her. She was always giving them people food goodies in spite of my request not to. It wasn't much, she would tell me, and they loved it. Of course they did.

By the time we decided to hit the road, Andy, Norm and I were completely wired on caffeine. We headed out in Andy's Ford Fusion. Once, when we were talking about car purchases, he'd told me that he'd had a hard time choosing between his favorite Ford Fusion colors, Dark Side Metallic and Sterling Gray Metallic. To me his Ford was the color of a gravel road. But I suppose the name Gravel Gray wouldn't sell cars.

"We will be driving right by Paige's house," Norm said as we got under way.

"You know where she lives?" I asked with just enough exaggerated innocence to let him know that I'd figured out they had some history.

"Okay," he admitted. "So I went out with her, you know, once."

"You went out with Paige?" Andy said. "You never mentioned it."

"It didn't go anywhere. She's not really my type. But I ran into her at a party, and, well, one thing led to another, you know how it goes."

Yes, I knew too well how it went. And on the Island it was hard to keep that sort of thing a secret. It was better to go off-island for a fling than try to avoid both the person and the ensuing gossip after the fact. So, I was surprised that Andy hadn't known about Norm and Paige, even if it was only a one-nighter. He apparently hadn't noticed Norm blush when Cynthia alluded to Paige's attraction to bad boys.

There were several houses along the dirt road leading to Paige's small one-story, pale yellow house. It was set back from the road, tucked behind a row of bushes and evergreens. The curved driveway was lined with tall rhododendrons. About half were in bloom. Magnificent purple blossoms cascaded from the tops of the plants, ending inches above the ground.

When we could finally see to the end of the driveway, Andy slowed to a stop. There were two cars in front of the one-car garage. One was a blue Honda that looked like it had recently gone through a car wash. The other was an old white Toyota Corolla, sides streaked with dirt and windows edged in golden pollen dust.

"I don't think she has two cars," Norm said.

"But if the Toyota is Morey's car would he be that obvious?" I asked. "She could have a visitor that isn't Morey."

Andy pulled over. "Let's find out."

"You mean hang out and watch?" That didn't sound like fun to me. Who knew how long it would take?

"No, I mean that Norm should go up to the house and say 'Hi. Just passing by.' or some such thing."

"No way," Norm said.

"I like it," I offered. "Direct, simple, transparent."

"Then why don't *you* do it?" Norm challenged. "You already talked to her once, you could come up with some loose end you wanted to check on."

Damn. It was the last thing I wanted to do, but in some way it made more sense than to have Norm suddenly appear on her doorstep. "Okay, I'll do it." I made a face at Norm for suggesting it, but I accepted the assignment. "You stay in sight,"

I ordered as I got out of the car. "I want her to know that I'm not alone." Just in case, I thought. Just in case Morey was there and was the bad guy we suspected him of being.

"Fair enough," Andy said. "Should I keep the motor running?"

"Very funny." Or, maybe not.

Andy and Norm got out of the car and watched as I walked down the driveway. They looked nervous, as if they were uncomfortable sending me into the lion's den on my own.

It didn't take more than a couple minutes for the whole plan to fall apart.

Moments after someone peeked out the window at my approach, Morey burst from a side door and ran over to the Toyota. At that moment, Norm was closer to the driver's side of Andy's Ford than Andy was. He jumped in but didn't get the car started in time to block Morey's exit. As Morey accelerated down the driveway, he swiped the back end of Andy's car and knocked it sideways, leaving a huge dent in the fender, and in our egos.

How were we ever going to explain this to Grimes and Crane?

Chapter 16
Nothing is Ever Simple

As I rushed back toward the car, Norm was yelling for Andy to get in. Andy managed to leap into the passenger seat seconds before Norm hit the gas. I screamed for them to stop, to wait for me, but it was too late. I just hoped that they didn't catch up to Morey on their own. For all we knew, he could be armed.

I immediately got on my phone and called Grimes to explain what had happened. I told him that we had come across Morey at Paige's, and he had taken off in a white Toyota when he saw us. Andy and Norm were in in pursuit. I didn't know where they were headed, but they had turned east when they left Paige's.

"That all you know?" Grimes asked. I barely had the "yes" out of my mouth before he hung up.

At that point I realized there was another voice yelling . . . *at me.* It was Paige, and she was not a happy camper. She was standing on her front porch screaming obscenities. I wasn't sure whether I should try to calm her down or just leave.

It wasn't a hard decision. Since I didn't have a car, I wasn't going anywhere in a hurry; I might as well see if I could deal with Paige's anger. As I got closer, she stopped yelling and started crying. Then she collapsed on the top step of the stairs leading to her porch, her shoulders shaking as she sobbed. Damn. Was she an accomplice or another victim? There was no way to know for sure. But she wasn't trying to escape, and she looked and sounded truly heartbroken. I couldn't simply walk away.

"I'm sorry, Paige," I said, stopping a few feet short of the steps. "He didn't have to run."

She lifted her tear-streaked face to look at me. "Yes, he did. You know he did. They're trying to frame him."

"Who is 'they'?" I asked.

"You and your friends." She sniffed loudly. "And the police."

"You do know he stole cash and jewelry from his mother?"

"No, he didn't. She gave him money." She looked puzzled. "What jewelry?"

"Sounds like he left out that little detail, huh?" I knew I sounded unnecessarily sarcastic, but it was time she started dealing with reality. A bigger concern was that Grimes might not be happy that I'd let that piece of information slip out. "So, what reason did he give you for why the police were after him?"

"Like I said, they're trying to frame him."

"Okay, so you're saying he claims he didn't *do* anything . . . to his stepfather or to anyone else?"

"Well, he didn't murder his stepfather, if that's what you're getting at."

"What about the threats to Andy, Norm and me? Did he mention anything about that?"

She paused, looking down. "He did tell me about the coyote."

"What about it?"

Her head came up and she looked intently at me, as if on the verge of an explosion. When she finally spoke, her voice was shrill with anger. "You're all for those stupid coyotes, you and your friends. None of you gives a damn about people's pets."

"That's what he said about us? Is that what *you* think?"

"He thought it served you right."

"Did he write threatening notes to us?"

She didn't say anything, just sat there glaring at me.

"What about the coyote? Did he hang a dead coyote by my door?"

She suddenly looked apprehensive, like she was worried that she had said too much.

"I admit, we came here looking for Morey. We just wanted to ask him a few questions, that's all. We could have called Deputy Grimes when we saw his car parked in your driveway, but we didn't." She didn't need to know that we hadn't known the Toyota belonged to Morey.

"What kind of questions?"

She had me there. "Well, did he tell you about our exchange at Nigel's?"

"What if he did?"

"I just wanted to understand why he was so upset with me. They kicked him out before he had a chance to explain why he thought my views on wilding had anything to do with his stepfather's death. That didn't make any sense to me. Did you talk about that with him?"

"He told me that he came back to make amends with his stepfather. For his mother's sake. But before he could talk with Jake, someone opposed to wilding killed him."

"Morey told you that he believes whoever killed his stepfather was an anti-wilder?"

"Well, what do you think? Look how many pets have gone missing. Or have been attacked. Wild animals should be in parks and zoos, not here. There's no place for them here on the island."

It sounded as though she'd accepted everything Morey fed her on face value. But it was difficult to believe that Morey cared all that much about the pets on the island, or even about his mother's missing cat.

"What about his drug problem . . . did you talk about his drug use?"

She looked down at her hands. "He's trying to break the habit. He'd been clean for months. Then, recently, he's had a relapse."

Was she speaking from first-hand knowledge? "Have you kept in touch while he's been gone?"

For a moment I thought she was going to lie to me or get defensive about his addiction. Then, for whatever reason, she seemed to change her mind. "No," she admitted. "I haven't seen him since he left the island."

"He just showed up out of the blue?"

"He didn't want to burden his mother, and he needed a place to stay and . . . thought of me."

"Was that before or after Jake's death?"

She hesitated, then said, "After."

Was she lying? Her eyes had darted up and to the right, but that wasn't necessarily a reliable indicator. Still, I sensed she wasn't telling me truth, or not the whole truth. Would she lie to protect a man she barely knew? "If he wanted to avoid the police," I said, "why did he leave his car out in plain sight in your driveway?"

"We'd had a tarp over it; but he'd run an errand and hadn't put it back on yet."

"When did he run his errand?"

She suddenly stood up, and the muscles around her mouth

tightened her lips into a rigid pout. "I don't think I want to talk to you anymore."

"It's either me or the police," I said, knowing full well that it wasn't an either-or situation. The police would likely show up any minute.

She looked down the driveway. "You've already called them, haven't you?"

"Yes," I reluctantly admitted. "I had to tell them about the car chase."

"Why did you have to stick your nose in?" she yelled. Before I could respond, she turned and rushed back into the house, slamming the door so hard it felt like the glass in the front window might shatter. But it didn't. The sound echoed in my mind as everything grew quiet.

In many ways I felt sorry for Paige. Maybe I could have handled things better. But if she'd had a thing for Morey back when, and he'd been aware of her feelings for him, then there probably wasn't much I could have done. She probably felt flattered when he turned to her for help. And now everything had fallen apart. I suppose it was easier for her to blame me, Norm and Andy for her troubles than it was to blame Morey for what he had done.

I headed down the curving driveway out to the road. Either Andy and Norm would come back for me or Grimes would show up. It was a matter of time. The question was whether I would be better off waiting or heading for town on foot. I could probably run it in under a half hour. On the other hand, I could call a friend.

JJ answered on the second ring. "Lew, what's happening?"

"It's a long story. And if you don't mind coming to pick me up, I'll buy you a cuppa and tell all."

"Did your car break down?"

"No, I was with Andy and Norm, but they had to leave in a hurry."

"And they left you *where?*"

I gave him my location.

"What the hell?" he said. "Did they just drop you off? What did you do?"

"Why do you think *I* did something . . . no, you don't have to answer that. Just come get me, okay?"

JJ assured me he would be there post haste and rang off.

While I waited, I thought about Morey using Paige's place as a safe haven. Obviously he had been aware of her feelings for him or he wouldn't have asked to stay with her. Had he ever given her encouragement, I wondered, or had she lived on fantasy and hope all these years?

And Morey. In my mind, childhood trauma doesn't excuse adult behavior. Not for anyone. Nor do I accept any form of drug or alcohol addiction as an excuse. That said, I generally prefer treatment to punishment. But even if he wasn't responsible for all the things that had happened to us, in my opinion, Morey had crossed the line when he robbed his mother.

I couldn't remember who had written that "simplicities are enormously complex," but it seemed to me that the events of the last week clearly demonstrated that principle. Jake had enemies because of his views on the wilding of Vashon. That might or might not have been the reason someone killed him. Possibly he had other less visible enemies. Maybe it was as simple as a son and stepfather fight that ended in tragedy. Then there were the threats against Andy, Norm and me. In someone's mind, we represented the pro-coyote contingent on the Island. Could that individual possibly think that by thwarting us, the coyotes would magically go away? And then there was Paige, willing accomplice or gullible love-sick woman? In affairs of the heart, nothing was ever simple.

Bogged Down

Yes, simplicities were definitely enormously complex.

Chapter 17
Oh Deer

I hadn't heard from Andy and Norm nor from Grimes when JJ arrived to rescue me. "Where's your shining armor?" I asked.

"It's in the shop for repairs."

"Oh, you must rescue a lot of damsels in distress."

"That's my lot in life. No damoiseaux, just demoiselles." He pursed his mouth and gave me his best French gentleman look.

"Spare me, please."

"Hey, I haven't whined about my love life or lack thereof for a long time."

I was about to zing him on the meaning of "a long time" when my phone started howling. It was Grimes. "Where are you?" he said abruptly when I answered.

"JJ and I are heading off to get something to eat."

"Are Andy and Norm with you?"

"No, I haven't heard from them since they went after Morey."

"Damn!"

"You haven't heard from them either?" I'd been hoping he had.

"No, and, well, I don't want to worry you. Let me call you back."

"Hey, hey" I yelled into my phone. "Don't you hang up after saying something like that. What's happened?"

"Well . . ."

"Come on . . ." I was starting to feel that dread that I so often experienced in Afghanistan just before things turned sideways.

"Look, there's been an accident on Vashon Highway, just past the bicycle tree, but I don't know yet who's involved or how serious it is. As soon as I find out I'll let you know."

"Do you have reason to believe it could involve Andy and Norm?"

"I don't know yet. Seriously, I'd tell you if I knew. I shouldn't have called, but I was hoping you'd heard from them."

"Call me as soon as you find out." I tapped the off button and turned to JJ. "Head out Vashon Highway, south of the High School, past the bicycle tree. There's been an accident. No one has heard from Andy and Norm. They were chasing Morey."

JJ didn't have to think about what to do once he knew where we needed to go. That's one thing I've always liked about him—he never wasted time jawing about something when action was called for. Before I'd finished telling him what had happened, he'd made a turn down a side road that, hopefully, was a shortcut. We bumped along the gravel surface, creating a plume of dust behind us.

The bike-in-tree was a Vashon landmark, a bicycle, complete with wheels and handlebars, fully imbedded in a good-sized tree, about six feet off the ground. There were several stories to explain how a bicycle had been left there long enough to be eaten by a tree, some more fanciful than others.

Its origins might be myth, but everyone knew where the tree was, and it was often cited in directions by islanders.

I filled JJ in on what had happened while he drove like a madman, tires skidding around curves.

"More than twenty miles over the speed limit could get you a pretty big fine," I said.

"Want me to slow down?"

"No, I'll cover the cost of the ticket." It felt like a safe promise since both Evans and Grimes were most likely at the accident site. If so, there was no one else to issue a ticket. Unless some overly conscientious resident made a video and took it upon themselves to turn us in. There are lots of walkers, bicyclists and horseback riders on the roads to watch out for, so it wouldn't be unheard of for someone to report a reckless driver.

At that speed, it didn't take long to get there. I recognized Andy's Ford Fusion from the distance. The car was smashed up against a telephone pole. "Oh no. No!" I may have screamed the words; I'm not sure.

"Don't jump to conclusions," JJ said in an even voice that was most likely intended to calm me down. It was a nice try, but it didn't work. I felt about to burst with anxiety.

There was a Medic One vehicle next to the Ford with a Fire Rescue truck parked off to the side. A man dressed in jeans and a sweatshirt was in the middle of the road waving cars past. JJ pulled over across the street from the accident. I couldn't help myself. I leapt from the car and would have run across the street in front of oncoming traffic if JJ hadn't leapt out after me, grabbed my arm and held me back until it was safe to cross.

Grimes and Evans were standing next to the Medic One vehicle. They were talking to someone in an official looking white, short-sleeved shirt with a dark shoulder patch.

As we reached the other side of the street Andy stepped from behind the aid car. "Thank god," I said. I was suddenly aware of the tension in my shoulders and took a deep breath to gain control of myself.

Grimes turned toward us as we approached. "I was just about to call you." He shook his head and rolled his eyes as if to indicate that he couldn't believe what he was about to say. "Norm apparently thought he was Steve McQueen, engaged in a high-speed chase down the highway, and swerved when a deer ran onto the road. Car skidded, spun out and slammed into that pole. Damn stupid thing to do." Grimes sounded really angry, but although I tended to agree with his overall assessment of the situation, I felt nothing but relief.

"Where's Norm?" I asked. Andy was okay, but where was Norm?

"Over here," a voice called from inside the aid car.

We went around and looked in. "They think I may have a broken arm," he said. "Damn deer."

"But you're okay?" I asked.

"I just said I may have a broken arm. That isn't okay."

The EMT told Norm to hold still and stay calm. Norm took a deep breath then said, "The creep got away."

"Well he can't get that far," JJ said. "It's an island, after all."

Norm let out a loud sigh. "I'm just so . . . so mad. We almost had him. Then that deer charged across the road."

"I assume Morey didn't stop to see if you were all right," I said. Not that I would have expected him to. It was just one more black mark against him.

Grimes joined us. "I've got people looking for him at both ferries. He might have slipped aboard the Pt. Defiance ferry a few minutes ago, but if so, he'll be stopped at the other side."

We waited around while Norm was checked out. Andy

decided to ride in the Medic One vehicle with him to the clinic where they could do an x-ray. JJ and I offered to follow and drive them home from there, but Andy said they weren't sure how long they would be. He would call us if they needed a ride.

Before we left we checked out Andy's car. They had been traveling south when the deer had run into the road. The car had turned almost completely around before sliding into the pole. The front part of the passenger side looked unscathed; the brunt of the impact was on the rear door, the seat where I would have been if I'd managed to get aboard in time.

Just a few feet away, the twisted and bloodied body of the deer lay alongside the road.

"They were lucky," JJ observed.

"My thoughts exactly." Except for the deer, of course.

On the way back to pick up my car, JJ and I stopped at Zombiez for something to eat. I was starving, and JJ is always hungry. While we were stuffing our faces with plump, juicy burgers and crispy onion rings under the watchful yet dead eyes of several zombie figures, we speculated about what Morey would do next.

"Paige implied he might have hung the coyote next to my door," I said. "But she didn't actually admit he did it."

"Somehow shooting a coyote and kidnapping a pet seem like two different things to me. One shows a total disregard for animal life. Whereas at least on the face of it, the kidnapper took good care of Boner."

"People can love their dogs and still enjoy hunting," I said. "That's why there are dogs bred for the purpose."

"I know you're right. I guess I just don't like to think that there's someone on the island who would get their kicks by shooting a coyote, or any animal for that matter."

"Hey, someone killed Jake; that's the ultimate disregard for life."

"And for all we know, Morey may be taking something that is making him aggressive or even paranoid."

"Did I mention that he had a big fight with his mother and robbed her?" I said

"He what?" JJ stopped eating and stared at me.

I filled him in on the details Grimes had shared with us. Then I told him that Grimes had made us promise not to tell anyone, so he needed to keep mum. I didn't add that I'd already let part of the secret out of the bag when talking with Paige. I would deal with that detail when and if the time came that I had to.

"I can do that," JJ said. "Now, don't yell at me for what I'm about to say, but I almost feel sorry for him, assuming he's innocent of everything except the theft."

"Why on earth would you feel sorry for him?"

"I have some sympathy for addicts," JJ said. "They're so lost, so pathetic. There's a reason they start taking drugs in the first place."

"That doesn't excuse behavior."

"I agree, just saying that he could be a lost soul rather than an SOB."

"I'm still leaning toward SOB. But I'm willing to throw in lost soul as an extra."

We finished our meals and sat there letting the calories spread throughout our bodies. Finally, my brain started to work again.

"Andy, Norm and I were going to talk with a couple of Morey's high school buddies this afternoon. I suppose I should call them and let them know we won't be dropping by."

JJ brightened up. "Hey, the two of us can do that."

"We could," I said, considering. On the one hand, it seemed to me that the circumstances had changed, and talking to people who knew Morey back when was moot. The police would catch up with him and question him about all of the crimes he was potentially responsible for. On the other hand, you never knew what you might learn by talking to someone until you talked to them. "Oh, why not?" I concluded.

Chapter 18
Not a Bad Dude

One of the downsides to being a more recent islander is that you aren't part of the network of long-time residents. These were people who had grown up together, attended the same schools, played on the same teams, marched in the Strawberry Festival Parade, shopped at the same places, supported local causes, on and on, for as long as they could remember. Norm and Andy had that advantage, but JJ and I didn't. Still, we could legitimately claim to be their emissaries; and we did live on the island.

Our first stop was at the home of Tanner Jacobs. He, his wife and their four children lived in a sprawling farmhouse surrounded by animals. As we drove up to their house, we saw chickens of various types and colors running free in the large fenced front yard. To the left was a pen containing compact, dusty brown goats. A couple of donkeys were wandering off to the right. A barking dog of mixed breeds greeted us as we parked. He was wagging his tail, but we still hesitated before getting out of the car.

I had seen Tanner around, but we had never been introduced. He came out on his front porch and called for his dog to "hush up." He was short and had shoulders the same width as his waistline. But for some reason he didn't look fat, just straight up and down. He was wearing a blue plaid work shirt and jeans with holes in both knees, probably not strategically placed designer holes. He was smiling. That was encouraging.

"You with Andy?" he asked as we approached.

"Yes and no," I said. "I'm Lew." I extended my hand, and we shook. "I was going to come with Andy and Norm, but they were in an accident. Andy wasn't hurt, but he had to go with Norm to the clinic. Norm may have broken his arm."

"Oh, that's too bad. How'd it happen?"

"Deer on the road. Norm was driving Andy's car and swerved to avoid hitting it." I left out the part about it being a high-speed chase in pursuit of Morey.

"Damn deer. They are a nuisance at times," Tanner said.

"I've had more than a few close calls," I agreed. "Anyway, hope it's okay that we came ahead without them. We can pass along what you tell us."

He nodded what I took to be agreement, so I introduced JJ and they shook hands. I noticed that Tanner seemed to squeeze JJ's hand extra hard and for what seemed like a long time. JJ has told me that happens to him a lot with some men. As if they think they can tell whether he is gay or not by his handshake.

Tanner led us to a table and chairs in the shade of a tree, clapping his hands to shoo away a couple of chickens. He asked if we wanted anything to drink, but we declined.

"I'm not sure how much Andy told you," I said, easing into the topic. "But we are trying to learn a little about Morey Lawton, what he was like when he lived here, who his friends were, that sort of thing." I was deliberately vague; I didn't want to steer him in a particular direction.

"Well, like I told Andy, I'm not sure I can tell you a whole hell of a lot about what Morey's like these days. We hung out a bit back when, but he took off before our senior year."

"You haven't seen him lately?"

"No, not for years."

"What was he like when you knew him?"

Tanner laughed. "We were all a bit foolhardy back then. Liked to sneak a drink and a smoke. Chase girls. You know."

I didn't really know, but I thought I had a pretty good idea. "Did he like school?"

"None of us liked school much, tell the truth."

"What about animals, did he like animals?"

"Now that's a strange question." Tanner cocked his head to one side and waited for me to respond.

I made a quick decision. "I'll be honest with you, Tanner. We are trying to figure out whether Morey is responsible for a few, uh, threatening acts against Andy and me."

"Threatening acts?"

"Someone hung a dead coyote next to my door, presumably to let me know they disapprove of preserving coyotes on the island. And someone, maybe the same person, kidnapped Andy's dog."

Tanner sat up a little straighter. "Not Boner," he said with feeling. "The dog Andy brings to town with him?"

"Yes," I said. "But he was returned this morning."

"Well, that's a relief. But why kidnap a dog?"

"The note said it was to make Andy feel what it was like to lose a pet. Possibly someone opposed to the wilding of the island did it to make a point. Do you think that's something the Morey you knew back when would have done?"

Tanner shook his head. "He wasn't exactly political. And not a bad dude, just liked a bit of fun, you know."

This was the second time someone had used the label "dude" to describe Morey; Nigel to indicate his strangeness, Jacob to defend him. I could use the word in a sentence but didn't think I ever would.

"What about drugs?" I asked. "We know he's had a drug problem. Do you know if it started when he was in high school?"

"We all smoked a little weed, but that's about it. He did sometimes drink too much, but it was the thing to do, you know?"

"My understanding was that his father was pretty hard on him."

"No kidding. He used to beat the crap out of him. But then his mom remarried, and Morey didn't like Jake much either. Not sure why. Jake was a nice guy." Tanner suddenly looked uneasy. "Hey, you two aren't connected with the cops, are you?"

"No, no connection," I assured him. "We're just trying to figure out who's doing this stuff to us so we can put a stop to it."

————

David, the guy we talked to on our second stop didn't enlighten us much either. His description of what Morey was like in high school was almost a perfect match for what Tanner had said. Young guys acting out their insecurities by pushing the limits of what the community would tolerate. But nothing that included anything political or mean-spirited.

We were just getting back in our car when my cell howled. It was Andy. If we were still available, he and Norm were ready to be picked up and needed a ride.

When we arrived at the clinic, the two men were waiting outside for us. Norm had his arm in a sling, but he looked calmer than he had at the scene of the accident. They climbed in the backseat. Andy immediately asked if we had heard anything from Grimes about catching Morey. I checked my phone just to make sure I hadn't missed a text. But there were no messages from Grimes.

"How's your arm?" JJ asked Norm.

"Apparently nothing's broken," Norm said. "Just a few bruises and a sprained wrist."

"That's good news," I said. "When I saw your car up against that pole, I was sure you were both goners."

"Well, my car certainly is," Andy said. "First Morey rams it and then tiger here slams it against a telephone pole."

"We would have caught him if that damned deer hadn't interfered."

"I'm curious," JJ said. "How fast were you going when you spun out?"

"Faster than I've ever driven before," Norm said. "I couldn't believe Morey's old wreck of a car could go that fast. We barely kept up."

"I've never much cared for my Ford," Andy said. "But I would rather have traded it in."

"What have you two been up to while we were at the clinic?" Norm asked, changing the subject.

I filled them in on the conversation I'd had with Paige and the ones JJ and I'd had with the two men who had gone to high school with Morey. "Everyone seems to agree that he was wild but not motivated by anything other than having a good time," I said.

"What about the coyote?" Andy asked. "What did David and Tanner think about the possibility of Morey shooting a coyote to send us a message?"

"They didn't think it sounded like him. But then, they haven't seen him for a while. After talking to them, I think kidnapping Boner wasn't something he was likely to have done either. He's been gone too long. And no one describes him as the subtle type. Whoever took Boner was a planner. Not a 'grab the jewelry and run' kind of person."

"So, you think Morey ran away because of the theft?" Norm asked.

"I'm not ruling anything out completely, not even the murder."

"But if he didn't make the threats, then that means there are *two* maniacs out there," Norm said. I didn't like that possibility any more than Norm did, but that didn't mean it wasn't the case.

"My money is still on Morey," Andy said. "For all of it. Especially if he's using."

"Hey," Norm said, "speaking of that, let's swing by and have a chat with Chewie. I'm up for it."

"You're only up for it because they gave you a pain pill," Andy said.

"Chewie?" JJ and I echoed. It was the first time I'd heard the name of Norm's marijuana contact.

"Like in Chewbacca," Norm said. "He's got a lot of hair. You should see him without his shirt."

"I don't think so," I said. Then, turning to JJ, I added, "But hey, maybe this will be your Mr. Right."

JJ made a face and just kept driving.

After considerable discussion about whether it was a good idea to go by and see Chewie, we finally decided to give it a shot. Norm gave JJ directions, and we changed course. It was agreed that Andy and JJ would stay in the car so as not to overwhelm him. I got chosen to accompany Norm because Chewie likes "big women." I know I'm tall, but I don't think of myself as a "big woman." Nevertheless, I was curious about this Chewie person, so I let the characterization stand.

Chewie's place was in an area of the island not serviced by main roads. Rather, it was at the top of a small hill with unmarked intersections and dirt roads that seemed to randomly head off with no clear destination. My guess was that the entire hill had probably been owned by one person at some point, and as the land was sold off, they'd improvised on ways to subdivide in order to give access to the new individual properties.

His driveway was a long winding dirt track that ran through a thick bank of overhanging firs. There was so little light filtering down through the branches that it was like driving through a tunnel. At the end of the tunnel the trees opened up into a large clearing. A red barn with white trim dominated the open space. There were large double doors in the front of the barn with crisscrossed white two-by-fours that were either for structural support or intended to create a particular look. A normal house-sized door to the left looked like an afterthought. Both doors were closed.

On the left-hand side of the barn, about halfway between the barn and the trees, was a large RV, maybe an old Airstream. It was shaped like a silver bullet. Beyond the RV was the remains of a shed. As we got out of the car, the only sound was the trickle of water from a tiny stream to our right as it chased itself down the gradual slope covered in knee-high grass.

"You're sure this is where he lives?"

"I think he sleeps in the RV, but the barn is where he usually hangs out."

As we approached the smaller door of the barn, I noticed there were several cameras mounted above the two larger doors. It would be difficult to get close to the barn without being spotted. *If* there was someone looking.

I didn't see the two Dobermans until we were within a few feet of the entrance. They were wearing spiked collars, sitting immobile, just to the left of the smaller door. Like two guardians of hell.

"Should I say nice doggies?" I whispered to Norm.

"Oh, it's okay. They won't attack unless Chewie tells them to."

"That's good to know."

The door opened when we were still a few steps away. "Norm," a voice said from within. "Good to see you, man. Who's the hottie?"

First I'm a big woman, now I'm a hottie?

Chewie stepped out into the light. He was at least six-foot six, big boned, and, as advertised, very hairy. He had on a sleeveless, wife-beater T-shirt that showed off the dark bushy growth that ran down his arms onto the backs of his hands. More hair sprouted up around the stretched-out neck of his T-shirt. His thick head hair was slicked back from a widow's peak in front and fell down to his shoulders.

"This is Lew, Chewie. She's a friend."

"Lucky you."

"We have a couple of questions," Norm said. "Do you have a minute?"

"Sure. Over here." He led us around the side of the barn to some chairs barely shaded from the waning sun. "What happened to your arm?" he asked.

"Minor car accident. You should see the deer."

"Damned deer." That seemed to be a common refrain on the island. It wasn't long after a deer ate all of your vegetables or prize roses or ran across the road in front of your car at night that they ceased being lovable.

We sat down, and I crossed my legs, hottie fashion. Norm gave me an eye roll and then got down to business.

"This is totally off the record, Chewie. We're having some trouble with a guy and want to know what we're dealing with. We know he's a user, but we don't know what he's using. We're hoping you might have some information on him or know someone who can tell us something."

"Maybe. Depends." He waited for Norm to continue.

"You may know Morey Lawson. He's been gone for a while, but he's back."

Chewie smiled and rubbed his chin. "You're sure this is off the record?"

"Absolutely."

"Well, I do happen to know of the guy. He came by the other day and went batshit on me when I told him I couldn't supply him with what he wanted. He kept waving a wad of money around and saying he could pay. I almost had to sic the Spikes on him."

"The Spikes?" I said.

"Spike and Spike," he explained, aiming a thumb at the two dogs who remained at attention just a leap away. "Can't tell 'em apart, so I call 'em both Spike."

The two identical dogs had followed us from their position in front of the barn. Now they were sitting about six feet away, staring at us as we stared back at them. There was something very unsettling about the way they were studying us. Like two undertakers assessing us for embalming.

"Can you tell us what he was looking for?" Norm asked.

"He's either freebasing or injecting, not sure which. No one on the island deals in heroin, especially not that black tar crap that he was asking about. It's cheaper than the good stuff, but it can be contaminated." Chewie paused and looked at us for a moment with the same intense stare as his dogs. "But," he continued, "there *is* someone who comes over from the city, from time to time. Serves what you might call a select clientele. I gave Morey his name."

"And will you give *us* his name?" Norm asked.

Chewie looked at Norm, then at me, then back at Norm. "It ain't too healthy to give out this guy's name."

"But you gave it to Morey" I said.

Chewie smiled at me. "Yeah, I did. Probably shouldn't have. Felt sorry for him. Thought he might as well get his drugs here as taking his chances in the city."

"From your point of view, just how unstable was he?" I asked. "Did you think he had the potential to be violent?"

"'Potential to be violent'–that's cute." Chewie smiled again. "Was he a hothead with a bad temper and a short fuse? Uh huh. Right on."

"But you still gave him someone's name so he could get more drugs?" I hoped I didn't sound too judgmental, but it's hard to keep your tone neutral when an inner voice is yelling "what were you thinking?"

"Hey, Morey had the money and was pretty determined. The contact can take care of himself."

"Well," Norm persisted, "if we wanted to get in touch with this dealer, how would we go about it?"

"It's not that I don't trust you," Chewie said, looking thoughtful. "But I can't have any of this coming back on me. Sure, I sell a little weed on the side, good stuff, but I'm hoping to get a license so I can sell it in the open. You understand that I can't be associated with someone selling illegal drugs. I'd never get a license."

"You have my word that no one will know where we got the information."

"And mine," I added.

He looked at us, his gaze as direct and unnerving as that of the two Spikes. The message was clear, we'd damn well better keep to our end of the bargain.

"I'm not writing anything down," Chewie said. "I'll tell you a name and a number. You want to write it down, that's your business. As far as I'm concerned you two were never here." Then he relaxed and turned to me, grinning. "But, hey, sweet-cakes, *you're* welcome to come back any time you like."

Sweetcakes? Was he jerking my chain or just being himself? What the hell, he was doing us a favor, and I've been called worse.

He gave us the number, slowly, repeating it twice. Then he gave me his own number and said to feel free to call any time. I didn't plan on it, but I memorized it anyway. If I ran into someone who wanted a little weed, I might pass it on. It was probably cheaper to buy from him than from the local store. And it might be better product.

We thanked him and headed to the car. The Spikes watched us go, totally motionless, ready to spring into action given the slightest excuse.

We didn't give them one.

Chapter 19
Pistol Packin' Mama

Norm and Andy were hungry, so we stopped to pick up a pizza at the Saucy Sisters before heading back to Andy's office. Andy was still pumped up from the morning's events, and Norm was feeling no pain. Neither felt like going home to rest, even if that was the smart thing to do.

"What now?" Norm asked with his mouth full of pizza. Even with only one hand he was managing to wolf down all of his share and more. Although I wasn't hungry, the smell was enticing. I picked a piece of pepperoni off a slice and Norm slapped my fingers with his good hand and smirked. "Watch it, *hottie.*"

"You don't scare me," I said, filching another pepperoni.

"I bet no one takes pepperoni off Chewie's pizza with the two Spikes staring them down," Norm said.

"Morey's lucky to have come away from Chewie's with his limbs intact."

"Okay, everyone. Time to get down to business," Andy said. "Who wants to call the dealer?"

"I don't think he will tell us anything," I said. "At least nothing we don't already know."

"Can't see what's in it for him," JJ agreed. "Unless you want to pay for information."

"Then why bother getting his contact information?" Andy asked.

Norm and I looked at each other. "It seemed like the thing to do," Norm said, and I nodded agreement.

"Besides," I added, "if he sold Morey illegal drugs while thinking Morey is mentally unstable, why should he tell us? Wouldn't that just incriminate him? And we already know Morey is doing some weird stuff."

"So, if we don't call the dealer, where does that leave us?" Andy asked.

"No place I ever wanted to be," I said.

Except for Norm's chewing noises, like thongs slapping a muddy beach, we sat there quietly contemplating our options. In my mind, there didn't seem to be much of anything we could do at this point to determine for sure whether Morey was responsible for any of the things that had happened to us. And if he wasn't the one, and it was someone else entirely, then we were back to square one.

JJ finally broke the silence. "Seems to me there's not much you can do on your own at this point. You need to goose the officials to get some answers."

"Goose the officials?" I said. "Anyone in particular?"

"You know what I mean." JJ hit my shoulder with his fist, his dark brown eyes flashing mock disapproval.

Andy sighed. "Let's just hope Grimes catches Morey. That would be a step in the right direction."

"I've thought about talking to Morey's sister," I said.

"We could," Andy said. "But Grimes told me he talked with her already. It was a dead-end. Said they were never close, and he isn't exactly on her Christmas list these days."

Norm was still working his way through his pizza, making

some new sounds that reminded me of a dentist tamping down an amalgam filling.

"You really need to work on your table manners," I said. Half serious.

"Hey, I only have one hand."

"And that means you have to chew with your mouth open?" It crossed my mind that it was none of my business, and a tacky thing to say as well, but it was too late for second thoughts.

"It's a guy thing," JJ said, whether in Norm's defense or to retaliate for my goosing comment.

"Yeah, a guy thing," Norm said, leaning forward so I could practically see his tonsils as he chewed. Sometimes he can be a real class act.

Trying to lighten the downer mood I'd created, I grabbed another slice of pepperoni off his pizza and said, "And it's *my* thing to steal food." I popped it in my mouth and chewed vigorously with my mouth open. "There, just want to fit in."

JJ groaned. But Norm laughed, and I joined in.

By the time we finally called it a day, I was exhausted, not physically but emotionally. What I wanted to do was go home and have a run to unwind, but I wasn't sure that was a good idea. We had agreed that we would be extra cautious for the next few days. And being out alone as it got dark didn't seem too smart. It had been hard enough to convince JJ that I was safe walking down the path to my house on my own. Even with a Glock in hand.

When I pulled into the walk-in parking area, I didn't get out immediately. Instead, I took a few minutes to look around and assess the situation. There didn't seem to be anyone nearby, at least no one I could see. With my hand on the pistol in my pocket I got out of my car and headed down the path toward home.

As I walked rapidly along the graveled foot path, I found

myself mouthing the lyrics to an old Willie Nelson song: *Lay that pistol down Babe*. Damn he's good. He can take a simple song of revenge and give it soul.

The moonlight was bright enough to make me feel comfortable on the narrow path even without a flashlight. Most of the lights in the houses I passed by were off. Even Beatrice's house looked all dark and buttoned up for the evening. A bit early for her, but maybe she was watching television in bed. I knew it was a stereotype, but I pictured her glued to a repeat of a Miss Marple mystery.

It was almost a letdown when nothing happened. No one shot at me, no one attacked me, no one even yelled at me. The trip from my car to my front door was totally a non-event. But once I stepped inside it was a different story. I was immediately bombarded . . . by cats, two of them to be precise. Natasha and Dilly were not happy with me, and they were damn well determined to make sure I knew it.

I locked the door behind me, wishing I had a deadbolt. And bars on my windows, and an alarm system with cameras, and a pair of matching Dobermans. A lot more than two dilettante cats. Those two were even unlikely to defend me against an attack by other cats, unless I was opening a can of Blue Buffalo Wilderness Chicken Grain-Free cat food.

After checking to make certain there was no one else in the house and that all the windows were securely locked, I finally set my Glock aside while humming *lay that pistol down, Babe*. Then I fed my insistent feline companions and tried to decide if I was hungry or not. After searching my cupboards for snacks, I decided I wasn't hungry enough to actually go to the bother of fixing something, so I poured myself a glass of wine and ran the water for a bath.

It was unfortunate that the only bathtub in the cabin was upstairs, but the original owners probably used my spare room as their main bedroom. All I had downstairs was a small bathroom with a tiny shower and the bare essentials.

From my point of view, there's nothing more relaxing than a glass of wine and a good soak. When the tub was full I got in, leaned back in the hot water, and was just starting to relax when I thought I heard a distant rattling sound. I told myself it was the cats, probably up to no good, expressing their peevishness because I'd locked the bathroom door.

On the other hand, what if someone was trying to break in? It crossed my mind that if I was a character in a movie, this might be the moment when the eerie music started playing and people in the audience were yelling, "Look out!"

Listening for all I was worth, I thought I heard another sound that I found difficult to attribute to my cats. It wasn't much, but I couldn't get it out of my head that there could be someone trying to break into my cabin. I forced myself to leave the comfort of the steaming water, threw on some clothes and pressed my ear against the door. Nothing. Still, I was damn sure I had heard *something*, something that didn't fit with the typical noises my house made at night.

If I'd just thought to bring the pistol in with me, I'd have been a lot happier, but I hadn't. It was on the sideboard in the hall downstairs. A foolish place to leave it under any circumstances. If someone broke in, they would undoubtedly see it there. Bloody hell. I didn't want to be shot with Beatrice's handgun.

My clothes were sticking to me because I hadn't taken time to properly dry myself, and I didn't have any shoes. I'd taken them off when I came in and left them at the front door. I felt both stupid and vulnerable. My situation reminded me again of my time in Afghanistan. Just when you started getting comfortable, that was when the bad stuff always happened. Instead of trying to relax, I should have remained vigilant. Now I was paying for my mistake.

I don't know how long I stood there listening. Logic told me I was better off staying in the bathroom rather than exposing myself to whoever was out there. *If* there was someone there. On the other hand, I couldn't just stand there indefinitely trying to decide what it was that I'd heard. If someone was in the house or was trying to get in, I had to do something.

The bathroom stretched from midway along the front of the second floor to the side of the house. There was no deck accessible from the bathroom, and it was a straight drop to the ground from the single opening window facing the woods. But it wasn't more than a couple of feet from the window to the sloped roof. Although I had never tried it before, I thought I might be able to get out the window and swing onto the roof. It seemed worth a look. Better than staying shut up in the bathroom all night waiting for something to happen.

The window was already cranked part way open, but I had a screen up. I slowly cranked it open all the way, surprised and relieved there was no sound. Next came the screen. It popped out with a soft tinny ping that I hoped didn't sound like what it actually was—*if* there was anyone listening. It was then a matter of pulling myself into a seated position on the windowsill and leaning out to assess the situation.

Getting from the window to the roof looked like a stretch, but not impossible for someone my height. I took a deep breath and pulled myself into a squat, then slowly leaned out until I could reach for the roof. I pride myself on my flexibility and overall strength, but it was awkward finding a place to grab on. Once I found a hold, however, it wasn't that hard to swing a leg over the edge of the roof and pull myself up. The gradually sloped roof was easy to climb up and over. Being barefoot was an advantage in that I didn't make any heavy-footed galumphing sounds. Once on the other side I was careful to ease myself off the roof onto the deck next to a wall rather than in front of a window.

My goal had been to reach the deck. I hadn't planned what to do after that. I had no phone and no weapon. And I had carefully locked all of the doors and windows from the inside. If someone had broken in, they had either picked the lock or forced the door open with a tool. Even if I could get in, that might not be the smartest move under the circumstances. And the same held true if they were up to some sort of mischief outside my cabin.

I stood there for what seemed like forever, probably a couple of minutes in "standing in the dark listening and waiting for someone to attack" time. Finally, I made a decision. Before trying to get Beatrice's attention and asking to use her phone, I would check out the parking lot to see if there were any strange cars around. I knew the ones driven by the full-time residents and frequent weekenders. Of course, a car I hadn't seen before could always belong to a visitor or one of the weekenders who didn't come often. But it was a place to start. And it was action that would take me away from a potentially hostile confrontation.

The dangerous move, if there was someone lying in wait, was crossing the deck to grab the old pair of sneakers I leave there for gardening. Then I'd have to run like hell around the small, fenced garden and into the woods that covered the steep hillside behind my house. Breathing deeply, I prepared myself for the sprint, praying that no one with a gun was watching. Once I was under way the entire effort probably took less than thirty seconds, but it seemed to take forever. By the time I was hidden among the fir trees, I was experiencing an extreme adrenaline rush. I paused long enough to see if there was anyone in pursuit, and, seeing no one, I pulled on my shoes, tied the laces, and headed off toward the parking lot.

I often ran this route through the trees to the parking area, both for exercise and because it was fun. There wasn't quite a path, but I had taken that route enough times to be familiar with the terrain and to know how to avoid or deal with some of the most challenging obstacles. If someone was following me, I doubted they would find the landscape as friendly.

The hillside was steep in places, but it occasionally leveled off. There were some large alders that had recently come down in a windstorm and quite a few smaller branches that had to be maneuvered over or around, but the underbrush was sparse, mostly ferns, bracken and salal, so it wasn't an incredibly difficult run. At one point there was a small stream, but it was narrow enough to leap across with solid footing on the other side. As I got near the parking lot the foliage became thicker and the descent steep. I had to slow down and watch my footing so as not to trip and fall.

Because we had all decided to be as alert as possible about our surroundings, I had paid particular attention to the cars parked in the lot and along the road leading to the walk-ins. Slowly moving past the line of familiar cars, it seemed to me that nothing had changed. But I only had to be off by one car to be horribly wrong. It was possible someone could have parked on the hill above and walked down, although that seemed unlikely. There was no place to quickly hide with a vertical embankment on one side and a steep ravine on the other.

I had just about decided to sneak back through the woods to Beatrice's when I saw someone making the turn from the walkway to the parking area. At this distance in the dim light I couldn't see who it was, so I ducked down behind a car. Friend or foe? And had they seen me or not?

When I peeked around the end of the car, I saw the man

stopped about half way across the lot, looking in my direction. Now what?

"Hello," he said tentatively. "Anyone there?"

I recognized the voice. It was a neighbor's uncle, a visitor I often passed the time of day with when we met on the path. I stood up. "Hi, just me, Lew. You frightened me."

"And *you* frightened me," he said, moving toward me.

"Sorry, but I had a bad experience the other day, and I've been a bit nervous since then."

"I heard about the dead coyote someone left at your place," he said. "Did you find out who did it?"

"No, not yet. That's why I'm feeling jumpy." I didn't feel like explaining the evening's scenario to him, but him turning up was a stroke of luck. "Any chance you have your cell on you? I've locked myself out and want to call a friend who has a key."

"Yes, I do." He immediately reached into his pocket. These days it seems that everyone is a single movement away from their phones. He handed me his iPhone and I punched in the familiar number. Would JJ answer when he didn't recognize the number I was calling from? I was relieved when I heard the tentative "hello."

"JJ? I've locked myself out and need you to come let me in. Can you do that?"

"I thought you had a spare key under a rock out back."

"Un huh, that's right. So, you can come over? I'm in the parking area."

"Let me see if I understand. You don't have your phone with you, so you're using someone else's, right?"

"Yes."

"Are you in danger?"

"No."

"But you want me to come over there."

"Yes."

"Okay. I'll leave immediately."

"Thanks." What a great friend. Picks up on the smallest cues and is willing to take a request on faith.

I handed the cell back. "I appreciate that. My friend's on his way."

"Want me to wait with you until he arrives?"

"That's nice of you, but I'm fine." I wasn't sure that was entirely true, but I didn't plan on standing out in the open after he drove off and left me there alone.

Ten minutes later JJ drove up and pulled into a parking spot. I came out of the woods and walked over to his car. He apparently didn't see me coming, so when he started to get out of the car and caught sight of me, he yelped and leapt back, banging into the door frame. "Dammit," he said, rubbing his head. "You scared the hell out of me."

"Sorry. You okay?"

"Yes, are you?"

While waiting for JJ I'd had time to think and had concluded the cats were the most likely source of whatever I'd heard. Or it could have been an animal sneaking around outside, maybe an otter. They were brazen critters and always looking for a new place to take up residence. I had probably ruined my evening and JJ's for no reason. But I still needed to be certain. I explained the situation to JJ, what I'd thought I heard and why I was now doubting myself. We agreed that it was best to check it out on our own and not bother Grimes unless we needed to. As a precaution, he got a baseball bat and a tire iron out of his trunk and handed me the bat.

"Not much against a gun," I said.

"And you have to be quick if attacked by an otter."

I settled the bat across one shoulder and said, "Well, let's go find out."

As we drew near, JJ put his hand on my arm and whispered, "Want to go in the front or the back?"

"Might as well go in the front door," I whispered back.

To my relief, the door was still locked. "That's a good sign, isn't it?" JJ asked. He used his key and pushed open the door, quickly stepping inside and to the left, the tire iron at ready. "Anyone home?" he yelled into the silence.

No one answered. And there was no other sound.

I stepped inside and closed the door behind me to avoid being silhouetted by the outside light. We stood there and listened.

"Room by room search?" he asked as two sleepy cats came out of nowhere and began rubbing themselves against his legs. He bent down and petted them each in turn. I can never understand why they seem to like him more than they do me when I'm the one who feeds them.

My Glock was right where I had left it. I picked it up, checked the clip, and left JJ to guard the stairs while I went from room to room on the ground floor.

No one was there. And nothing looked like it had been disturbed.

We crept up to the second floor, the cats trailing behind us, our entire entourage searching each room in turn. The bathroom was the only place we couldn't check out because the door was locked, from the inside. Wouldn't you know it, I didn't remember ever having a key to unlock it from the outside. It had never come up before.

"This is a problem," I said. "Want to wait while I go back in through the window from the outside?"

"Do you have a ladder?"

"I think I can get back in the way I got out. Over the roof and through a window."

"Just like Santa, huh?"

"Something like that. Wait here; I shouldn't be long."

It was surprisingly easy to get back inside. In no time at all I was in the hall with JJ. "I'm sorry," I said. "But at the time I really did think I heard someone trying to open the door."

"Well, otters are usually less direct," JJ said. "But let's go check something." We went downstairs and got a flashlight. He used it to examine the outside of the door. "No scratches," he said. "No indication that I can see that anyone tried to break in."

I leaned close and studied the unblemished surface around my doorknob.

"There's one other possibility," JJ said. "Maybe they were going to break in and tried the door, but something scared them off. If so, you were lucky."

Perhaps, but somehow I didn't feel all that lucky. Getting spooked like this was becoming a habit. And just because there was no one there this time didn't mean my luck would hold.

Chapter 20
A Very Bad Dude

J J spent the night but had to leave early the next morning. When I turned on my computer, I saw that I had a message from a new potential client. A referral. Most of my work comes from referrals. The message didn't provide any particulars, but there was a phone number. I decided to call right away; I needed a distraction.

When the HR person asked if I could come to Seattle to meet with her that afternoon, I agreed to do so. I could go into the city early, run a few errands. Maybe I'd be able to spend a normal day instead of one constantly looking over my shoulder.

As I was about to get in the shower the phone howled. It was Beatrice.

"Are you okay?" she asked.

"Of course. What's up?"

"Well, last night I thought I saw someone on the path, and, well, I was worried."

"Worried?"

"I didn't want to disturb you if it was nothing. But I wanted to make sure you weren't in trouble. When I found your door locked I decided everything was just fine. Then this morning I started worrying again. I'm just glad you're locking your door at night."

I didn't know whether to laugh or scold her for going out at night to check whether I was tucked in safely. "Beatrice, you shouldn't be going out at night alone."

"You do," she pointed out.

"But I have your gun," I said, feeling guilty. "And if you don't mind, I'd like to keep it a little longer."

"No problem."

"But you have to promise me that if you have any concerns, any at all, you will call me instead of coming over, agreed?"

"All right, that makes sense. I'll call next time."

JJ was going to give me a bad time about this one. Although I *had* heard someone testing my door. Beatrice, she was a really good if imprudent neighbor.

Dilly and Natasha didn't protest as much as usual when they realized I was leaving, and they were staying inside. Either they'd become used to the idea or they had a secret exit that they used when I wasn't around. It would be just like them to keep up a pretense to make me feel guilty and squeeze as many rewards out of my guilt as they could.

On my way to the car I texted the people I thought needed to know about my day plans, an increasingly long list. I wasn't used to having to account for my actions to anyone, but under the circumstances it seemed appropriate. First JJ. Then Andy. Then Grimes. And Beatrice. She'd probably seen me pass by and would feel better knowing where I'd be during the day.

Even with a concealed weapons permit, which I didn't have, I wasn't sure it was legal to take a gun on the ferry. But I doubted anyone would ask to look in my purse. It had never happened before, and I felt more secure knowing I had a weapon as back-up.

Minutes after I drove on the ferry my phone yelped. It was

Crane. When he found out I was on my way to Seattle, he asked me to stop by. I quickly said yes. Maybe I could "goose him" into action. Or at least find out where they were in their investigations.

No matter how many times I took the ferry I almost always enjoyed the trip. Sometimes I get out and walk around, either inside the main cabin area or outside on the deck. Other times I sit on one of the green vinyl benches and gawk at the scenery. But most often I stay in my car and read. I always keep a book handy. It's a great twenty minutes of enforced calm. I like it best when I'm parked where I can see out. Frequently there are cormorants perched on the wood pilings at the docks, sometimes fanning their wings as if waving to the passengers. Occasionally there are marine mammals nearby. Dolphins arcing out of the water, seals swimming this way and that, purposeful looking sea lions, and, infrequently, a whale blowing mist into the air. Today I ended up in the middle row. That meant I would be one of the early cars to disembark, but there was no view. Still, I didn't feel like getting out, so I stayed where I was and thought about what I wanted to ask Crane.

———

It was a breeze driving through West Seattle, but when I hit Seattle's frequent stop-and-go traffic I silently cursed some of the big companies for bringing in so many people to work in the area, even though some of those very same big companies provided me with consulting income.

Unfortunately, Crane's office was close enough to downtown Seattle to make parking a nightmare. Early birds and people with parking karma got the convenient spots. I didn't mind walking a fair distance, but I would have liked to be able to park without having to cope with heavy traffic while searching for a lot or a garage that didn't have a sign out that said "full." One time a couple of months ago I had to pay for the time I spent inside a garage looking for a space in order to raise the bar at the exit. I'm still seething about that one. As for on-the-street parking, well that would be like winning the lottery.

The good news was that I finally found a garage that claimed to have parking available. It was about half way between Crane's location and my potential client's. The bad news was that it was an older garage with darkened cement walls and narrow stalls and a generally gloomy atmosphere. I kept winding up and up to the next level, getting excited each time a parked truck tricked me into believing I'd finally found a space, only to discover that the stall on the other side of the truck was already filled by a short car. I reached the stratosphere before finding a place to leave my Prius. So much for running any errands; there was no way I was going to give up this parking spot. Oh well, it was an excuse to walk through Pike Place Market between meetings, maybe just wander around, have something to eat.

I made sure no one was around before stashing the Glock under some tools in the tire well in the trunk. Not readily accessible, but then I wouldn't need it until I returned to the island. At least I sure as hell hoped I wouldn't. Although the parking garage felt like the perfect place for an ambush, rationally I knew it would have been next to impossible for anyone to have followed me around the city while I was looking for parking. And since I hadn't known in advance where I would end up, there was no way they could have beat me there. I felt safer than I had in days.

Major Crimes was located in a building that had once been voted the ugliest government building in the county. A lot of buildings have gone up since the mid-1970s, many of them unattractive, but with its honeycomb walls and boxy exterior, if this one didn't still hold the ugly-building title, it was surely a serious contender.

The inside of the building wasn't much better. It was dingy, cramped, and had a musty smell reminiscent of the countless number of bodies that had walked the narrow halls over the years. Crane sent someone down to escort me to his office. She took me up a creaky elevator and led me through rows of cubicles with four-foot-high cloth-covered modular walls, past tiny glass-enclosed conference rooms with white boards stained by years of use, and across a large room filled with antiquated wooden tables that looked like they served as makeshift desks.

I could see Crane through the large floor-to-ceiling glass panel next to the door of his office. He looked up as we drew near and waved me in. I had to maneuver around a small table piled high with files to get to a chair that had seen better days. Somehow Crane looked even thinner seated behind his desk, his ears outstretched as if by flapping them he could soar around the cage-like room.

He thanked me for coming in and said that he was pleased to be able to give me an update in person. Then he launched into a series of generalities about how he and his detectives were making progress, good progress, fine progress, lots of progress. He reminded me of a politician running for office, someone who hoped to create a good impression without getting specific. Personally, I didn't find it at all reassuring.

"Have you caught up with Morey yet?" I asked when he stopped talking.

"Not yet, but soon." His attempt at an encouraging smile looked more like a dyspeptic pursing of the lips.

"Did you learn anything from the note about Boner's kidnapper?" I asked.

"I'm afraid we didn't."

"So, you asked me to come by for—" I started to say a pep talk but stopped myself. "For a general update, nothing specific."

"I understand that you and your friends have been concerned, especially after the car accident, so I wanted you to know that we are making progress." There was that word again —progress.

Determined to pinpoint him on what he meant, I asked, "Making progress on finding Jake's killer or making progress on discovering who instigated the incidents involving Andy, Norm and me?"

"Both. We assume they're connected."

I waited for him to add something, but when he didn't, I asked, "How?"

"Because it seems very likely that the same person killed Jake Williams, shot Detective Forester, left a dead coyote at your doorstep, and kidnapped Andy's dog."

"You don't mean Morey, do you?"

"Yes, that's who I mean." He seemed genuinely surprised that I would even ask.

"But why did he kill his stepfather?"

"As I'm sure you know, there was no love lost between the two."

"I understand, but he left home a long time ago. Why come back now and kill him?"

"As soon as we catch him, we'll ask him that."

I wasn't sure why I was arguing with Crane. Given the evidence, it was entirely possible that Morey was responsible for all of those things. But it just didn't feel right to me. Not that I wouldn't be happy to find that he was the sole person guilty of all of those crimes. But the more I'd thought about it, the less likely it seemed. It was too neat, too tidy. Like assuming the butler did it.

"Most of the people we've talked with say that even if he's on drugs, he isn't . . . uh, a bad dude." Had I really said that?

"Oh, believe me, he's a very bad dude." Crane's dark eyes drilled into me. "He may not have specifically returned to kill his stepfather, but, since he was forced to steal to support his habit, well, you just don't know what someone like that might do."

I agreed with him there.

"And no one else appears to have had as strong a motive," he added.

"What about the anti-wilders? They're pretty passionate about their cause."

Crane shook his head. "Do you really think an anti-wilder would murder Williams just because he was trying to save a few animals? I mean, it's a public policy issue. In small communities, people write letters to the editor, maybe get riled up during a public meeting. But kill someone . . .?"

He obviously had no idea how strongly some islanders felt about the issue, no matter which side they were on. Although given the way the facts were lining up, he might be forgiven for considering it practically a closed case. And if that huge stack of files on his table was any indication of his workload, you couldn't blame him for wanting an easy answer.

I felt awkward asking the other question I had for him, but he had dragged me all the way down to his office for next to nothing, so I went for it. "Did they find out anything from the bullet in Forester's leg?"

He seemed to hesitate, then said, "It passed through, and they didn't find it at the scene."

It was my turn to hesitate. I couldn't help wondering how hard the team had actually looked for the bullet. At the same time, another more sinister thought occurred to me: what if they had found the bullet and made it disappear? The bullet would have told them what kind of gun it came from. And a careful examination of the wound might have suggested it was self-inflicted. Would Crane have gone along with a cover-up? Or would loyal colleagues have done it in secret to protect one of their own? On the off chance that they hadn't found the bullet due to incompetence rather than misplaced loyalty, I would have to go back there and have a look around for myself.

When I stood up to leave, Crane also stood and said he would see me out. As we walked past the row of tables, he said, "I do appreciate all of your help. And I'm sorry you've had to go through this." He sounded sincere, but I couldn't help but feel his words were scripted, something he often said to victims to help them move on. Even so, it was good of him to say something like that. I didn't envy him his job.

As I followed Crane toward the elevator, I saw Detective Wyatt Forester coming in our direction. He was limping slightly and frowned when he saw me. I smiled to let him know there were no hard feelings on my end, just because he blamed me for his own incompetence. It crossed my mind that a big smile would probably irritate him more than anything else I could do or say, so I added a few teeth to my grin.

He acknowledged his boss with a nod, then as we edged past each other, he nodded at me and said my name: "Lew." It sounded like half a sneeze.

Before he could disappear, I asked, "How's your leg, Detective?"

"Fine, just fine, thanks," he said over his shoulder.

When we reached the main hall, Crane shook my hand and said, "Stay safe."

Yes, I thought, as I departed, I intended to do just that.

From there I walked to Pike Place Market, checked out the various farmer's stalls, and stopped to watch the fish vendors tossing salmon around to the delight of potential customers. I was always tempted to point out to bystanders that handling the fish that way bruised the flesh and also destroyed scales which in turn encouraged bacteria, but, so far, I had held my tongue. Let them enjoy the show. They probably didn't know what good fish tasted like anyway.

The aroma of food finally got to me and I bought a pierogi filled with spinach and potatoes. Then I bought some chocolate-covered blueberries and ate the entire bag while walking around looking at the crafts for sale.

My meeting was in one of my favorite buildings on the central waterfront. The wood stairs were worn, the brass railings rubbed smooth from use. All of the floors seemed to slope, the walls were chipped in places, the interior paint yellowed like an old photograph. Still, there was something appealing about this historic structure, its hallways lined with rows of pictures depicting its past. Unfortunately, the building was destined for renovation, perhaps eventually for demolition. Now that the unsafe waterfront viaduct had been removed and a waterfront park established, it was inevitable that rents in this valuable view property would skyrocket. Building owners would eventually sell to developers. People working for peanuts to support good causes would lose out to high-paid employees who wouldn't put up with stained walls and slanted floors. Starbucks would probably open a coffee shop on the ground floor.

The meeting went well, although based on what they told me, I wasn't sure I would be able to discover more than they already knew or guessed about their employee's complaint. It's true, however, that people will often be more forthright talking to an independent consultant than to an insider. And frequently the process of formalizing a complaint can lead to a solution. Even so, in my experience, I'm often called in to verify and document what is already known. I'm not complaining; it keeps me employed and solvent.

After a relatively easy drive back to Fauntleroy, I just missed a ferry. While waiting for the next one, I kept going over the arguments for and against Morey as his stepfather's murderer. Although there was a lot of circumstantial evidence to suggest he might indeed be the guilty party, we needed answers to a few key questions before I would be willing to convict.

As Crane had said, they would learn more when they caught him. While he hadn't been apprehended getting on or off a ferry after the car chase, it was certainly possible that he had slipped away since then. Still, to me it seemed more likely that he was holed up somewhere on the island. Having grown up on Vashon he probably knew every inch of it. But it also seemed unlikely he could stay hidden for long without help. The island was rural, but not that big. Had his mother forgiven him for stealing from her and provided a place to stay? Was Paige sticking her neck out for him a second time? He didn't seem to have other loyal friends on the island, at least none that we'd come across so far. If I had to bet, one of the two women, either his mother or Paige, was providing assistance.

The more I thought about it, the more I leaned toward Paige as his accomplice. Morey was Jeannie's flesh and blood, but he had caused her a lot of grief, in the past and in the present. Paige, on the other hand, was convinced he was a victim and not a perpetrator. Under the circumstances, however, she could hardly let him stay at her place. But as a long-time resident, she probably had friends or relatives on the island. Maybe someone who had a cottage they would loan her, or a rental property she could say was for an out-of-town guest. She might even know of a vacant rental house or an abandoned building where he could squat without being noticed.

There were a lot of hideouts that I wouldn't be able to track down, but if Paige had a friend or relative with a rental property or a house up for sale, then my real estate friend, Marie, might know about it. I didn't want to reveal why I was asking though. That didn't seem fair to Paige. She might not be guilty of helping a fugitive. Whereas manipulating a friend, well, that might not be fair either, but if she didn't know she was being manipulated, it wouldn't matter.

Luckily Marie was in the office rather than out showing someone a property. I explained that I had a friend who was looking to buy, but also needed a place to stay ASAP. "Someone said a friend or relative of Paige Thoreson's has a house about to go on the market, maybe something she could rent for a while. I couldn't get through to Paige; just wondered if you know anything about that."

"Nothing that I know of. Maybe they were thinking about Paige's aunt. She just moved into assisted living while recovering from a hip replacement. She might be willing to rent her house short-term. Want me to check?"

"Where is it?"

"On Smith Road. Good location."

"If my friend is interested, I'll have her get in touch. Thanks." I started to say goodbye and then added, as if an afterthought, "I think I met her aunt once at the grocery—what's her name again?"

"Linda, Linda Holden."

"Yes, I did. A nice woman. Too bad about her hip."

As soon as I hung up, I went online and looked up Linda Holden's address. There it was, right there on the County's real estate parcel map. Could it really be that easy?

Once I got off the ferry it wasn't too far out of my way to swing by the Holden house, a relatively minor detour. Like many houses on the island, the Holden home was tucked back away from the main road in a thickly wooded area, mostly second growth evergreens and alders with a few vine maples sprinkled in here and there. The rational part of my brain told me that I should wait until I had someone with me to check things out, but I didn't want to wait. It was *my* lead, and I wanted to see it through. I promised myself I wouldn't do more than take a quick look to verify or disprove my suspicion.

I drove by and parked down the road and around a bend, again wishing my car was less conspicuous. Then I opened my trunk and dug out the Glock from my tire well and headed back up the road with the gun in my jacket pocket. There was no reason to stay out of sight until I got to her property. If I saw someone I would wave as if I was simply out taking a walk, just another islander getting a little exercise. Once closer to the house, I would take yet another short-cut through the woods and see what there was to see.

Before disappearing into the woods, I looked around to make sure no one was looking. After that, getting from the road to the Holden house through the trees didn't take long. The land was flat, the undergrowth sparse, and there were several animal paths that I was able to follow for a way. As the trees thinned out and the grass took over, I could clearly see the side and part of the front of the house. But there wasn't much to see.

If there had been a dog in the yard. If there had been a car parked in the driveway. If the side door to the garage hadn't been so accessible. If, if and if . . .

It was just too tempting to approach the garage from the blind side of the house. I told myself that only if there was easy access would I peek inside. Then I would leave, no matter what I found.

I was on a roll. There was a side door that opened without resistance into what I anticipated would be the garage. I stepped inside and found myself in a workshop, walls lined with tools above a long workbench. There was another door, however, on the other side of the workshop. It was standing open, providing a perfect view of the inside of the garage . . . where Morey's white Toyota was parked.

Bingo.

Without waiting around to see if Morey was there, I went back outside through the workshop door. Staying a fair distance away from the house, I circled around to get a better look at the layout before calling Grimes. What I saw gave me pause. The front door to the house was standing partially open. Why would Morey choose to hide out here, put his car in the garage, and then leave the front door open?

Something wasn't right.

As a safeguard, I called JJ and told him where I was and what I was about to do and why. I kept my voice low, barely above a whisper, my body slightly turned away from the house.

"Don't, Lew. Don't do it." JJ's voice seemed unnaturally loud in the silence surrounding me.

"I'm just going to have a look inside through one of the back windows," I said softly. "And that will be it."

"I'm serious, Lew, please don't do anything stupid. Morey could be in there. We don't know what his state of mind is. He may be dangerous."

"You call Grimes and let him know where Morey's car is, okay?"

"Why don't *you* call Grimes?" JJ asked. Then: "Oh, right, if *he* tells you to back off, you'll have to do it."

"Thanks, JJ, you're a pal."

I turned my phone to mute and slipped it in my pocket. Pistol in hand, I moved through the trees to the back of the house. It was only about twenty feet between the house and the edge of the woods. I took a deep breath, ran across the open space and flattened myself against the side of the house. When

I didn't hear any movement inside, I slowly inched my way around to a window and peered over the bottom of the sill into the interior of the house. There were no lights on, but I had a clear view of the living room.

And a clear view of Morey, spotlighted by a dim stream of light from the window. He was lying in the center of a brown shag rug, legs straight out, arms askew, head to one side. Morey might indeed have been a very bad dude. To me, however, he also looked like a very *dead* dude.

Chapter 21
Suspect Roulette

After checking inside to make sure Morey was dead and the killer wasn't still in the house, I barely had time to make a quick trip out to my car and back to get rid of Beatrice's gun before Grimes and Evans arrived. Evans was driving. They stopped about 50 yards away from the house. Then they apparently saw me standing there, waving them forward. I hadn't bothered calling to report what I'd seen since I knew they were on their way.

They pulled up to where I was standing, and Grimes lowered his window and raised his eyebrows in question without saying anything. "It's okay to talk," I said

"He's already gone?" Evans asked, leaning across Grimes to better see me.

"No, he's here, all right. In the living room."

They got out of the car, pulled their guns, and headed for the front door.

"You won't need those weapons," I said, following right behind them up the porch steps. "I'm 100 per cent certain he's dead."

They both paused and turned to look at me. "Dead?" Evans said.

"I saw him lying on the floor from the back window. I went in to check just to make sure. In case I needed to call an ambulance."

"Okay," Grimes said. "You stay here."

I didn't respond and continued in right on their heels. No way I was staying outside.

They still had their guns drawn, and as soon as the body came into sight, Grimes told Evans to check out the rest of the house. I didn't mention that I'd already done that since I wasn't sure they would be pleased. Although if they thought about it, anyone with half a brain who saw a body on the floor would check to make sure there wasn't a killer with a gun still lurking nearby waiting to pounce.

I'd been in a hurry before, but now that I had more time to examine the body up close, I noticed how dark the red smear of blood on his chest was. He'd probably been dead at least an hour or more. And given the spatter on the rug, he'd been shot right there where he was lying.

Grimes knelt down and felt for a pulse, then said, "Doesn't look like he's been dead long."

I couldn't help wishing I'd figured out where he'd been hiding sooner. I might have been able to save him. Then we would have had some answers instead of yet another question.

Grimes stood up. "How'd you know he was here?"

"Well, it seemed to me that if he was still on the island, he'd need help to stay hidden. Paige has a thing for him, and she apparently believes everything he tells her, including the part about trying to kick his drug habit. I decided she was a likely accomplice."

"Dang fool woman."

"I agree. Anyway, this place belongs to her aunt who recently suffered an injury and has temporarily moved into assisted living. Paige may have suggested this was a good place for him to stay, or he may have known about her aunt and come here without her permission." I doubted the latter was the case, but I really wanted to give her the benefit of the doubt.

"We'll see about that."

Evans returned. "No one here."

Grimes got on the phone and called Crane. He stepped out on the porch for the conversation, so I only heard bits and pieces of what was said. But I could tell from the tone of his voice that it wasn't a pleasant exchange. Evans and I walked around the room, observing without touching anything. When Grimes returned, he said, "We need to clear out of here and wait for the crime scene team to show up."

Once outside I asked, "So what's Crane's problem?"

"He's ticked that we didn't locate Morey before he was killed. And he's doubly ticked, pissed, in fact, that you were the one to find the body. He told me you hadn't mentioned anything about knowing Morey's whereabouts when you met with him this morning." Grimes was glaring at me.

"I didn't know then," I protested. "And even after I guessed that he might be here, I had no way to be sure until I saw his car in the garage."

"But you had a look inside before you bothered notifying us."

"Yes, but . . .," I began.

Grimes held up one hand to stop me. "Don't say any more. It's okay."

Grimes might say it was okay, and Crane couldn't prove I'd lied to him, since I hadn't. But I was wondering what Marie was going to think when it occurred to her that I had used subterfuge to get her to tell me about Paige's aunt. Would she accept the rationale that I had been trying to protect Paige? At the time it had seemed like a good idea to make up a story about a friend needing a rental. But didn't that imply I didn't trust Marie to be discrete? I hoped she would accept my apology.

"Frankly," he continued. "I'm glad you figured it out. Not that I'm happy he's dead. But we weren't getting anywhere with our search for him."

Evans interrupted, "This means he's no longer a suspect in his stepfather's murder, doesn't it?" His voice trailed off into uncertainty.

"Not necessarily. Maybe his mother found out he killed Jake . . ." I paused. "No, I can't picture Jeannie killing her own son." I thought some more. "What if . . .," I said, trying to jump-start my brain with the familiar brainstorming phrase. But I couldn't think of anyone who benefited from Morey's death.

"Maybe this is drug related," Evans offered. "A drug deal gone bad."

"But there hasn't been any indication that Morey was a dealer, just a user. Do drug dealer's kill their customers?" I asked

"Might have been money related," Grimes said. "We know he was having a hard time supporting his habit. Maybe he tried to cheat his dealer and they came to blows."

"Or maybe he figured out who killed his stepfather and was blackmailing the killer to raise money for drugs," Evans said, looking to me for approval.

I was impressed; I didn't think Evans had it in him to come up with such a convoluted theory. "I can see that," I said. That won me a big *look how smart I am* grin from Evans. "But if that's true," I added, "then we are back to square one."

We sat down on the steps and continued playing the "what if" game, considering anyone and everyone who might have had a reason to disapprove of, dislike, or resent Jake or his stepson Morey. We kept spinning the wheel, but we didn't land on anyone.

Finally, I pointed out something that had been at the back of my mind, something I'd been avoiding thinking about. Someone needed to tell Paige and Jeannie about Morey. Cowards that we all were, we decided to leave it to Crane.

When we heard a car approaching, we all stood up at the same time. It was too soon for Crane's team to have arrived. "Think it's Paige?" Evans said. Maybe one of us would have to tell her the bad news after all.

Then the car came into view and I remembered that I had turned my phone off. "I forgot to let JJ know I was all right," I said.

JJ pulled his car to within inches of the porch and leapt out. For a moment I thought he was going to throw something at me, then that he was going to hug me, then both at the same time. "Damn you, Lew," JJ said. "What was I supposed to think when you didn't pick up your phone?"

"That I was distracted. That I forgot I'd turned my phone off." When it didn't look like he was going to accept my excuses, I added, "That I'm a shit and don't treat my friends with the respect due them?"

"Now you're talking." JJ scowled at me. "I was worried."

"Thank you." I surprised JJ by going over to him and giving him a hug. I may tolerate but I never initiate a hug. JJ's a hugger, and I should have called him. It seemed the least I could do.

Once he calmed down, we quickly brought him up to speed on the situation. He asked if I was going to hang around until Crane's team showed up. Grimes said, "Not necessary. We know where to find you."

Evans surprised me by looking at me and saying, "You should be careful."

"Don't worry," JJ said. "I'm not letting her out of my sight."

"That's sweet but unnecessary," I protested.

"We can talk about it over dinner. I saw your car down the road. I'll take you there and you can follow me to my place, okay?"

I didn't argue. I could call Beatrice and ask her to stop by and feed my cats again. She wouldn't mind, and they would be pleased.

———

While JJ was chopping veggies for an exotic dish he was preparing for his friend who didn't deserve it, I sipped a glass of Syrah and went through all of the probable suspects out loud, moving on to improbable suspects, and then to wild guesses.

"I'm leaning toward Morey trying to blackmail the killer," JJ said as he tossed veggies into a large fry pan of sizzling oil. "Even though Evans came up with the idea."

"Why?"

"Because that sounds like the jackass kind of thing Morey would do."

"But that means he figured out who the killer was when no one else could. Do we give him that much credit?"

"Or suppose you're wrong about him," JJ continued, ignoring my question. "What if he was motivated by something other than money? What if he was trying to investigate to help his mother find closure? Have you considered that he may have come back because he wanted to see his mother? Maybe make amends?"

"That's a very generous notion, JJ. But it doesn't explain why he ended up stealing from her."

"You've got me there," JJ said as he stirred the veggies.

"You do have a point though. *Why* did he return and why at this particular time? Had something changed? Did his mother ask him to come? Or was it just about the money?"

"It doesn't have to be an either-or," JJ said. "He could have come to make amends with his family and still have acted on his need for money."

My phone barked. I didn't recognize the number. "Hello," I said.

"It's me, babe," Chewie sounded like we were old friends. "Don't say my name," he added before I could respond.

"Okay." Why wasn't Chewie using his own phone, and why didn't he want me to call him by name? Did he think my phone was bugged? Or JJ's house? Maybe he just wanted to make sure that nothing incriminating was being recorded.

"There's something you need to know."

I almost said "I'm all ears," but then a vision of Crane came to mind. Instead I said: "I'm listening."

"I could have told you this before but didn't. But the more I've been thinking about our conversation, the more I've felt like I should have told you. Anyway, Jake came to me to talk about Morey. He thought Morey was trying to clean up his act and wanted me to promise I wouldn't, uh, wouldn't give Morey anything, you know. Or help him out. That was two days before Morey stopped by my place."

"Which means they had either talked or had been in contact."

"Sounded like it to me."

"Thanks. Anything else I should know?"

"That's it." The phone went dead.

JJ was about to serve what looked like a delicious stir fry. "More wine?" he asked. I held out my glass. "Was that who I think it was?"

I raised my eyebrows in question.

"Chewie," JJ said with confidence.

"How did you figure that out?"

"I'm psychic," JJ laughed, serving me a large portion of

aromatic veggies and noodles. "And . . . I could hear a bit of his side of the conversation."

"You know what that means?" I took a big forkful of food. "Oooohhh," I said, my mouth full.

JJ pulled my plate away. "Finish your thought or no more food."

I pulled it back. "No thoughts, just want food!"

We ate in silence for a few minutes, savoring each bite. Then JJ said, "If Jake thought his step-son was trying to get clean and was making sure he couldn't get more drugs on the island, then he must have known he was coming back."

"That, or Morey was back earlier than we thought."

"But how did Jake know to go to Chewie? And do you think he sometimes sells more than marijuana?"

"Hard to know for sure, but somehow I don't think so. At least not now. I believe he wants to go legit." I shoveled some noodles into my mouth, chewed briefly and swallowed. "It's a small island. Jake may have simply asked around."

"But if Jake was trying to help, why would Morey kill him?"

"Maybe Morey didn't want to give up his habit and resented Jake's interference, or maybe he did and then changed his mind. He could even have lied to Jake as a ploy to get money from him." To me it always seemed to come back to the money.

"The problem with that theory is that Morey got shot. If Morey killed his stepfather, then who shot Morey? Don't tell me that Vashon Island has more than one killer on the loose. Hard to believe."

"Enter big bad city drug dealer guy," I said dramatically. "He goes to deliver drugs to Morey. Morey doesn't have any money. Morey tries to get drugs for nothing. Maybe he even tries to rob the bad guy. Bad guy shoots him. Like that scenario?"

"You're suggesting Morey killed Jake, and the drug dealer took out Morey. Plausible."

"Or, maybe the drug dealer killed Jake so he couldn't report him for selling drugs to Morey."

"Now that sounds a bit far-fetched," JJ said. "And if Morey didn't shoot the coyote and kidnap Boner, then who did?"

"Okay, let's say that Morey used the coyote and Boner to make a point about the wilding of Vashon, and the drug dealer in turn popped off both Jake and Morey. I guess that makes some kind of sense."

We both considered our conclusion while enjoying what remained of our meal.

"Some kind of sense, maybe," JJ said, pausing to sip his wine. "But there are still too many unanswered questions."

"Like what on earth was Jake doing with a Seattle drug dealer in the bog?"

Chapter 22
The Post Hoc Fallacy

E arly the next morning I got a call from Jeannie. When cleaning out Jake's office she'd come across a pile of papers that included some stuff Jake had been working on. She wanted to know if I'd be interested in looking through the papers before she packed them up.

"You asked me about what local issues he was involved with, in addition to the wilding controversy," she said. "Maybe these will be helpful."

"Have you looked them over?" I asked.

"Just briefly. I can't . . . I'm having trouble concentrating. That's why I'm packing things up—it's keeping me occupied."

I thanked her, mumbled a few words about how sorry I was about Morey, and said I would be over within the hour.

The reason I'd originally asked Jeannie if it was possible Jake had upset someone about something other than wilding was that there were any number of controversial issues that various groups of islanders were passionate about. School funding. Farmers versus horse owners. The increasing cost of real estate. Lack of sufficient health services. Lack of on-island jobs. Speed limits on the Vashon Highway. The annual deer hunt taking over the Central Forest for almost a month. The increasing number of part-time residents. Protecting the island's limited water resources. Taxes for the Fire District. On and on. Some of the issues seemed trivial to me, but it was hard to judge what someone else considered of earthshaking importance. Jake's papers just might provide a new line of inquiry.

———

Jeannie looked tired, quickly handed over the box of papers and didn't encourage me to hang around. I thanked her again and left her to grieve alone and in her own way.

I was so anxious to see what was in the box that I drove to a nearby park and started going through the contents in the parking lot. The papers weren't organized and covered a variety of topics. I knew that I needed to do a more thorough reading, but this first time through, I was simply hoping something would jump out at me. It did strike me that there seemed to be a disproportionate number of notes and items related to the bog. Had Jake been acting on behalf of the Island Land Stewards on something bog related? If so, why hadn't this come up before?

Once I'd given the contents an initial search, I put everything back in the box and headed for the Island Land Stewards' building. Unfortunately, when I arrived, Andy was with someone. While I waited, I studied a giant map of the island taped to the back wall. The bog was not well delineated, even on the map created by the Island Land Stewards, but it showed approximately where it was without being too specific about the surrounding area. Part of the script for bog tour guides had to do with how the Island Land Stewards hoped to acquire more land adjacent to the bog or to protect more of the surrounding area with easements.

The existence of the bog depended on the pond of water

captured in the narrow valley that had been left behind by receding glacial ice. Unfortunately, the tiny streams that fed that pond and the one that carried water away ran across private land. The concern was that changes to those adjacent private lands could alter or divert the flow of water and potentially drain the bog, destroying the 13,000-year-old eco-system. But my recollection was that there were fairly sound agreements with nearby landowners and that there was no imminent threat. That's what I wanted to verify.

When Andy was free, he motioned me into his office. "What's up?"

"I have a question about the bog."

"Sure."

"Did Jake mention that he was looking into something related to the bog and the properties surrounding it?"

"No. Why?"

"Well, Jeannie gave me a box containing some of his papers. A lot of them concern the bog."

"Nothing's changed, as far as I know. We've had extensive discussions with those landowners over the years, and I think they all understand the uniqueness of the larger piece of real estate and the impact changing something on their individual properties could have. They know we would be interested in buying their land if they get to a place where they want to sell. Of course, what we'd really like is for them to leave their properties to us in their wills. But that's a big ask."

"But what if someone was offering them a lot of money for their property. People can get greedy."

"I see where you're going with this, but I think Jake would have mentioned it to me if he'd come across anything like that. And I don't see how that's related to Morey's death."

"Maybe it isn't. But I've been thinking. There's something called the correlation fallacy, after this, therefore because of this. Otherwise referred to as post hoc ergo propter hoc. Think about it in this instance: After a number of years away, Morey comes home, and immediately after that, Jake dies. Then, shortly after Jake dies, Morey dies. We automatically assume each one of these things somehow caused the next. That they must be connected. The point is, maybe they aren't. When you consider each independently, there are some diverging lines of inquiry."

"Okay," Andy said thoughtfully. "What I hear you saying is that the timing of Morey coming home may not have had anything to do with Jake's death. And Jake's death may not be linked to Morey's. It just appears that way."

"It's even possible someone is using our assumptions against us."

"You mean the killer is trying to deflect our suspicions away from him by making us think Morey was the one threatening us?"

"Something like that. The only problem is that Morey's dead."

"Yeah," Andy said. "If someone other than Jake's killer did Morey in, the killer can't be happy about it. It makes it harder to believe in the one killer theory."

"But it's equally hard to believe that there are two killers with two separate motives for murder right here on the island."

"I know. It doesn't seem too likely, does it?"

"A week ago I wouldn't have thought it likely we would have two *murders* on the island," I said, "let alone two *murderers*. But if Jake's killer was trying to make us think that Morey was the one threatening us, doesn't Morey's death change that?"

"Assuming he . . ."

"Or *she*," I interrupted.

Andy smiled. "Assuming he or *she* still wants everyone to

think that the issue was about the wilding of the island, then we may still be targets."

"You're probably right. In any case, we need to approach Morey's death with fresh eyes," I said.

"*We?*" Andy raised his eyebrows and sent me a meaningful glare.

"Okay, okay. I know that Crane and his team are trying, but they don't have the same skin in the game that we do. And we aren't his only case. He's a busy man. You should see the stacks of files in that guy's office. So, let's call Grimes and run this past him. He can give us some perspective and decide whether to pass our thoughts along . . . or not."

"I do think that's the best approach," Andy said. I wasn't sure I agreed entirely, but I was willing to talk with Grimes. After that I could decide what I personally wanted to do next.

Andy got Grimes on the phone and explained that we wanted to talk to him about some thoughts we had on the two murders. Grimes suggested we come on over to his office. Both he and Evans were there and available.

It's easy to convince yourself you are on the right track when the pieces seem to fit together. Even when you know that in complex situations pieces can come and go and even change shapes. But it's surprisingly hard to remain skeptical once you think you have the answer.

Grimes met us at the door and led us back to his office. Evans was there, occupying the only comfortable looking chair in the room. He didn't get up to shake hands when we came in. Maybe he was afraid we'd try to take his chair away. I had to settle for a straight-backed wood chair that looked like something that once belonged to a vintage Victorian table dining room set. Back when butts were smaller and posture more rigid. Andy grabbed another ancient chair that may have had another life in a doctor's office waiting room.

The conversation did not go well. It wasn't that Grimes and Evans weren't willing to listen, but, like Crane, they were convinced Morey had killed his stepfather and was responsible for the threats against Norm, Andy, and me. Morey's death was being attributed to a drug deal gone bad. If not that, then maybe he tried to sell what he'd taken from his mother and the buyer decided he didn't want to pay for the loot. Grimes assured us that kind of thing happened more often than we might imagine.

When we left, Andy turned to me. "They could be right. And if they are, then our nightmare is over."

It *was* possible. Maybe I was being paranoid for no reason. After all, I had thought there was someone trying to break into my home when it was only a neighbor checking to make sure I was okay. On the other hand, there was something that still didn't feel right to me.

"Don't start leaving your doors unlocked at night yet," I said as I waved goodbye and headed home.

Chapter 23
Shoot First?

As I drove off it occurred to me that if the police were now looking at Morey's death as the result of a drug deal, then I'd better warn Chewie. If they traced Morey back to him, I didn't want him to think we'd given them his name. Maybe I was experiencing some kind of honor-among-thieves mentality, but I didn't see what harm it could do to give him a head's up.

Chewie had given me his phone number, and I could still recite it using the rhymical chant I'd used to memorize it. But I decided not to call. If the police went after Chewie, I didn't want my phone number to show up on his phone records. It was better to drop by, even though Chewie's place wasn't exactly on my way home.

There were a lot of out-of-the-way places on the island hidden down long winding roads. But Chewie's piece of land was definitely off the beaten path. The uneven gravel and dirt road leading to it was narrow and riddled with potholes. It was also incredibly dusty due to the long dry spell we'd been experiencing. As I drove up the hill, dust swirled upward and fanned out to coat the brush alongside the road. Looking back, all I could see was a fantail of brown haze. My poor car was going to be filthy.

When I reached the clearing there were two cars parked between the barn and the RV. Chewie had company. Maybe this wasn't a good time. On the other hand, I couldn't assume that everyone who came by to see Chewie wanted to buy marijuana. And by now I was already on camera; I might as well make my presence official.

I knocked on the side door to the barn, and just as I was about to give up, Chewie opened the door a crack. "Sorry," he said. "I haven't put your order together yet. Can you come back tomorrow?"

There was something about not only *what* he said but the way he was saying it through the tiny opening that sent the message that something was very wrong. "Dammit, you promised," I replied, playing along.

"Like I said, ma'am, I'm sorry. Tomorrow, okay?" He started to close the door.

Ma'am? If I'd had any doubt before, it was gone. "I'll expect a discount," I yelled through the rapidly closing space. Then I turned and quickly returned to my car.

In spite of my misgivings about Chewie's situation, I wasn't at all sure what to do. Call Grimes and wait for him to arrive? Call JJ for back-up? What if Chewie was in immediate danger? Hell, I couldn't just leave or wait for the cavalry to arrive. I had to *do* something.

There wasn't much room to pull off along the narrow, dusty road, but I didn't think it mattered if I wasn't legally parked. If there were any other cars, they could squeeze by if they needed to.

As I headed back to Chewie's on foot, I called JJ and got his voice message. I told him where I was and that I was fairly sure something was wrong. I added, "If you don't hear from me in a half hour, call Deputy Grimes." I turned my ringtone to vibrate and put my cell in my pocket. Poor JJ. I was doing it to him again. I owed him big time when this was over. But Chewie had gone out of his way to help us, and if he was in trouble, I needed to return the favor. Although, that didn't necessarily mean he wanted me to call in the cops. I needed to figure out what was going on first.

Avoiding the cameras in front of the barn, I circled around to the back and was relieved that there didn't seem to be any cameras there, none that were obvious at least. The only way in was a normal-sized door off to the side nearest me. There were no windows. Whatever was supposed to be in the barn originally didn't need windows. And probably whatever Chewie did in there now didn't require them either. Unfortunately, if the door opened directly into the big open area of the barn like the front door did, I would be visible to anyone and everyone in there.

My initial thought was that if I couldn't get in unseen through the back door, I might at least get close enough to hear something. Beyond that I wasn't sure what I would do. As I drew near, another thought crossed my mind: where were the Spikes? They might not like an intruder who came in unannounced.

I didn't know whether to be pleased or disappointed when I saw that the back door was ajar. Was it a trick? There was no way to know for sure, but I had to take a look inside.

The Glock in my hand suddenly seemed heavy, an invitation to whoever was inside to take a shot at me. *If* they had a gun, and *if* they saw me before I saw them. What was I going to do, shoot first or ask to be shot by telling them to put down their weapons or else. I wasn't in Afghanistan, so I could shoot to maim, not to kill. But that would be taking a risk that I wasn't sure I was willing to take. And it depended on who was in there, how many there were and what they were up to. Dammit, I hoped I knew what I was doing.

I pushed the door open a few inches. There were voices coming from inside. One was Chewie's. He sounded angry and, yes, scared. The other voice was cold and menacing. Or so it seemed to me. Suddenly a few words leapt out loud and clear: "Down on your knees." The voice was not Chewie's.

I rushed inside, holding the gun in front of me, ready for action. But I wasn't in the main area; I was in a grow room. There were rows of plants on long tables with bright lights overhead. There was another open door just across the room. I cautiously moved forward. As I got closer, I could see what was happening. And it wasn't a scenario that favored the good guys.

The Spikes were nowhere in sight. Chewie was on his knees, and a skinny guy with long hair and a big pistol was standing in front of him with the semi-automatic pointed at Chewie's head. "You gave my name to a crazy smackhead who tried to rip me off. What I want to know is who the hell else knows about that, huh? Tell me that and you can live."

Why didn't I believe him?

There were a million thoughts racing through my mind at once as I stood there trying to assess the situation. It was obvious there was no time to call for back-up. And I had absolutely no doubt that if I yelled for him to put the gun down, he would just turn it on me. But if I did nothing, he would shoot Chewie. As I saw it, I only had one option and one chance to pull it off.

From the doorway I squared my stance, took careful two-handed aim, and pulled the trigger. The shot was loud in the high-ceilinged barn, echoing off the walls. As the shot reverberated in the barn and in my head, I saw Chewie jump up and throw himself at the other guy. He was twice the other guy's size, but the other guy was still holding onto his damn revolver.

I raced across the floor of the barn. Chewie had the guy down with his arms outspread. Giving it everything I had, I stomped on his hand. He screamed and spread his fingers. I quickly scooped up the revolver.

Armed with two mean looking weapons I yelled for them to stop. Chewie took one more punch at his opponent's head before rolling away from him. The other guy lay there, moaning and shaking his head, cradling the hand I had stomped on.

I handed the semi-automatic I'd retrieved to Chewie as he stood up. "Here."

"Nice shooting," he said. "Although you could have aimed higher."

I looked down at the guy on the ground. His left leg was covered in blood. "By higher I'm assuming you mean at this hand." I'd considered that but the leg was an easier target. And I didn't have much experience with the Glock.

Chewie grinned. "Well, maybe a little lower than that."

"Very funny," I said. "Is this who I think it is?"

"You got it."

"We need to call the police."

Chewie hesitated. Then he said, "He killed Morey, didn't he?"

"That would be my guess."

The guy suddenly seemed to focus on what was happening and attempted to get up, swearing loudly at Chewie and me.

"Hold it right there," Chewie said, pushing him back down with his foot while waving the semi-automatic in his face. The guy collapsed back on the ground.

"I know why you're hesitating," I said to Chewie. "I came in through the back. But I don't think we have a choice."

"They'll take away my livelihood. I'll never get a legit license."

"Better your livelihood than your life."

Chewie looked at the guy on the ground. He was following

our conversation like someone watching a ping-pong game, back and forth, wondering what the next volley would bring.

"I can pay you," the guy on the ground said suddenly. "Make it worth your while."

Chewie looked at me and smiled. "I guess there's at least one thing we agree on." I smiled back. "Okay, let's turn this scumbag over to the authorities."

"I'm on it." I got out my cell phone.

"Tell them to take their time getting here," he said. "I wouldn't mind letting him bleed out a little more."

The two sheriff's deputies chose that moment to come bursting in through the front door of the barn, guns pointed at us. "It's about time," I said, spreading my arms and slowly putting my Glock and phone on the ground. Chewie did the same with his assailant's revolver.

"She shot me," the guy on the ground yelled. "That crazy bitch shot me."

Grimes looked at me.

"Damn right," I said. "He's lucky I aimed for his leg." Chewie flashed me a grin.

Evans said, "You shot him?" He seemed truly surprised.

"I can explain."

In spite of the fact that Chewie was facing jail time and a hefty fine, he was smiling. "She's a damn good shot," he said. "Saved my worthless life."

Evans took a good look at the blood on the guy's leg and got on the phone to call for an ambulance. Grimes kicked the two weapons off to the side, looked at me, and said, "Okay, then explain."

JJ suddenly appeared and came rushing over to me. "Are you okay?" he asked. I couldn't chastise him in front of the two deputies for not waiting a half hour before calling the police, but I frowned to let him know I was displeased. If our situations had been reversed, I would probably have done exactly the same thing.

I assured him I was fine.

The guy on the ground wasn't through complaining. In a whiney voice he said, "She stomped on my hand. She shot me." Then he looked up at me and said in a louder voice, "Bitch."

"She saved my butt," Chewie told JJ.

"She was about to explain what happened," Grimes interjected. "Let her talk."

I had just started telling them about the sequence of events when Evans interrupted. He had wandered toward the back of barn while placing the call to the ambulance. "Holy crap," he yelled back at Grimes. "Wait until you see what's back here."

Grimes looked questioningly at me. "No bodies. Just some plants." I started in again. Before I could get to the part about having no choice but to shoot him before he shot Chewie, Grimes himself interrupted. "This is the guy who shot Morey, isn't it?"

"That's what we're thinking."

"He admitted that to me," Chewie said. "And he was about to kill me." That had obviously made an impression on him.

"I'd keep my mouth shut," I warned Chewie. "You might be in a position to trade information for leniency."

"You can't give him legal advice," Evans said.

"I think she just did," JJ offered. Turning to Chewie, he said, "And I'd take it if I were you."

"Is everyone on this drug dealer's side?" Evans asked.

"It's just marijuana," JJ and I said in chorus.

"Finish your story," Grimes said with an exasperated sigh. "I need to call Crane, and I want to know what I'm talking about when I do."

I gave him an overview of what had happened, and he called Crane. Then we left Evans behind to keep an eye on the cuffed and hastily bandaged alleged drug dealer/murderer while the rest of us went outside to wait for the ambulance and the major crimes team.

"Where are the Spikes?" I asked, suddenly remembering that I hadn't seen them anywhere.

"They're okay," Chewie said. "He had me put them in the RV. Said they made him nervous. In retrospect I think he was worried that he couldn't shoot both of them fast enough to avoid having one of them go for his throat. If I'd known what he was up to, I would have sicced them on him."

The ambulance arrived within fifteen minutes of being called. The EMT quickly assessed the dealer's wounds as non-life-threatening. The bullet hadn't hit anything critical. They patched him up and settled in to wait for backup. Crane was sending someone to ride in the ambulance with the EMT on the trip to Seattle.

We waited. Chewie asked if it was okay for JJ to get us all beers from his fridge in the RV. JJ and I thought that was a great idea, but the others declined because they were on duty. "Sorry," Chewie said with a wicked smile, "but I don't have any lemonade."

As JJ headed toward the RV, Chewie yelled, "Oh, don't worry about the Spikes . . . unless you want to live a little longer." JJ stopped in his tracks. "Okay if I go to the door with him?" Chewie asked Grimes. "I won't go inside."

"You should let him," I said. Grimes had never seen the Spikes, but he reluctantly agreed.

It was really hot out, the sun beating down relentlessly in the clearing. Everyone had beads of sweat on their foreheads. Grimes and Evans had taken off their jackets and laid them across a nearby old piece of fencing, eyeing our cool beers with envy.

"I have a friend who can take care of the Spikes," Chewie

said. He handed me a card. "Will you see that he comes and gets them?"

I agreed, grateful that he hadn't asked me to take them. I'm not sure what I would have done if he had. I was confident that Natasha and Dilly wouldn't have approved.

It took the rest of the day to sort things out. Crane himself turned up with several members of his team. They took possession of the drug dealer/murderer and his weapon and put Chewie under arrest. Crane still wasn't entirely convinced that I hadn't withheld information, but he was pleased to make two arrests.

Crane of course asked why I was there in the first place, stopping just short of asking whether I was a customer.

JJ jumped in before I could say anything rash. "We were here before, trying to get information about Morey's drug connections." He quickly added that Chewie hadn't sold anything to Morey and had tried to help us.

Crane seemed dubious but backed off, warning me that he expected a full accounting of my actions after they got everything sorted out. Then he confiscated Beatrice's Glock and informed me that he expected me in his Seattle office first thing in the morning.

Grimes and JJ walked me to my car, and Grimes took the opportunity to lecture me on why I shouldn't be taking dangerous risks. Then he went on to thank me for helping catch Morey's murderer and preventing a third murder, apparently oblivious to the irony of his two very conflicting responses to what I had done.

JJ squeezed my arm and grinned. Under his breath he murmured, "You *big women* are awesome."

Chapter 24
The Road to Hell

After apologizing to Beatrice about the hopefully temporary confiscation of her Glock by the police, I promised to get her another more appropriate weapon soon. Then I went home and apologized to my cats for keeping them in prison, ignoring them, not giving them enough treats, for every sin I'd committed against them. Next, as if it were Halloween for Cats, I showered them with goodies. At that point I became invisible to them as their lust for food took over.

The box of Jake's papers Jeannie had given me was on my desk. I knew I should go through them again, this time more carefully, but I wasn't feeling up to it. Nor did I think that I could concentrate enough to actually do some of my own consulting work. I finally decided it was time to binge on Netflix movies and popcorn. Tomorrow I would get back to life as usual.

If I hadn't decided to watch The Descendants, a movie in which a man is being pressured by his family to sell off some pristine property on Kauai that had been in the family for generations, I might have been able to relax for the rest of the evening. It was satisfying to know that Morey's killer was in custody. Even if we didn't have all of the details, and we still didn't know if Morey had killed Jake. Realistically, tomorrow would not be life as usual, not until we had more answers.

The movie was fairly entertaining, but all of its talk about land trusts got me thinking about the bog again. Since I first saw the hand poking up out of that pond, I had believed that there had to be a reason Jake was murdered in the bog.

When I couldn't get that thought out of my mind, I dragged myself away from the TV and opened the box of Jake's papers. As I removed each piece of paper, I scanned its contents and placed it in a pile on the floor, grouping them by topic. When I was through, the stack related to the bog was impressive. There were notes on past meetings with various landowners, minutes from meetings where the bog was discussed, maps of the area, descriptions of the spring and water drainage, a geological history. It was a virtual compendium of information, but nothing that indicated any current concerns.

I also came across some handwritten notes that had been ripped carelessly from yellow pads. The top edges were ragged and uneven. The writing was also sloppy and there were lots of abbreviations. It was difficult reading. One page in particular caught my eye. It was a list of short phrases: "$50,000 offered." "First in on sale." "Finalized with title." That sounded suspiciously like he was taking notes on a real estate agreement. What if it was related to one or more properties adjacent to the bog? I could probably go online and identify which, if any, properties near the bog were involved. On the other hand, there was a faster way to at least narrow the search.

I hadn't yet apologized to Marie, my realtor friend, and it seemed pretty callous to apologize and then ask her for a favor in the same breath, but that's what I did.

"I can't believe you didn't just tell me," Marie said. "I would have given you the information."

"I'm really sorry, but I didn't exactly have standing in the investigation. And it was a longshot. I didn't want to implicate Paige if she wasn't involved." I threw out all of the reasons I had come up with; maybe one or more would stick.

Marie seemed to consider. "Well," she said finally, "I can see that. But . . . you should have called me right after it happened."

I laughed. "I decided to wait until I had another favor to ask."

"Come on, seriously?"

"Seriously."

"What this time?" Her curiosity apparently won out over her pique. That was what I'd been counting on.

"It's about the land around the bog," I explained. "I need to know if any developers have been sniffing around lately."

Marie thought a moment. "Why are you asking?" This time she wasn't taking any chances. But I was in the same position as before. I didn't want to show my hand too soon.

"It's about a rumor I've heard. We think the landowners near the bog are committed to its preservation, but if some developer is trying to pull a fast one, we need to get ahead of that."

"By 'we' you mean the Island Land Stewards."

"Right." Although I trusted her ability to be discreet, I couldn't quite bring myself to be totally transparent. If I turned out to be right again, this time I would at least call her immediately. Maybe by combining the truth with a lie the outcome would be palatable. And if I was wrong, no one would be the wiser.

"That makes sense," she said. "I'll check around and get back to you."

I thanked her and hung up. There wasn't much I could do until I heard back from her, so I clicked the movie back on. But I had trouble staying focused. There was something nagging at me, something trying to break through my brain fog into the open. I kept watching the movie without really taking in what was happening on the screen.

There were lots of people looking to purchase land on the island. People looking for vacation homes, retirement homes, acreage for farming and animals. People looking for development opportunities. Like Rene Hubbard. But she was doing it openly, through one of our most popular realtors, and she was supposedly going to build low-income housing. There were cheaper and better options than land near the bog for that.

Suddenly it hit me. There was a serious problem with what I had just done. If I was on the right track and some real estate developer really was responsible for Jake's death, I might be putting Marie in danger. Dammit. I hadn't thought things through very well at all.

When I called her back Marie answered on the first ring. "I had my hand on my phone," she said. "I was about to start making a few calls for you."

"Look," I said, "I just realized that I need to talk to a few of the residents near the bog before I have you asking around. It might make things awkward for the Island Land Stewards if I don't talk to them first." It was lame, but it made sense on the surface. "Sorry to have jumped the gun like this. I really appreciate you being willing to help. I'll get back to you in a day or two, okay?"

She agreed, and we left it there.

———

Wednesday morning, I went into Seattle to give my statement to one of Crane's team members. I considered mentioning my latest theory about the possibility of a clash between Jake and a land developer, but the person taking my statement didn't seem interested in any speculation, and neither Crane nor Forester was available.

On my way back, I called JJ while waiting at the ferry dock, but he didn't answer. Then I reluctantly called Grimes and asked if he had a few minutes for me when I got back. I wanted to run my theory past someone, expose it to the light of day, test its credibility. On the one hand, I was afraid that Grimes might simply tell me to let it go, but on the other hand, if I was right, it needed to be on law enforcement's radar.

Grimes invited me into his office, and since Evans wasn't around, I got the good chair. I asked him if he'd seen the movie The Descendants. "George Clooney is in it," I added. "Great scenery."

"No, I haven't. Is this a social call?"

"There's a point," I said. I took a deep breath and explained how I'd been watching the movie, got the idea about real estate developers putting pressure on people to sell and made the leap to Jake and the bog. "I'm thinking about asking some of the nearby residents if they've been approached by a developer interested in buying their land. What do you think?"

"I think this isn't something *you* should be doing."

"But is it something that *someone* should be doing?"

Grimes thought about it for a minute. "You're convinced that the fact Jake died in the bog is significant, aren't you?"

"Absolutely. Think about it. It's highly unlikely Jake and his killer just happened to wander that far into the bog. Or that the murder happened elsewhere, and the killer carried him all the way in there. There are much easier places to dispose of a body. Although it doesn't exactly explain why they would be there in the first place. But don't you think the possibility deserves consideration?"

"Okay, you've got me there."

"Then it can't hurt to ask, right? And I can do it on behalf of the Island Land Stewards. There are several parcels bordering the bog where development could have huge impact. In particular there are a couple of areas where drainage into or out of the bog is critical. If a developer has been asking around, or if someone is thinking about selling on the QT, it would be good to know."

"You *could* ask around. But if I sanctioned that, Crane would have my badge. What if I put Evans on it?"

I was torn between wanting to stay in control of my idea and knowing that it was better if the police did the questioning. Reluctantly I agreed to let Evans run with it. I would go home, get back to my project work and take care of Natasha and Dilly in the style to which they used to be accustomed.

If the road to hell is paved with good intentions, then within five minutes of leaving Grimes, I had started down that road. Did I really believe that after killing Jake the developer had been knowledgeable and reckless enough to send the threatening notes to us, hang a dead coyote at my doorstep, and kidnap Boner? Or was this another case of a correlation fallacy at work? Maybe Morey had been responsible for some of it after all. Or maybe there was still one more bad guy lurking out there, someone who really was motivated by opposition to the wilding of the island.

Before I made a conscious decision, I found myself detouring past Paige's house. I didn't know if she was home or not, but if she was, maybe she would feel differently about answering a few questions about Morey's involvement in what had happened, now that he was gone.

I saw her peek out from the edge of the blinds as I approached her house. It was even money whether she would answer the door or not. I was definitely not on her favorite person's list. When she didn't respond to my persistent knocking, I found myself feeling unreasonably irritated. In her position, I might not have answered either. Nevertheless, I pounded on the door and said loudly, "Come on, Paige, answer the door. You know that I know you're in there."

When she finally opened the door and I saw her red eyes and unkept appearance, I felt my heart soften a tiny bit, but then she said," What the hell are you doing here?" My heart immediately hardened into cold cynicism.

"I'm here for answers. I'm getting damn tired of constantly looking over my shoulder and having to carry a weapon around. You going to come out or invite me in?"

She stepped aside and I went directly over to the couch and sat down. She took a seat on an overstuffed chair across from me, slouching down as if all of her resistance and hostility had suddenly drained out, leaving her limp and defeated. "I don't know anything other than what I've already told you."

"It's like this," I said, trying to sound calm and reasonable. "I know you're grieving for Morey, but I need you to be clear-headed for a moment and think hard about anything he may have mentioned that indicated what he was up to."

"Like I just said, I've already told you everything I know."

"Let's talk about the threatening note that Andy got. Did Morey ever mention anything about that?"

"Well, yes," she admitted.

That was a start. "Did he put the note on Andy's desk?"

After a moment's hesitation, she nodded.

"And the notes on our doors?"

She nodded again. "He only wanted to scare the three of you. His mother was really upset when her cat, Woody, went missing. He felt like he was getting some revenge for the cat's disappearance by writing those notes."

"And did he try to ambush us the night of the coyote survey?"

A tear gathered at the corner of her eye and threatened to

roll down her cheek. "I don't think so. I mean, I didn't think so at the time. Now I'm not so sure. He had a gun, and he told me he was a good shot. He used to go prairie dog hunting in South Dakota. And he liked hunting generally. But I don't think he would have shot a person . . ." She paused, then said, "If he did it I'm sure he didn't mean to actually shoot anyone, just get you to back off. He wasn't a bad guy. He just couldn't seem to get his act together." She wiped away a tear with the back of her hand.

"What about the coyote someone hung next to my porch. Did he do that?"

She looked down at the floor and nodded. "That one he did do. He really hated those coyotes."

"The timing bothers me," I said, falling quiet when Paige put her face in her hands and started sobbing. I didn't know what to do, so I just waited until she got herself under control.

"I need a glass of water," she said. She got up and headed for the kitchen. I got up and followed her.

I waited until she took a sip of water before asking something that I should have thought of before. "Did you help him with the coyote?"

She put the glass down and took a deep breath. "Will I get in trouble?" she asked. "I mean, he was the one who trapped it and shot it. He even carried it over there beforehand and left it in the bushes. It was all ready to go. All I had to do was hoist it up while he was at the party. He wanted to make sure people saw him there, as an alibi." She collapsed on a kitchen table chair. "What was I thinking?" she said, shaking her head back and forth. "What on earth was I thinking?"

"That's the problem, Paige. You weren't thinking." She had believed him and supported him. It was too bad he hadn't been a better person. "Did you also help him kidnap Boner?"

"No." She sounded indignant. "I would never have agreed

to that. Andy's a nice guy, and everyone knows how much he loves that dog. Although since the dog wasn't hurt . . ." She looked thoughtful. "But I'm sure Morey would have told me if he'd kidnapped Boner. And he would have needed a place to keep him."

"He didn't tell you about his mother's jewelry," I pointed out.

Paige looked own at her bare feet with their pink polished toenails. For a minute I thought I'd lost her to the world of pedicure fantasy, but then she looked up at me and said, "I could tell he was lying to me about that. He was embarrassed. If it hadn't been for the heroin, well, he just couldn't help himself."

"But you still don't think he was responsible for kidnapping Boner."

"No, I'm almost positive he wasn't." The tears started running down her face. "I loved him," she said. "But I wasn't able to help him. And now he's . . . dead."

"He had a serious drug problem, Paige. There wasn't anything you could have done."

She sat there, silently crying. It was enough to crack the most cynical heart, even mine. I've done things in my life that I'm not proud of. And I've made some stupid mistakes. I've even fallen for the wrong guy a time or two.

"What's going to happen to me?" she finally asked.

"You're going to put the past behind you and get on with your life," I said. "That's what we all have to do."

"But the coyote . . .?"

"As far as I'm concerned, Morey hung it there. No one ever needs to know otherwise."

Chapter 25
The Number One Suspect

The first thing I did when I got home was pour myself a glass of merlot. I would have preferred a cab, but the merlot was open. Red and dry, a full-bodied merlot goes well with the sound of begging cats.

After attending to Natasha and Dilly I called Andy and told him that Morey had been responsible for the notes and the coyote, maybe even the shooting, but probably *not* for kidnapping Boner. And if Forester had shot himself, as I still suspected, then that meant Morey hadn't actually followed through on his threats, except for the coyote. He had, however, played into the killer's hands by providing an excuse to use Boner's kidnapping to keep people thinking Jake's death was related to the wilding of the island.

Andy had to go to a meeting, so I was saving my latest theory for when he called me back later.

Norm didn't answer his phone, so I left him a message to give me a call.

JJ answered but was rushing off to meet a client and said he would get back with me later.

I had no option but to try to focus on paying work. It wasn't

as if I didn't like my work—I did. I liked investigating compli-
cated situations and making sure the good guys came out on
top. And I felt good when I nailed someone for abusing the
power they had over others. A lot of my harassment cases were
about people in power preying on those too timid or too inse-
cure to speak up. Until the victim finally reached a tipping
point. And then things often got ugly. At any rate, it was time to
set up a series of interviews with employee peers of the alleged
victim of my latest assignment.

One moment I was thinking about harassment, and the
next Rene Hubbard flashed through my mind. What if—? I
quickly got online and looked up her company. I should have
done it before, but she had seemed so transparent about what
she was looking for on the island. But there it was—a glaring
contradiction. Her company specialized in high-end development projects, big money-makers, not public-spirited stuff.
Maybe her initial thought was to capitalize on the bog's mystic
appeal to attract people willing to pay extra for a condo on an
island within commuting distance of Seattle. The key question
was, when did she start looking for property to build low-
income housing? Before or after Jake's death?

My phone interrupted my speculation. It was Marie.

"I have news," she said, sounding pleased with herself.

"About what?" I asked.

"About the developer you were curious about."

I felt my heart rate increase. "You haven't been asking
around, have you?"

"Well, you aren't the only one who cares about land preservation on the island. And you won't believe—. Oh, oh. Sorry.
I've just been signaled that there's someone here to see me, so I
have to run. I'll call you back, okay?"

"No, Marie. I . . ."

"Catch you later."

"You need to listen to me." My tone was half command, half plea. But it was already too late; Marie had hung up. I called her back and got her answering machine. Then I called her office. By the time someone picked up the phone it was again too late. Marie had just left with a client. The receptionist didn't know her name. But she was a well-dressed woman with perfectly coifed hair.

It only took me a few minutes to lock everything up and rush to my car. Twenty minutes later I was at Marie's real estate office. She still wasn't answering her cell. No one knew where Marie had gone with her new client. Ignoring the protests of an associate at the desk across from hers, I began rifling through Marie's files.

"You can't do that," the associate protested. She was a soft-spoken woman who always seemed to wear something pink. I racked my memory banks for her name.

"Janice, right?" I said, glancing up.

"Yes."

"Well, Janice, it's critical that I get in touch with Marie right away." I've found that using someone's name tends to give you more authority over them. But in this instance, it didn't work.

"I'm going to have to ask you to leave," Janice said.

"Sorry," I said without looking up. "But I need to figure out where Marie went. Either help me or leave me alone."

Janice stood there a moment, watching. Was she waiting for me to do as she asked, or was she about to get physical?

Her indecision gave me just enough time to figure out that I wasn't going to find the information I needed on Marie's desk. I did, however, come across a scrap of paper with my name on it and another name written beside it: Hubbard Development LLC. Rene Hubbard. Well dressed and stylish. Damn.

"Okay," I said as if agreeing that she had been right all

along. I held my hands in the air in surrender and took a seat in the waiting area. I needed to think. Maybe I was wrong; maybe it was a different well-dressed woman looking for real estate on the island. I called Hubbard's office, but surprise, she wasn't in. And that was all they would tell me, other than that I could leave a message.

I tried to convince myself that everything was fine. Rene Hubbard had come openly into Marie's office. Even if she had been responsible for Jake's death, there was no reason to suspect that Marie was in danger. Was there? Unable to shake a feeling of dread, I went out to my car and called Grimes. He wasn't in. His admin told me that he had been called home to fix an emergency plumbing problem.

When he picked up his home phone on the seventh ring he said, "This better be good."

"Sorry to interrupt . . ."

"Oh, that's all right. I was just lying on my back under the kitchen sink with water dripping on my forehead."

"Well, it may be nothing, but it could be something," I said.

"You're going to have to do better than that."

"Well, I mentioned to Marie, my realtor, that I thought there was a developer trying to buy land next to the bog. Then I had second thoughts about her looking into it and asked her to hold off. But she didn't. And now, she thinks she knows who that developer is. In fact, she's with her now. Only she isn't aware that Jake was looking into it before he was killed."

"Dammit, Lew. That wasn't too smart."

"I know. I was trying to warn her, but she didn't give me a chance. I'm at her office. She isn't answering her phone. No one knows where she went or the name of the person she went with. But I suspect it's Rene Hubbard, the developer Annie Regis was showing properties to."

"Stay there. I'll change clothes and be there as soon as I can."

By the time Grimes joined me, I'd called Marie half a dozen times and left as many messages. We went into her office to see if there was something I missed. Janice glared at me as we passed by, but seeing that I was with Grimes, she didn't say anything.

We looked around, opened a few drawers, and went over the papers on her desk. Then Grimes punched Marie's number into his phone to see if he could get through. Seconds later I heard a phone ring down the hall. Then I heard Marie's voice in stereo as she came around the corner into her office. Grimes looked up at her, and she stared back at him as they realized they were only a few feet away from each other while talking on the phone. Grimes actually said "goodbye" as he hung up. That told me he had been as worried as I had.

"Were you with Rene Hubbard?" I blurted out.

"Yes, what's going on?" Marie looked truly bewildered.

"But isn't she the developer who was looking at bog properties?"

"That's the reason I wanted to talk with her, although I let her think it was to show her a farm house with a barn and horse paddock that's for sale." Marie looked pleased with herself. "Annie told me she was also looking for a vacation place where she could keep a horse."

"Sit down," Grimes ordered. "Let's take this from the top."

Marie dutifully explained that when she started asking fellow realtors about anyone who recently showed interest in the bog area, Annie had admitted that's what Rene Hubbard had originally been looking at. Then she'd changed her mind and started searching for properties to accommodate low-income housing.

"That just didn't ring true to me," Marie said. "No developer of high-end projects switches over to a limited profit margin project overnight. So, I decided to feel her out. It isn't unheard of for a client to use a realtor to locate properties of interest to them and then go behind the realtor's back to make an offer directly to an owner."

"So, she came over to look at a farm and you asked her if she was still interested in property near the bog?"

"I used a little more finesse than that, but, yes, that's what I did. She informed me, rather firmly, that she had given up on the bog development idea some time ago. Said she realized right away it wasn't feasible. And, after I showed the farm to her, she said she was interested in making an offer. She wants to show it to her family first."

"So, you believe her?" I asked.

"Yes, I do. She seems to genuinely want to buy vacation property here. She talked a lot about her family and her daughter's love of horses."

"And the low-income housing project?"

"She said that's on hold. But not completely off the table."

"She didn't happen to mention meeting Jake, did she?"

Marie looked startled. "No, why would she?"

"Marie, I'm sorry," I said. "I should have told you that I was looking for a link between Rene and Jake. That's why I had second thoughts about having you ask around."

"There's no proof," Grimes interrupted. "It's conjecture. But I would ask both of you to avoid any further inquiries into her transactions. Understood?"

"Yes," Marie said. Then she looked at me. "Lew, you've got to learn to trust people."

"I'm really sorry. I was trying not to involve you." That was the truth, but there was also some truth in what she was saying about trust.

Annie Regis had an office just a couple of miles down the road toward the ferry. Grimes called her to let her know we were on our way. When we arrived, she asked, "What's this about?" We must have had the look of two people on a mission.

"Why don't you tell us about Rene Hubbard's interest in buying land adjacent to the Whistling Pete Bog?" I asked before Grimes could say anything.

Annie seemed surprised by my question. After a brief hesitation, she said, "Rene was very specific about not wanting me to talk to anyone about it. She knew the project wouldn't be popular with a lot of islanders. She told me she wanted to get through all of the preliminary studies and paperwork before it became public."

"And how did you feel about that?" I asked.

"Not good," she said. "I think it's a mistake to develop that property. But it isn't my decision."

"What about the landowners involved?" I asked. "How did they feel about selling to a high-density land developer?"

Annie took a deep breath. "I don't think any of the landowners are particularly eager to sell right now. But I understand she offered several of them $50,000 in cash in exchange for an option if they decide to sell. That might look like a pretty good deal to some of them. She's also optioned some of the open water rights."

"She must have known that the county or the state could deny her the permits necessary for the project," I said.

"She seemed to think she could get approval. There's spring water on some of that land. And as you know, most of the objections about development on the island are because of lack of water. But to be honest, I was relieved when she changed her mind. That's when I showed her the Winchell properties."

"And the emphasis changed from a high-end development to low-income housing, just like that?"

"Well, yes."

"Didn't you find that strange."

"Not really. She said she realized that development near the bog wasn't feasible, which it probably isn't. Then she learned there was a need for low-income housing on the island, which there is. It all made sense to me."

"And you didn't think her initial interest in the bog was something the police might want to know about?" Grimes sounded peeved.

Annie looked stunned as one possible reason we were asking these questions about Rene Hubbard suddenly hit her. "I heard that Morey killed his stepfather." She paused, obviously hoping for confirmation.

"We haven't closed the door on other possibilities," Grimes conceded.

Annie cheeks flushed red as poppies. "You don't think . . .?"

"We aren't sure what we think at this point," Grimes said. "We are gathering information. But you'd be advised to keep your mouth shut until we finish our inquiries."

I felt sorry for Annie, but that didn't mean I approved of her decision to keep mum. Even if she'd believed Morey had killed his stepfather, she'd owed it to the community to warn them about such a sensitive land grab.

———

On the way back to pick up my car, Grimes informed me that as soon as Evans interviewed a couple of the landowners to confirm Marie's story, he would turn over what we had learned to Crane. "But keep in mind that being an unscrupulous realtor doesn't make her a murderer."

I agreed, it didn't make her a murderer, but it made her my number one suspect.

Chapter 26
The Deadly Developer

The first thing I did the next morning was call Grimes and ask if it was okay with him if I went with Evans to talk to the landowners near the bog. "Someone from the Island Land Stewards will have to talk to them at some point," I said. "We need to see if their positions about preservation of the surrounding area have changed. Might as well combine the two lines of inquiry." Besides, the more I'd thought about it, the more convinced I'd become that Rene Hubbard was more than unscrupulous. But I needed evidence.

"That makes sense," Grimes said. I wasn't sure if he agreed or just didn't want to argue with me about it.

"Did you get your plumbing fixed?" I asked to be polite.

He sighed. "Someone's coming today." His tone suggested my attempt at politeness hadn't been appreciated.

When I followed up by calling Evans, he told me that he had already made an arrangement to meet with Sam Davies, one of the land owners adjacent to the bog. If I could be at the office in a half hour, I was welcome to tag along.

I may have exceeded the speed limit a bit—35 mph on the island's rural roads is difficult to comply with under the best of circumstances—and I got there with time to spare.

Bogged Down

On the way to Sam's place, I filled Evans in on the little I knew about Sam's background. He was one of the property-owners that the Island Land Stewards were fairly certain they could count on to give them an option to buy if he decided to sell. Sam had retired from an engineering job at Boeing some years ago and moved to their vacation home on Vashon after his wife passed. He was an avid birdwatcher and a member of the Vashon-Maury Island Audubon Society.

Evans was pleasant enough on the drive over. He had apparently forgiven me for sidelining him the day Jake's body was discovered as well as for my other minor transgressions since then. I went out of my way to be pleasant in return. It's always a strain for me to make small talk, but when I discovered he was an avid sail boater, it became a lot easier.

We heard the dogs barking from inside the house the minute we pulled up. They sounded big, like their barks came from deep down in cavernous chests. So, when Sam opened the door and two tiny dust mops started jumping up on us, I almost laughed.

"Hey, Fritz, Casper, get out of here." Sam didn't sound like he meant it, and the dogs kept on pawing at us, begging for attention. I leaned down and rubbed Fritz or Casper, which-ever dog was going to town on me. Evans, on the other hand was shaking his leg and backing up to get rid of his attacker.

Once the dogs lost interest in us, we went into the living room and sat down. Evans opened with a direct question: Had Davies talked to Rene Hubbard about selling his land? Davies glanced guiltily in my direction before replying.

"It was a financially appealing offer," he said. "I needed to consider it."

"When did she approach you?" Evans asked.

"It was about a month ago."

"And what's happened since then?"

"Nothing. For a while she was all gung-ho, then she seemed to lose interest."

I got impatient and jumped in with the question that was at the forefront of my mind. "Did you mention her offer to Jake?"

"Yes, I did. I thought I owed him a head's up. I knew how concerned he would be if the land was developed. He was the one from the Island Land Stewards who first approached me about preserving my property. He emphasized how redirecting drainage water could destroy the bog. But the developer said they would make sure that didn't happen."

"When Jake was killed did it occur to you that Hubbard might be a suspect?" I asked.

Sam seemed taken aback. "A woman? Overpower Jake? No way. Besides, I thought Morey killed his stepfather." The grapevine had apparently convinced more than one person that Morey was the guilty party.

The next two stops produced little new information. Hubbard had definitely made the rounds of the landowners in the area, promising them sweet deals if they would give her the first right of refusal if and when they decided to sell. She'd come on strong then suddenly seemed to lose interest. Everyone assumed she'd done her homework and realized how hard it would be to get county permission to build near the bog. End of story for them, but confirmation of my suspicions for me.

After talking with JJ to get his buy-in, I made an appointment with Rene Hubbard for the following afternoon at her firm's office in Seattle. Supposedly to talk with her about a development project for a client. If she looked me up, she would know right away that I was from Vashon Island. That might put her on guard, but I didn't think that would help her sidestep what JJ and I had in store for her.

_____

When we arrived at Hubbard's fancy suite of offices, the well-dressed receptionist's bright red lips puckered with disapproval. "You can't bring a dog in here."

"He's a service dog," JJ said, oozing charm out of every pore.

"Where's his vest?" she asked, softening a tiny bit.

"He doesn't like to wear it. But don't worry, we'll just sit over here and wait. You won't even notice we're here." JJ jerked Boner over to a line of chairs and pushed at his behind to get him to sit down.

Now it was all up to me.

Rene Hubbard's office was set up just like we'd hoped it would be with an impressive desk center stage and two client chairs in front. The desk had a middle panel that was about a foot off the floor, perfect for my plan. She got up long enough to shake my hand before retreating behind her desk. I sat down and said something inane about why I was there. Then I opened my purse, took out a pen and clumsily dropped it. "Oh," I said as I bent over to ostensibly pick up my pen. At the same time, I shoved a mesh bag filled with dog treats under the desk toward Rene's feet. To a dog's sensitive nose, they smelled strongly of meat, specifically lamb and pepperoni. Gross, but Boner is wild about them.

The next move was up to Boner.

"Sorry," I said as I straightened up in my chair. "Darn, my phone is vibrating. Just a sec." I took out my phone and hit send on the open text message to let JJ know everything was in place. Then I smiled to let Rene Hubbard know I was ready to talk.

I heard a female voice say, "You can't go in there," just as Boner appeared in the doorway. He sniffed the air briefly and made a beeline for Rene Hubbard. JJ was hanging onto his expandable leash, pretending to try to reign him in, pulling him up short just before he betrayed what he was actually after. Rene Hubbard looked sufficiently horror struck to convince me we were on the right track.

"I didn't realize that you'd met Boner before," I said.

Boner struggled to get closer to Rene Hubbard as she pushed her chair away from him.

"You can't have a dog in here," the strident voice of the receptionist said from the doorway.

"It's okay. I'll take him out." While everyone was focused on JJ and Boner, I used my foot to retrieve the dog treats and leaned over quickly to scoop the bag into my purse.

Rene Hubbard was having difficulty regaining her composure. "I can't imagine . . .," she began, obviously unsure how to finish her sentence.

"Boner *never* goes to strangers," I said emphatically. "But he has a good memory for people. You must have been super nice to him for him to be so happy to see you again."

"I don't know what you mean."

"I think you do." I paused meaningfully. "Let me spell it out. We know you had an appointment to meet Jake. He made a note of the meeting on his calendar." Not true, but she couldn't know that. "And the police will be able to prove you were on the island the day he died. There are cameras on the ferries, you know." I wasn't sure how long they kept recordings, but she probably didn't know either. "There are also records of ferry ticket purchases." Again, I wasn't sure how much data was collected and saved, but I was counting on her not knowing any more than I did. "And we've talked with the owners you approached to buy land near the bog."

She started to interrupt, but I held up my hand. "And don't try to tell me that it's a *coincidence* you changed your mind about purchasing their land the day after Jake died." Only she would know the timing of her decision not to pursue the bog properties, but from the look on her face it was a darn good guess.

"You can't prove anything," she said. Her unnecessary denial screamed guilty to me. And she'd turned pale under her carefully applied makeup.

"I'm here to give you a chance to turn yourself in."

"Just because that dog recognized me doesn't prove anything."

"You weren't listening. You had motive and opportunity. Boner was just the finale."

For a moment I thought she might simply ask me to leave. Then her shoulders sagged, and tears started forming at the corners of her eyes. "It was an accident," she said softly. "An accident." I hoped my phone recorder had caught her confession. I could hardly ask her to speak up.

"I'm sure you didn't intend to kill him," I said, trying to provoke her into saying more.

"Of course, I didn't." Her voice wavered with emotion. Then she suddenly seemed to realize what was happening, stood up and squared her shoulders. "Please leave. I have nothing more to say to you."

I remained seated. "It's over. I'm giving you a chance to go to the police on your own. Accidents happen. You need to come clean." Had I really used a cliché like "come clean?"

She blinked but didn't say anything.

"We know you took Boner to make everyone think an anti-wilder was responsible for Jake's death. The fact that you took good care of him tells me that your heart is in the right place." Sure, right between your lungs.

She looked so pathetic I almost felt sorry for her. Almost.

"Please go."

"If that's what you want." That was okay by me. I felt confident I had enough to goose Crane into action.

———

Crane wasn't as pleased with what JJ and I had done as I thought he should be. The recording might not stand up in a court of law, and a dog can't be a witness, but we'd handed him a confession that he could use for leverage. Didn't that merit a heartfelt thank you? Apparently not.

Meanwhile, Dilly and Natasha were being fed on a regular basis, and Chewie worked out a deal with the authorities. He got probation and a fine in exchange for his testimony about the drug dealer. Without his testimony they would have had a hard time tying the dealer to Morey's murder. And the drug dealer turned out to be a very bad guy who law enforcement officials were pleased to nail.

Andy, Norm, and I finally managed to do our coyote howling survey. It was an interesting evening with a star-filled night sky overhead and the mystical vocalizations of our much loved and equally hated coyotes. We even heard one pack exchanging howls with coyotes across the water on the mainland, perhaps a long-distance call between distant relatives. The information we gathered that night, combined with wild cam data, database reports and scat analysis, indicated that all four packs on the island were probably doing well and actively breeding.

There were still several loose ends. One was Beatrice's Glock. The police said they would return it when the case was finalized, but that could be a while. In the meantime, I bought her several pepper spray cannisters of different sizes and gave her a certificate for a self-defense class being provided on the island for older women. With luck she wouldn't need any of it, but it made me feel better.

Another loose end was the missing bullet that went through Detective Forester's leg. I did manage a trip to the area where he'd been shot and examined every inch of ground on my hands and knees, turning over leaves and pushing aside cones from fir trees and twigs to check underneath. All I found was a tarnished penny and a pile of deer scat. Determining whether he'd actually shot himself was apparently going to be a loose end that remained loose. But if Paige was right that Morey had been the shooter and was simply trying to scare us, a self-inflicted shot seemed the most likely explanation.

Rene Hubbard hired one of Seattle's finest criminal lawyers and entered a plea of involuntary manslaughter. Her story was that Jake persuaded her to take a look at the bog to get a better picture of what was at stake if she developed the nearby land. When he lost his balance and slipped off the log into the pond, he'd hit his head on something and was unresponsive when she tried to help him. Convinced he was dead, she panicked and ran away. After that she was afraid how it would look if she admitted being with him when the accident happened.

Given my jaded view of human nature, I had a different version of events. In my story, she agreed to go with Jake to the bog to gather facts that might be useful in creating more hype about her development's location. Then, when they reached the log, I could picture her telling Jake that, in spite of everything he'd showed her, she intended to proceed with the development. I could also envision her turning back toward the trail, Jake reaching out to stop her, her jerking away or even striking back at him. Maybe there was even a brief scuffle. Maybe she pushed him, perhaps not intending to do him serious harm. Then Jake, off balance, slipped off the log into the pond, hitting his head on something that caused the intercranial bleeding that resulted in his death. Whatever the particulars, in my version, she left him there without knowing for certain that he was dead.

Whichever narrative represented what actually happened, it was entirely possible Jake was dead before being submerged in the pond. Apparently, the lungs and airways of a corpse can passively fill with water after several hours. It could have all happened exactly the way Hubbard said it did. Or it could have happened as I imagined it. Either way, she was guilty of not calling for help as well as for attempting to cover up her involvement with Jake's death.

The press dubbed Rene Hubbard the "deadly developer." She fought back by giving a local reporter an interview in which she was seated in the family living room, her husband and two kids off to one side, the family dog lying at her feet. She may indeed have had a soft spot in her heart for dogs, but I couldn't help wondering if she'd considered doing Boner in after about the hundredth time he'd humped her leg.

I ran into Grimes one day in the hardware store. "I've been meaning to get in touch," he said. "You know, without your persistence, we might not have picked up on the Hubbard connection."

"Is that your way of saying *good job, Lew*"? I kidded.

"Something like that," Grimes said with a smile. "Thanks. Oh, one more thing. Woody is back."

"Jeannie's cat came home?"

"Well, someone recognized him from the posters Jeannie put up. He was on Maury Island. No idea how he ended up there. But a happy ending is a happy ending."

I had no argument with that.

Epilogue

A month later I decided to throw a small party. I invited
Marie as a peace offering, and she accepted. She
brought her current boyfriend who turned out to be the life of
the party. He brought his guitar, a good voice, and a loud laugh.
Nigel was also there and came up with enough one-liners that
Marie's friend had plenty of reason to laugh. Andy came alone
and was feeling no pain after a couple of beers. Norm brought a
ditzy but nice young woman who flirted with all of the men,
including JJ. Darryl and Lisa managed to find a babysitter for
their three kids and showed up ready to party. Beatrice came
early, said she would only stay for a half hour, and ended up
being one of the last to leave. I had included a couple other
walk-in neighbors, a woman I had worked with on various local
events, and a guy JJ wanted to get to know better. They all
came, and everyone seemed to have a good time.

At one point we toasted our "safe community" with a bottle
of champagne I had been saving for a special occasion. We
didn't dwell on the two deaths but toasted the fact that both
murderers had been off-islanders. Somehow that was reassuring. We may have been invaded by a couple of bad guys, but
they weren't "family."

We snacked, laughed, drank, and whooped it up until the cats came home. Natasha and Dilly had sneaked out when Marie and her friend arrived. I was relieved when they made it back unscathed. I promised them that I would let them out during the day, in spite of the eagles and other potential dangers, but they needed to understand that their cat door was going to be locked up tight at night. I wasn't sure my plan would keep them completely safe from coyotes, but I assume they agreed that imprisonment once the sun went down was a good compromise.

After the others were gone, JJ and I were sitting on my deck finishing up the Syrah and the remaining local goat feta and crackers. "It must feel good to have helped out the police when they were *bogged down*," JJ said. He wiggled his eyebrows and grinned.

"You've been working on that one for a month, haven't you?"

"Give me another month and I might come up with something even better."

"Well, I have one for you. To quote one of my favorite feminist authors, Miles Franklin, 'Friendship is warmth in cold, firm ground in a bog.' Thank you for being my friend."

JJ gave me a hug and let me have the last word.

Acknowledgments

There *is* an ancient bog on the island, but not in the location I've described. Just like the fictional bog, the real bog is very fragile, and visitors are discouraged. The homes and owners near the bog in my book are also fictional and do not represent the attitudes of those living near the actual bog. Nor is there an organization called the Island Land Stewards. However, the coyote packs and coyote counts are real. And there *was* a cougar, although he was not interested in living in harmony with the domestic animals on the island and was removed.

There have been several other changes since I wrote this book. Sadly, the quirky Zombiez is no longer in business, replaced by a "normal" family eatery. Nevertheless, from my point of view, the character and atmosphere of the island community remains consistently appealing. If not a bit weird. What other community elects a goat or a dog as their unofficial mayor? What other community boasts having a rusted bicycle suspended inside a tree trunk over 8 feet off the ground? And what community has an annual parade that includes a shopping cart drill team from the local grocery?

Vashon Island is a great place to live and to visit. I hope I have captured at least some of its unique flavor in *Bogged Down*.

About the Author

Award-winning author Charlotte Stuart PhD writes mysteries that fall into a number of different sub genres: cozy mysteries, character-driven mysteries featuring a female PI, a laugh-out-loud comedic series, as well as more traditional mysteries. She's also coauthored a legal thriller with Don Stuart.

In general, she favors twisty plots with a dollop of adventure. Before she started writing full time, she left a tenured faculty position to go commercial salmon fishing in Alaska, spent a year sailing and exploring in the Washington and Canadian San Juans, became a partner in a management consulting group and later a VP of HR and training.

After living on boats for over a decade, boating and forays into wilderness areas often find their way into her stories.

Charlotte lives on Vashon Island in the Pacific Northwest and is the past president of the Puget Sound Sisters in Crime and a member of the Mystery Writers of America and the International Thriller Writers.

facebook.com/charlotte.stuart.mysterywriter

instagram.com/cstuartauthor

bookbub.com/authors/charlotte-stuart

goodreads.com/goodreadscomclstuart

Other books by Charlotte Stuart include:

The Discount Detective Mysteries

The John Smith Mysteries

The Macavity & Me Mysteries

Raven's Grave

Midnight for Justice, a legal thriller by Charlotte Stuart and Don Stuart